SONG OF MEMORIES

A Story of Eurydice and Orpheus

MOLLY TULLIS

The Bibliophile Blonde LLC

Copyright © 2023 by Molly Tullis / The Bibliophile Blonde LLC

All rights reserved.

Editing by Damoro Design.

Cover art and design © 2023 by Damoro Design.

No part of this book may be reproduced in any form or by any electronic or mechanical means, including information storage and retrieval systems, without written permission from the author, except for the use of brief quotations in a book review.

For everyone who's needed a little help pulling themselves out of the Underworld. You're not alone.

A NOTE FROM THE AUTHOR

The beauty of mythology is how it transforms as it is retold, from generation to generation. *"Song of Memories"* focuses on the infamous story of Orpheus and Eurydice from a fresh point of view. This story includes original plot lines and mythological references that do not follow existing accounts to the letter.

"Song of Memories" is a Greek mythological retelling that contains graphic violence, swearing, and sex scenes.

PROLOGUE

Pan was the god of mischief.

It was a gloriously fun part to play in the pantheon. He came by it honestly; Hermes was his father. Pan always thought he got the better end of the deal. While Hermes still had some semblance of responsibilities, Pan did not.

No one expected Pan to do anything but drink with the dryads and make appearances at Dionysus's festivals. He liked to view his role in the world as a consistent merrymaker. There was enough death and drama to keep Greece going until the end of days. Pan never took anything too seriously. There was always someone or something that would clean up his messes when things went too far. He lived his life on a knife's edge and never intended on slowing down.

Until Eurydice.

She was a daughter of Apollo and a forest nymph. She loved music and only rivaled Pan himself in her wildness. Her laughter was a melody that coaxed flowers to bloom and caused the trees to cry. The first time Pan laid eyes on her, his immortal heart stopped—to this day, he still wasn't sure if it ever resumed its steady beat.

After Eurydice, Pan's perspective shifted. His heart expanded to accommodate a world that had created someone as ethereal as Eurydice. Pan brought balance to the world, delivering on a sense of mirth and frivolity he believed necessary to human life—he no longer left trails of carnage behind him wherever he went. Instead, he brought joy to those who were hurting and blessed the wineskins and fields of those less fortunate. He stopped attending the parties of royalty and merchants and would pour drinks for the farmers until dawn.

Hermes made fun of him in the way that only a parent could. He poked fingers and threatened to tell Eurydice himself of Pan's love for her unless Pan did it himself. Pan was horrified by the idea. Parents were embarrassing whether you were eighteen or eighteen hundred.

The day Pan summoned enough courage to tell Eurydice how he felt, Eurydice met Orpheus.

Nothing had been the same in Pan's life ever since.

When she came to meet him in the woods at their favorite meadow, he expected to reveal his heart to her. She was bursting with excitement, telling him she had news of her own. He obliged her with a soft smile on his face, eager to hear about whatever had put such a spring in her step—literally, petals littered the ground wherever Eurydice walked.

She said Orpheus's name.

Pan's heart shattered.

The grass under his feet died, and a cold breeze swept through the clearing. The trees shivered, and the flowers' roots curled. Pan had never understood why humans drove themselves to despair and madness over lost love; now, he wanted to join them. All it took was a brief second, a revelation, and Pan's chest threatened to cave in. He wanted to pull at his hair, break his horns, and join the mourners.

It was only Eurydice's frightened expression that brought Pan back to the moment. He blamed the sudden outburst on surprise, and Eurydice waved it away. She went on to tell him of her love for Orpheus—for his music—and Pan knew that he could not compete with a nymph's love for a musician.

So Pan pushed aside his feelings. He buried them deeper than the spring bulbs and locked up his emotions tighter than the frozen streams on the mountainside.

The only thing that mattered was Eurydice's happiness. If she was happy, Pan could deal with the rest... Then she died.

Pan discovered that grief was a never-ending spiral. It was always waiting with new, unforeseen levels of hell to grip his heart like a vice. Orpheus was determined to rescue her, and for the first time, Pan appreciated him. That was a dedication that Eurydice was worthy of.

He failed.

Pan and Hades nearly came to blows over the number of times he attempted to sneak into the Underworld. Hermes, full of regret for his son, found a loophole. Pan was a god of the forests...and the forests of Asphodel were no different, were they?

Hades was more than happy to oblige Pan once Hermes confronted him. He didn't want to keep people apart; he was simply trying to keep cosmic order by keeping the veil between the realms intact.

So began the happiest times of Pan's life. He ran with Eurydice between the trees of the Underworld, cavorting with the other nymphs and dryads who had passed. He brought them wine and fruits from the mortal world and told stories of the latest human trials.

Forty years passed, and Pan was too scared to disturb the hard-wrought peace Eurydice had found in Asphodel. He never mentioned his feelings again.

Then Orpheus died.

I

I

Eurydice's life was simple. Life was easy when you were dead.

In her opinion, the simple things were the most glorious. Most mortals and gods alike never stopped to smell the flowers; she hadn't when she was alive either. Eurydice had created flowers with every footfall, but she had never stopped to enjoy them. In the Underworld, she had all the time in the world because time didn't exist at all.

The memories of her life in Greece were foggy at best, as if she was constantly trying to remember a dream. It didn't bother her because it didn't seem real. The only horrors she remembered facing were the first few days of her time in the Underworld.

Eurydice woke up in a small valley, near a stream, unsure of what she was supposed to be doing or where she was. The ends of her hair were damp, and the top of her tunic was soaked, but she couldn't remember going for a dip in the water. She wandered for two days, afraid to stray too far from the river, until Makaria found her and took pity on her. The goddess of blessed death was gentle and sweet, taking it upon herself to give Eurydice a tour of Asphodel. Eurydice had to be reminded she was dead.

    Luckily, part of Asphodel contained a great forest. Eurydice wept when Makaria showed it to her. It was full of the spirits of other nymphs and dryads who'd perished. They greeted Eurydice like an old sister.

    There were no chains around Eurydice anymore. Her lost memories faded. The idea of another life was merely like an aftertaste to her, something to soon be washed away forever. There was only the untamed wilderness of the forests of Asphodel, tended to by the creatures of the forests under Persephone's insistence. The Dread Queen's rise had not diminished her duality. She still took her obligation to the flowers and their spirits to heart.

    So Eurydice memorized the petals and what the tips of orchid stems looked like. She helped the trees grow and cataloged every inch of the forest. She filled her days with soft songs and softer melodies, creating a life that had only ever existed in her dreams until then. Erebus's darkness greeted them all like family, encouraging their night-blooming orchids and sleepy vines. The forest's denizens brought Hecate every herb or bud she could ever ask for.

    When Eurydice thought everything was perfect, it only got better. Pan arrived in the Underworld—still very much alive and immortal—after discovering a workaround that allowed him to visit Hades's realm. Eurydice wept for the first time since her death, brushing tears of joy off her cheeks, now that her best friend had returned to her. All of the nymphs and creatures of the forest belonged to Pan and she could never forget him.

    Eurydice finally had everything she had ever wanted.

    It was on a perfect, warm afternoon when everything started to change. Eurydice was lounging on a tree branch, keeping one sleepy eye on a chrysalis that was due to be reborn. Her lithe body was stretched out across the tree like an extension of it, the perfect picture of repose, while her long hair shone like copper in the light.

Telodice, one of Eurydice's good friends, was among the first nymphs that Eurydice met in the Underworld. She took a liking to her immediately, and they'd been thick as thieves ever since. Eurydice never asked her how she'd come to end up in the Underworld, but Telodice had never asked her either. It was an unspoken rule—it was offensive to ask and could be traumatic to retell.

At this point, I'm not even sure I remember... Eurydice struggled to put together a coherent string of thoughts regarding her own passing but never bothered to think on it for too long. There was always something more fun to be doing.

Telodice was currently sitting underneath Eurydice's tree branch, leaning against the trunk with her eyes closed. She was humming to herself and running her fingers through the grass before she shot straight up.

"Eurydice?" Telodice's voice was much too hurried for Eurydice's liking—she sounded upset. Eurydice glanced down at her friend, who was now nervously braiding her long blonde hair.

"Yes? Is something wrong?" Eurydice sing-songed. Her voice was melodic. It always sounded like she was going to break out into song.

"Did you ever send the herbs Hecate requested to her house? I've just realized I can't remember at all if I did it."

"Of course." Eurydice waved her hand like she was shooing a fly. "Is that what you're concerned about? I handled that a few days ago."

"Oh, thank the gods." Telodice giggled happily, a sated smile growing across her face once again. "I thought for a second that we'd forgotten."

"Do you think anyone forgets anything Hecate asks them to do?" Eurydice asked drolly, joining in with Telodice's laughter.

This was what the sum of their days looked like—fussing over requests for flowers and plants by the other citizens of the Underworld, lounging in the sun, or dipping into the cool streams that cut through the trees.

Eurydice and Telodice were musing about their plans for the upcoming summer solstice. Even in the Underworld, the celebrations were large enough to rival any of the other festival days.

"Is Pan going to join us?" Telodice asked, peering up through her thick lashes at Eurydice.

Eurydice blushed and nodded her head enthusiastically.

"I asked him last week. He said he wouldn't miss it. Apparently, he needs to make sure he stops at a few parties in the mortal realm first, but he'll be here by nightfall."

Telodice clapped her hands with glee. "Did Menidise decide on a menu yet?"

"She said something about not having enough figs..." Eurydice trailed off as a soft sweep of power rippled through the glade. It was a gentle, encouraging signature, and Eurydice knew exactly who to expect.

As if on cue, Makaria, the goddess of blessed death, appeared through the trees, her shining hair giving her away before she got too close.

"My friend," Eurydice said as a way of greeting. She propped herself up on one elbow, extending a hand to Makaria. "It's always good to see you. To what do I owe the pleasure? Do you want more irises for your home?"

"Were the last ones we sent the wrong color?" Telodice piped up.

"No, no." Makaria shook her head. "The ones you gave me were perfect. Thanatos loved them."

Eurydice smiled. *I highly doubt Death himself cared much for the flowers, but he does love everything that Makaria does, including constantly renovating that house of his.*

"Do you need something else for your garden?" Eurydice tilted her head.

Makaria didn't respond as she stepped fully into the glen. Telodice got to her feet and bowed slightly, addressing the goddess with the proper honorific. Eurydice sat up straighter, frowning when she saw the empty expression on Makaria's face. A cold shudder ran through Eurydice, something she realized she hadn't felt since she came to Asphodel...dread.

"What is it?" Eurydice's voice sounded breathy and frightened. It startled her how much she'd changed and how she didn't recognize the sound of her own anxieties. Telodice seemed to pick up on it too, quickly glancing between Eurydice and Makaria.

A beat of silence passed between them.

Makaria looked torn, as if she didn't want to tell Eurydice something.

What could have possibly upset a death goddess so much? Eurydice's brow furrowed farther. She knew the gods of the Underworld were not the heartless deities that Olympus would have you believe, but Makaria was resoundingly tough when she needed to be. Makaria took a deep breath and closed her eyes, all her words rushing out of her at once.

"I suppose there's no easy way to tell you this. Orpheus has died. He's on his way to the Underworld. Thanatos is with him."

There was a beat of silence, and Eurydice felt everything, all at once.

Except she didn't know what she was feeling. Her heart started to pound in her chest, and foggy remnants of sadness and betrayal started creeping up her spine.

"Who's Orpheus?" Telodice frowned, starting to bite at her nails, clearly picking up on the tension now cutting through the clearing. Eurydice and Makaria didn't respond. Eurydice's hands started to shake as she jumped down from the tree branch before she had a chance to fall.

Makaria was immediately at her side, reaching out to put a hand on her shoulder. "Do you... Do you remember Orpheus, my friend?"

Makaria was studying Eurydice's expression intently, looking for something. Eurydice didn't want to disappoint one of her companions, but she had no idea what Makaria was expecting of her. A quick glance at Telodice proved that she was just as confused about what was happening.

"H-he sounds like something from a memory," Eurydice whispered. Her face was pale, and some of the flowers closest to her started to droop. Makaria nodded as if that was very understandable and gently led Eurydice to a small pool, helping her sit down on one of the smooth rocks at the edge of the water. Telodice held her hand.

"You were married in Greece, Eurydice. Does that sound at all familiar to you?" Makaria spoke in low, soothing tones. Eurydice wasn't annoyed by it. She rather preferred it at the moment—even if it was somewhat infantilizing. Telodice gasped in quiet surprise.

Suddenly, flashes started going off in Eurydice's mind. She remembered her friends dancing with flowers in their hair, a great banquet, a winsome smile...and a snake?

Why do I remember a snake?

"You were bitten by a snake on your wedding day." Makaria prodded gently, and Eurydice realized she'd been thinking out loud.

"Oh. Yes, yes." Eurydice's heart started beating faster. "I was married. There was a wedding. We were so happy, but... Pan wasn't there. I was sad." Eurydice started massaging her temples as flashes of scenery started flickering through her mind like smoke, easy to see but impossible to grab and analyze. Something was burning in her chest like there was a hot coal sitting between her breasts.

"Shall we ask him?" Telodice piped up. Makaria threw her

a withering look and a raised brow, and Telodice quickly nodded and fell silent.

"I was married and then I died." Eurydice picked her head up and looked at Makaria for confirmation. She nodded her head.

"Do you remember anything else?" she asked, and Eurydice got the feeling once more that she was missing something.

"No?" Eurydice's voice rose as the missing pieces in her memory started to frighten her. "What else could I be missing? You only die once! I was married, and then I died, I died, I died..." Eurydice started to trail off, pulling her knees up to her chest and rocking back and forth.

"Ssh, that's quite enough. Don't worry about it," Makaria soothed, wrapping her arms around the nymph. "You don't need to remember anything. No one will force you."

"I remember Orpheus," Eurydice whispered, staring past Makaria and Telodice as though they weren't even there. "I remember Orpheus."

"Do you want to see him?" Makaria sighed, gently pushing some of Eurydice's hair off her face, the way a mother would tend to a child. "You don't have to. It's your choice."

"What if he wants to see her?" Telodice interjected, her eyes round and wide with curiosity. Makaria snapped her attention to Telodice and held a finger to her lips, indicating that Telodice's contributions were not helping.

"Does he want to see me?" Eurydice looked at Makaria, breathing heavily.

"It doesn't matter what he wants. What do you want?" Makaria looked troubled, as if this entire conversation wasn't going in the direction that she thought it would. If Eurydice hadn't been so completely overwhelmed, she would've pushed Makaria harder.

"I... He's my husband." Eurydice repeated the words robotically. Her fingers trembled, and some of her confidence ebbed away. "I want to see him. He's my husband. A bride should always want to see her husband, right?" Eurydice looked up at Makaria for guidance, trying to scan the goddess's face for any clues as to what she should be doing—but Eurydice had never been very good at interpreting what was happening between the lines.

"Eurydice..." Makaria started and stopped, letting out a long sigh. "If you want to see him, then I'll bring you to him. It's as simple as that." Makaria's smile was forced—Eurydice could tell—but she nodded anyway. Eurydice slid her hand into Telodice's and squeezed it, repeating the words as though saying them aloud again would ease some of the chaos in her mind.

"Yes, of course. I'm a wife. I want to see my husband again."

Eurydice's voice cracked, and some of the joy drained from her eyes as she said it. Makaria and Telodice were wise enough not to say anything else.

"I'll tell Thanatos that we're coming."

2

Orpheus shifted uncomfortably on the bed. The curtains were open, and a soft breeze drifted in. The sea was shining, and the smell of salt and citrus perfumed the air. The rooms that Orpheus occupied were massive. After a lifetime of adventures and fame, rivaled only by the gods, he could afford a lifestyle only matched by kings. By all means, he should be living out his final days in the upmost comfort, surrounded by loved ones. Instead, only contempt ran through Orpheus's veins.

The estate where Orpheus now resided was on the coast, on the isle of Lesvos. It was a sprawling property, covered in olive and lemon groves, with numerous outbuildings and stables. The main house consisted of two levels and boasted one-hundred rooms, all centered around a courtyard with fine in-laid mosaics and multiple roasting pits. It was famed throughout the region for hosting elaborate parties that lasted days or weeks on end. There was one particular feast of Dionysus where the partying lasted for thirty days straight—and this was the kind of opulence and indulgence that Orpheus used to navigate his way through life.

Now, none of it mattered. Orpheus was dying. It was his

time—he knew that. Besides, he could greet the gates of the underworld like an old friend.

How many people can say that? I've stood in Hades's throne room. There is no fear of death for me. Only this insufferable waiting.

"Someone! Fetch me a cup of wine," Orpheus yelled out to the empty walls, feeling his temper grow with every passing second.

Once he knew his health was failing, Orpheus fired most of his house staff. He had been chasing adoration and inspiration all his life, dragged down by the death of Eurydice.

Orpheus had tried to reach the level of fame that he once had standing next to Eurydice, but by the gods, nothing worked. Everywhere he went, his legacy was always coupled with hers. It was always the story of Orpheus *and Eurydice*. It chafed Orpheus's pride as nothing he did was good enough for him to stand on his own two feet.

He forced her from his memory and traveled with Jason. He wrote ballads that dominated all of Greece. He swam in riches of all kinds—money, treasures, travel, and women. There was nothing that was off limits to Orpheus, every day of his life. All of it left a bitter taste in his mouth, but he continued to chase the same high that he felt when he'd been standing next to Eurydice.

The gossip mongers had a field day with Orpheus's reputation. For a man whose story began with what was argued to be one of the greatest love stories of all time, his tendency to sleep and drink his way through the world didn't seem to line up. He championed himself and himself alone, living only in service to his own ego. Within a few years after Eurydice's death, Orpheus had all but forgotten her name.

But every verse, every coin, every maiden he pulled into his bed, none of it drove Eurydice entirely from his thoughts. He attempted to chase it away as though he could drown his broken pride with drink and accolades… Nothing worked. Orpheus wasn't above using her memory as a cheap ploy for sympathy, especially when cajoling other companions to his chambers.

Now, finally, as he yelled out into the halls of a half-abandoned estate, he knew his moment was coming. Death had finally come for Orpheus the way it had come for his wife, an entire lifetime ago.

Orpheus was dying, and for him, that meant he was ready to come alive again. How sweet would it be to feel Eurydice's adoration at his feet? Her warm presence by his side? Her influence on his songs? Would her return to him ebb some of the melancholy and lost time in his heart?

The gilded hallways were covered in expensive tile and tapestries, more mementos from his long life. The last two remaining servants heard Orpheus's demands and came running with a goblet and a plate of food.

"Do you think he's going to be in a better mood?" one of them asked anxiously, nearly tripping over a set of gilded armor in the hallway.

"I doubt it," his companion scoffed. "You know he only smiles when he's drunk or flirting. He's a nasty piece of work."

"There's no need for manners when you're a living mythical hero."

"A hero of what?" the server scoffed. Their voices lowered as they approached the entry to Orpheus's room. "He failed to bring Eurydice back. Everyone seems to conveniently forget that. Including Orpheus. He failed. It's not like he's Hercules. Hercules passed all of his trials and became a god. Hell, he became Hermes's consort."

"True, but not many men can say they've seen Hades face to face."

"Forget Hades!" the servant balanced his precarious tray of food, "It's Persephone that I want to lay my eyes on."

"We all will eventually."

"Luckily, this bastard is going first," the server grunted, plastering a fake smile on his face as he used his shoulder to open the door to Orpheus's chambers. "My lord!" he called out jovially. "We've brought you food and drink."

"I didn't ask for food," Orpheus wheezed, his voice sounding nothing like the melodious voice of legend. "I only wanted a fucking drink." Orpheus pushed himself up on his elbows, reaching one frail arm out towards the servant.

"Of course." The server bowed gently, handing the goblet over. "We wanted you to have everything that you require, my lord."

"That looks like shit," Orpheus grumbled, nodding his chin in the direction of the platter. The servers exchanged a quick glance, and one of them coughed awkwardly.

"It's all that is left in the pantries, my lord."

"What in the hell does that mean?" Orpheus snapped, sitting straight up in bed. "What do I have a cook for!?"

"You... Um, you fired the cook."

"When did I fire the cook? I did no such thing!" Orpheus grunted, his eyes going wide with barely contained rage. He had spent his mortal life living in extreme privilege and had developed a dangerously short fuse. There had never been a shortage of people waiting to tend on someone as legendary as Orpheus—cursed by Apollo and having escaped Hades!—and it had long warped his mind.

The servants took a well-practiced step to the side and dodged as Orpheus let out another anguished cry and threw his cup against the wall. Dark wine dripped down the plaster and stained it, joining a plethora of similar stains.

"Get me a new one!" Orpheus snapped. The servers quickly turned on their heels and left to avoid Orpheus's ire, making their way towards the wine cellar. The sound of their sandals slapping against the floor echoed in the halls, reminding everyone how empty the estate had become.

The servants looked at one another, and a heartbeat passed between them, slowly looking between their faces and the remnants of the once great house around them.

"Are you thinking what I'm thinking?"

"No one would know. We could spend a fortnight looting the house and go live like kings."

There was a nod of recognition as the servers busied themselves in the remnants of the stores, grabbing another goblet of wine for Orpheus. They moved with great care—more than they would normally take for someone they so despised—but now, that goblet of wine contained the fate of their lives.

It was silent as they reentered Orpheus's bedroom, the legendary bard now fast asleep and slouched against the pillows. The servers looked at each other once again, debating whether or not they should wake Orpheus up. They typically never would, but they were keen to watch Orpheus finish his wine so they could continue on with what they believed to be the rest of their lives.

"Sir?" One of them cleared his throat. Orpheus sat up with a sputtering of grunts and coughs, his eyes narrowing as soon as he saw the servants.

"What the hell took you so long?"

"You have a large and spacious estate, my lord."

"Shut up." Orpheus rolled his eyes, extending his feeble hand for the cup. "Keep your pretty words to yourself. I'm the only one around here that anyone wants to hear wax poetic." The servant said nothing but bowed graciously, handing the cup over to Orpheus.

The servers backed away slowly, disappearing from Orpheus's sight and hiding in the hallway. Orpheus raised the cup to his lips, drinking the entire cup in messy gulps. The wine trickled down his face, and he wiped it on his sleeve, letting out another dissatisfied grunt as he tossed the cup to the floor. A dark shadow enveloped the entire compound, and all throughout the property, torchlights and candles flickered out.

The servants bit back their shouts of alarm and huddled together in the hallway. There was a chill in the air, and they knew what it meant—Thanatos was nearby.

They had been successful.

"Horrible w-wine," Orpheus hiccupped. His breath started to feel shallow while he was completely ignorant to his home's sudden plunge into darkness. He lay back against the dirty pillows, humming half-composed lyrics to himself as his eyes fluttered closed. "I just need...need another nap," he promised himself, "then I'll finish that song."

Orpheus closed his eyes and died.

3

Eurydice asked to go back home to tidy up before they went to greet Orpheus. She didn't have much time. Makaria hadn't been kidding when she said that Orpheus was on his way with Thanatos. Eurydice thought she was going to be sick and desperately needed a few moments to herself before facing her ex-husband. Was he her ex-husband? What was the policy if you died on your wedding day?

Telodice and Makaria promised to wait for Eurydice at the edge of the woods and give her all the time she needed to prepare herself.

Eurydice's home was small, made of mud bricks and wood, perched in a small clearing. There were huge, open windows with sheer, billowing curtains that dominated most of the walls and very little furniture. If the weather was ever too harsh, Eurydice simply asked one of the weather nymphs to ease up. She couldn't bear to be kept from the forests of the Underworld, even inside of her own home. Her favorite spot in the entire house was the small rooftop balcony, with hanging tapestries dyed the colors of bright summer berries, oversized cushions, and two small braziers constantly burning frankincense. She spent most of her nights sleeping up on the roof, refusing to be confined to any space.

Eurydice sat in the bedroom that she never used, with a small hand mirror propped up against the wall. It was one of her favorite pieces—one of her few material possessions at all—and was carved with images of nymphs running in the forest under a full moon. It had been a gift from Pan. The fact that it appeared in her Underworld dwelling was nothing less than a kind, welcoming gesture on Hades's behalf.

Eurydice's hand was wrapped tightly around the end of her hair, her fingers shaky and palms sweating as she braided it. A part of her *knew* that she remembered Orpheus and their short marriage, but she had virtually no recollection of any of their time together. She stared at her reflection, trying to remember the woman in the mirror.

It shouldn't matter, should it? Makaria would warn me if Orpheus was dangerous. If I died on our wedding day, then surely, I should be excited to see him again? I must be. I am.

Eurydice took a long, slow, deep breath as she finished tying off her hair in a braid.

"I am excited to see Orpheus."

The words sounded dull and unenthusiastic as she forced herself to say them out loud. She tried to summon up some excitement or the thrill of love within her chest. Eurydice closed her eyes and waited for the feeling.

Nothing came.

Eurydice had never been a woman who fell in love too easily. In fact, Orpheus was the first serious lover that she'd ever had—she remembered that much, at least. Her life in the mortal realm had been mainly focused on the survival of her favorite trees and flowers and pushing for the balance of nature to remain untouched. She was born from a small creek in Northern Greece, pulling herself out of the waters and into creation, with Pan's blessing, when she saw someone polluting the waters with run-off from a forge.

Somewhere along the way, her connection to the land had been cut off. She wished she could remember why and how so she could avoid it again at all costs. Only since returning to the Underworld did she start to tend pieces of herself long forgotten, alongside the flowers and the saplings.

"I am excited to see Orpheus," Eurydice repeated herself, but she still sounded hollow.

Well, I suppose there's no apprenticeship for how to greet your long-lost husband. No time like the present.

Eurydice stood up and rolled her shoulders, stepping outside to join Telodice and Makaria. She could sense it in the air—the Underworld was nearly vibrating with anticipation. Eurydice fought back against another wave of nausea, feeling as though she was about to walk onstage in a play without having memorized her lines.

There was no pomp and circumstance when new souls arrived in the Underworld. There was no need. The souls of the recently departed arrived in a near constant parade to the banks of Styx, keeping Charon in perpetual motion.

When the word spread that Thanatos was returning with Orpheus, nearly all the residents of hell came to witness the reunion. Spirits, souls, and deities alike flocked to the banks to witness what would surely be the most talked-about arrival since Sisyphus.

Eurydice was trailing slightly behind Telodice and Makaria as they approached the banks of Styx, Eurydice keeping her head down. She was firmly focused on the small flowers that popped up wherever Telodice stepped and careful that she didn't tread on them as she followed. Makaria and Telodice stopped suddenly, causing Eurydice to nearly crash into them.

Makaria was wearing a simple gray tunic, but everything about her was illuminated, like oil in bright light. Telodice had managed to change too, and she was now dressed in head-to-toe pink, with roses pinned throughout her hair. Eurydice didn't think to change her outfit at all, and when she saw her friends, she'd paused and wondered why she suddenly felt ashamed. Unfamiliar emotions were the theme of the day for Eurydice, so she'd buried the notion and decided not to change her appearance after all.

Eurydice wore the same thing every day—a short, lilac tunic, that in the mortal world was more appropriate for young boys or girls. It was certainly not something for a grown woman to wear, or anyone with deity's blood, but it made Eurydice feel carefree and comfortable. What was the point of being dead if she couldn't wear whatever she wanted?

"Are you sure you want to do this?" Makaria's gaze was firm as she raised an eyebrow at Eurydice. Eurydice glanced between Makaria and Telodice. Telodice looked as excited as a sapling on a spring day. She was practically vibrating with excitement. If Eurydice didn't know any better, she would've assumed that Telodice belonged to Aphrodite.

In yet another unidentifiable feeling to settle in Eurydice's chest, she was suddenly burdened with the responsibility of Telodice's excitement.

A reunion for the ages, Telodice had said earlier. Eurydice widened her smile, trying to pull in her errant thoughts. *It must be. I'm only nervous. That's it. I'm simply nervous.*

"Yes, of course I want to do this." Eurydice's smile widened even further. Makaria said nothing in response while Telodice clapped her hands rapidly in excitement.

"Let's go then," Makaria nodded solemnly.

The banks of the river Styx were crowded like Eurydice had never seen before, and a strange wave of fear washed over her. She gritted her teeth and squeezed her hands into fists, wincing slightly as her nails dug into her palms.

Eurydice felt the weight of a thousand eyes on her shoulders as the crowd quickly recognized her. Everyone turned to stare at the legendary Eurydice, the muse of all muses, whose death had pushed Orpheus to the brink of insanity. The petals underneath Eurydice's feet started to wilt as she stepped forward, keeping her eyes down as Makaria cut a path through the crowd. Eurydice straightened up and suddenly found herself wishing that she had worn something more appropriate, something grander or prettier like Telodice did.

Eurydice was no longer Eurydice. She was Orpheus's Eurydice, and that palpable difference rocked her to her core.

Eurydice could hear the crowd's murmured whispers begin to grow louder and louder as they got closer to the river, all of them turning to one another and whispering whatever popped into their mind about Eurydice.

Eurydice tried to block out all of their voices, but the noise grew until she couldn't hear her own thoughts, replaced by the thoughts of a thousand others.

"She's not as pretty as I thought she'd be."

"Do you think she's excited?"

"She doesn't look excited."

"If I was going to see my husband, after all he did for me…"

Makaria abruptly stopped and turned around, wrapping her arm around Eurydice's waist and pulling her into her side.

"Walk closer to me," she encouraged, tossing a sharp glare out over the crowd. They responded instantly to Makaria, and the observers closest to them immediately took a few steps back. Makaria was a death goddess, after all, and very few deities commanded as much respect. Especially in the Underworld.

After what seemed like another eternity, the masses parted, and Eurydice found herself standing on the banks of the river Styx.

A hush went over the entire crowd, who suddenly got so quiet that Eurydice could hear the gentle waters of Styx running in front of her. Eurydice was holding her breath, her heart threatening to beat right out of her chest.

A pulse of cold magic whipped through the air, and several of the observers fell to their knees. The sound of heavy, leathery wings cut through the air. Thanatos.

"He's here." Makaria whispered, her mouth turned up in a small smile. Eurydice watched as Makaria's entire countenance brightened at the appearance of her lover, and another hot stab of shame pierced her gut as she realized she didn't even come close to how Makaria was feeling.

I'm nervous. That's normal. Eurydice forced herself to remember.

She was pulled from her thoughts as the sound of beating wings got louder, and a bright flash of light blinded everyone at the river. Eurydice squeaked and covered her eyes, turning away from the sudden brightness.

This is it. Her mind started to trip over itself. *He's here. When I open my eyes...*

"Eurydice," Makaria was whispering softly in her ear, "Orpheus is here."

Eurydice found a sudden burst of courage and opened her eyes without thinking, ignoring the swathes of people all around them. She pushed out and ignored everything that reminded her that they were not alone, and her eyes settled on Orpheus.

He's perfect.

It was Eurydice's first thought, and everything else melted away. The man who stood before her on the opposite bank of the Styx was smiling at her with an expression that she had seen a thousand times before. A collection of memories came rushing to the surface, and each tender moment Eurydice had ever had with Orpheus played in her mind. A great sense of loss and love surged through her veins, the strength of it sending Eurydice to her knees.

The crowd cheered, obviously pleased at the sight of Eurydice overcome, because this was the reaction they had hoped for.

Eurydice couldn't take her eyes off Orpheus. She could see his lips moving as his smile widened even further, mouthing her name over and over again. Eurydice couldn't even find the strength to respond, her hands shaking at her sides as she tried to comprehend the barrage of sensations inside of her.

Orpheus looked the same as he did in her memories. His golden hair was curling at his temples, and his long tunic was richly embroidered. There was a lyre looped over his shoulder, his opposite hand extended out to Eurydice as if he could reach her over the Styx. She retraced his features with her eyes and viscerally remembered how they felt. Orpheus's strong jaw and aquiline features were the things that sculptors themselves would envy.

Eurydice was so completely overwhelmed that she didn't even realize she was crying, unable to move while her knees sunk into the sand of the riverbank.

A great, booming voice cut through the cheers and tears and rocked the foundations of the Underworld.

"That's enough!" Hades himself emerged from the crowd. He had a white-knuckle grip on his bident and looked enraged.

"This is not Olympus, nor is the Underworld a colosseum," Hades growled, the echo of his voice causing the ground to shake. "The arrival of a new soul in the Underworld, regardless of whatever mortal status they achieved, is not a spectator sport. Depart!" Hades slammed the end of his bident into the earth, and a small shockwave rippled through the crowd. Within seconds, they all turned and started running back to wherever they had come from. Eurydice was still blinking in a mild state of shock as the banks of the Styx cleared out in under a minute.

"My deepest apologies." Hades's voice was suddenly much closer to Eurydice. She tried to clear her vision and realized she was staring at the hem of a black tunic with one extended hand at her eye level.

"Oh, thank you," she whispered, accepting Hades's hand as he helped her to her feet. She could barely keep her focus on the god as her eyes kept crossing the river, staring at Orpheus as he eagerly awaited his turn across the water.

"It's not my wish that you'd be the victim of such a spectacle today," Hades continued. "I would have arranged for a more...subtle meeting had I got wind of Orpheus's arrival in time."

"No need for apologies, my lord." Eurydice offered Hades a short bow. "You have always been kind to me and governed well during my time here."

"I should hope that your opinion remains unchanged," Hades replied before disappearing as quickly as he had come.

Eurydice looked back across the river and saw Thanatos greet Charon, who helped Orpheus step down into his boat. Thanatos laughed at something his brother said and then reappeared next to Makaria.

"You know where to find me if you need me," Makaria said by way of goodbye. Thanatos smiled warmly at Eurydice and grabbed hold of his consort and Telodice, vanishing on the winds as they cleared out the valley for Eurydice's reunion.

She could barely nod, her heart stuck in her throat, as she watched as Charon's boat hit the halfway point. Orpheus was still smiling wildly at her, saying things that she couldn't hear, beckoning for her with outstretched arms. He was stretched so far over the side that Eurydice worried he might fall.

Everything was happening to Eurydice in slow motion. Charon docked his boat, and Orpheus flew off it, running down the long pier towards Eurydice. The finer details of his features came into view, and Eurydice remembered how she'd traced each freckle on his cheeks in the summertime. The sweet warmth of a summer sun and memories of soft breezes and flowers flooded her memory. That was everything Orpheus was—he was springtime incarnated in a mortal man.

As Orpheus reached her, he stopped, his expression faltering when he realized that Eurydice had yet to move.

Eurydice was screaming inside of her head, telling her body to move, move, move. *Go to him!* Yet, something held her back.

Orpheus's smile softened but did not disappear as he held out his hand towards her.

"Hello, Eurydice."

4
40 YEARS EARLIER

Eurydice stretched her limbs out like a cat, enjoying the warm sensation of the sun on her skin. Her body buzzed with the smell of wildflowers and the sound of bees. The weather was perfect; it produced that kind of euphoric feeling that could only come from sunlight and a cool breeze.

Eurydice had taken Orpheus deep into the woods to one of her favorite glens, covered in wildflowers and far away from the prying eyes of other mortals or nymphs alike. It was a rarity for Orpheus and Eurydice to find any time alone together. Whether it was other wood folk trying to get a glimpse of the infamous poet that had tamed a nymph or other mortals trying to hear Orpheus practice, they attracted a crowd wherever they went. But not here, deep between the cypress trees, where Eurydice could close her eyes and listen to the quiet noises of Orpheus attempting to wrestle the creative process into submission.

Orpheus was murmuring something in her ear, lyrics and poems that she'd never remember, but he'd later write down all the words to.

His fingers weaved through her hair. He chuckled with

amusement every time he pulled an errant blossom from the strands. It amused him to no end, regardless of how many times Eurydice explained that she was a nymph, which meant sprouting petals was a constant occurrence.

"They're so pretty, Eurydice," Orpheus smiled, holding some of the petals up to the sunlight. Eurydice didn't answer while she studied his face. Orpheus had a perfect smile. He had won her over with a single look.

"I've told you this before," Eurydice rolled her eyes playfully, "I'm a nymph. Having flowers in your hair comes with the territory."

"I know," Orpheus groaned, dropping his head to her shoulder and pressing a line of kisses up her neck. "But I've never seen a woman who does that before. It's so...*exotic.*"

"Lovely." Eurydice deadpanned, closing her eyes and running her fingers through the grass. "You may be known for your lyrics, but compliments are not your strong suit."

"Are they not?" Orpheus chuckled, still embracing Eurydice as he hooked his leg around her calf and pulled their bodies closer together.

"I can't say I know many women who prefer to hear that they're 'exotic.' What's 'exotic' to you is completely normal to a nymph. You make me sound like a creature. An object."

"Do women not want to hear that?" Orpheus repeated himself, and Eurydice fought the urge to roll her eyes.

"Delicious, maybe..." Eurydice started trailing her fingers up Orpheus's arm. "I would take exquisite, divine, or your guiding star, if you're looking for a compliment." A soft breeze drifted through the clearing again, and Eurydice's eyes fluttered closed, enjoying the scent of crocuses on the wind.

"That's brilliant, Eurydice." Orpheus smiled. He sat up quickly, dislodging Eurydice and abruptly rolling her onto her back.

"*Oof,*" Eurydice exhaled sharply as she hit the grass. She straightened up, her brows furrowing as she looked over at

Orpheus. He had pulled a small scroll of papyrus and a reed pen from his kolpos, where he always hid them folded into his chiton. Eurydice tried to squash her frustration. There was no moment between the two of them that was safe from Orpheus's inspiration. He had been gifted an enchanted pen from Apollo, alongside his lyre, that never needed to be dipped in ink. It was a brilliant gift for someone who was blessed by the gods as a lyricist and musician. It was equally annoying for anyone who ever spent time with Orpheus since they could be interrupted at any time. Orpheus was not confined by the concept of needing to wait until he could sit down with ink to write.

"Did you need to write that down this instant?" Eurydice couldn't help but let some venom drip in her tone.

"Hmm?" Orpheus barely looked at Eurydice. She watched as he wrote down all the words she had used, each adjective, and penned them into something resembling a rough stanza. Her frustration simmered, wondering if this was what it meant to be a muse—to be a victim of theft, reduced to a beautiful object, not competent enough to create thought on her own, but must rely on the artist to cultivate her abstract thoughts into motion.

"I asked if you needed to write that down at this very moment." Eurydice sighed, watching as rose thorns began growing from her fingernails. She took a deep breath and forced herself to calm down, making the thorny appendages vanish.

"Oh!" Orpheus perked up. For a moment, Eurydice thought he was paying attention to what she said, but he was staring at her hands. "Can you do that again?" Orpheus stared at her, his gaze entirely focused.

Eurydice allowed herself to react, and the thorns burst forth again without hesitation while long vines and rose petals tangled themselves into her hair.

I wonder if he even sees me beneath the parts of myself that he considers wondrous—am I an actress to him? No, no, Eurydice chided herself and forced her thoughts back to the present. *This is what it feels like to be loved, right? To be adored? He accepts me. The wildness that fuels my blood.*

"It's incredible." Orpheus exhaled heavily, staring at Eurydice everywhere but her eyes, taking in the wonder that she was.

Part nature, part goddess, all woman.

There was a reason that nymphs had been at the center of stories for years. Their innate wildness was something that couldn't be fathomed by most mortals. It was as close to divinity as a mortal man could come, which meant that mortal men did what they often did when they came upon a treasure that was priceless. They found a way to make it their own— *their* creation—or they scorned it when they couldn't possess it.

"It happens when I am upset," Eurydice murmured, allowing Orpheus to hold her hand and turn it every which way. She waited patiently, and he failed to acknowledge the connection between her mood and the vicious thorns.

"Hm?" Orpheus seemingly stopped evaluating Eurydice's hands and picked his head up. "Who's upset?"

Some of Eurydice's carefully contained rage boiled over. Sharp thorns emerged up and down her arms, as sleek as a dangerous spine, and she exhaled heavily. *Is it always this impossible to speak to men?* She tried to think of all the positive traits that Orpheus possessed, which her fellow nymphs loved to remind her of. Orpheus's face merged into one of shock and awe as he stared down at her arms, once again becoming entranced with the way that she reacted.

"Ah, this happens whenever you're upset?" Orpheus blushed crimson, picking up his head and looking at Eurydice with a bashful expression. It finally seemed to get through his thick head that Eurydice was frustrated, and she could only shake her head at his apparently slow wit.

"It's a good thing you're pretty," Eurydice grunted, snatching her hand back from Orpheus.

"Hey now," Orpheus crooned, dropping his voice a little lower. He scooted closer to Eurydice, trailing his fingers gently up her arm, then across her shoulders, until he tilted her chin up so she was looking him in the eye. "I'm sorry, my love. I just can't help it."

"Sometimes it feels like you aren't even listening to me, Orpheus." Eurydice sighed, the thorns disappearing back into her skin at the placating tone in his voice. If there was any redeeming quality about Orpheus, it was that he always at least tried to apologize—and no one could grovel like a poet. It was practically what they were made for.

"How can I not get distracted by every little thing about you?" Orpheus murmured, leaning forward and pressing a series of soft kisses to Eurydice's cheeks. "You always amaze me. I can't even get through a sentence without being entranced by something new I learn about you."

Eurydice's heart picked up its pace and she flushed, trying and failing to hold onto some of the ire that he'd brought out in her earlier.

"It's that... You... *Oh.*" Eurydice sighed as Orpheus started kissing down her neck. "It's that you treat me...treat me like an object sometimes, Orpheus."

"Do I?" Orpheus made a noncommittal sound in between kisses. "I certainly don't mean to. How can I not stare at you like you're the most stunning thing at the market?" Before Eurydice could respond, Orpheus wrapped an arm around her waist and pulled her into his lap in a swift display of his strength. She settled over his lap, and Orpheus cupped her jaw with one hand, his other hand playing through the long strands of her hair again.

"You're my *muse*, Eurydice," Orpheus whispered, staring up at her as though she had hung the stars in the sky. "All I'm able to do around you is try to absorb everything that you are.

Do you know what a futile task that is? To try and capture everything about you that makes you...you?"

"Why does it need to be captured?" Eurydice raised an eyebrow, studying Orpheus. He only tossed his head back and started to laugh, a rich, joyful sound that flooded the clearing like the sunlight itself.

"Oh, Eurydice. What else would I do with you?"

"You could love me," Eurydice responded, wrapping her arms around Orpheus's neck, sliding their bodies closer to one another as the air around them grew thick with the scent of irises and crocuses once more.

"Ah, I could," Orpheus gave her a soft smile and nodded, "but immortalizing you is the greatest form of love I could offer, sweet Eurydice." Orpheus kissed her gently, tightening his grip around her waist. When he pulled away, his hand was full of petals.

"My sweet Eurydice, with petals in her hair." He gave her another dazzling smile, and she slid off his lap, while Orpheus started jotting down notes again—their conversation and her anger already long forgotten, a stanza that had already been written.

Eurydice lay back down in the soft grass, content to close her eyes and listen to the sounds of the forest, wondering if love always felt like surrendering parts of yourself to someone else.

5

Pan paced back and forth through the receiving room in Hades's hall. It was one of the finer rooms that he'd ever been in—and he'd partied in the most illustrious of places that both the mortal and immortal world had to offer—but that was what being a god of gemstones got you. It didn't matter the floors were practically glowing with dark obsidian tiles. Pan was always anxious whenever he was indoors.

Hades's sprawling estate was carved out of hell itself, cropping out from the stone walls and spreading over several different levels. It overlooked the banks of Styx, with a prime view of Charon and his infamous docks. From one of the thousands of windows carved into the impenetrable walls, Pan stared, walking back and forth and unable to take his eyes off the shores of the river.

The great hall was made of black stone and covered with inlaid jewels, with rich woven fabrics, the colors of gemstones, hanging from the rafters. There were tall basins in each corner, full of oil and burning with a dark flame, casting rainbows and flickers of color off the stones embedded in the walls. At one far end of the room there was a small dais with two obsidian thrones that looked as though they had sprouted up from the stone floor like trees.

Pan didn't think anything in the room counted as wealth—he measured wealth in entirely different terms than Hades. Pan's definition hinged more on how many different types of trees you could plant in one clearing or how long you could run in the soft grass without running into another soul. Pan was big, even by a god's standards, and appreciated wide open spaces where he could stretch out. He had thick, curling black hair, wide shoulders, and dark skin from his days in the sun. On more than one occasion, he'd been mistaken from behind for Hephaestus.

None of that was on his mind, however, as he ricocheted back and forth, passing in front of the tall, arched windows, still unable to tear his gaze off the Styx.

The air was filled with the sounds of excitement, people murmuring and shades gossiping with one another. It had been a long time since the atmosphere in the Underworld had been this electric. Pan knew why.

Orpheus is on his way to the Underworld.

Pan let out a long string of ancient curses under his breath, wringing his hands repeatedly as the sounds of his footsteps echoing off the walls started to drive him insane. In moments like this, his control started to crack, and his magic was unpredictable. Pan was switching back and forth between his satyr and fully human form, flickering like a flame, changing so rapidly that it was impossible to tell what he looked like.

If he was being honest with himself, Pan always preferred his fully human form, but it was possible to contain his magic at the best of times—and he was feeling particularly beastly on what was surely going to be a glorious day in the Underworld.

"Fucking Orpheus," Pan spat. "What a no-good, good-for-nothing *poet*…" Pan uttered the word 'poet' like it was a swear word, but a soft, feminine presence cleared her throat behind him.

"Are you cursing the poets now, Pan?"

Pan whipped around and let out a sharp cry that was half-scream and half-bleat. He hadn't heard anyone enter the room, and he assumed that most of the Underworld's inhabitants would be down on the banks of the Styx to watch the fateful reunion.

"Persephone!" Pan blushed crimson, offering her a short bow at the waist. "I didn't expect to see you here."

Persephone smiled, a knowing look crossing her face that Pan rightfully identified as being mixed with a fair amount of pity. Her long blonde hair was undone, with only a few small braids pulling it away from her face, and a red chiton trailed on the ground behind her. She looked radiant as both dark and brightly colored petals decorated the ground behind her. It was a notable trait that she shared with some of the nymphs. It was part of Persephone's role as the goddess of spring, but also as a fertility goddess, which was one aspect she shared with Pan.

That shared synchronicity between them had created somewhat of an unlikely but steadfast friendship between Pan and Persephone, especially if they were helping the other one cause a little bit of chaos. Pan was worried once Persephone's evolution into the Dread Queen was complete that part of their alliance would end, but he was happily proven wrong when Persephone showed that she was more likely to cause a stir than ever.

When Pan was looking for a way into the Underworld to visit Eurydice after her death, Hermes may have pointed out the loophole, but it had been Persephone who convinced Hades that it was to be allowed to happen. For that, Pan would forever consider himself in Persephone's debt—even if his serenity in the forests of Asphodel was inevitably set to be corrupted.

"I should have known I would find you here," Persephone sighed gently. "Although, I'm fairly certain that your treaty with Hades allows you access to the forests of the Underworld, not our throne room." Her tone was playful enough that Pan could tell Persephone was far from upset, but he cringed slightly nonetheless.

"I won't tell him if you don't?" Pan offered up, tapping some of his fingers together. Persephone burst into a fit of laughter, sounding as airy and unbothered as possible.

"Oh, sweet Pan, you should know by now that I could fill the caverns of the Underworld ten times over with the things I don't tell Hades."

"Is that right?"

Pan jumped in alarm for the second time that afternoon as Hades slipped through the heavy oak doors into the throne room. Persephone only raised an eyebrow in response, clearly challenging him to push her on the fact and seemingly not at all surprised to see him. A soft, knowing look passed between Hades and Persephone, and Pan's chest tightened at the sight. Sometimes it was additionally challenging to be in the presence of two people so irrevocably in love, and today was *definitely* one of those days for Pan.

Hades was wearing the same thing he always wore, an ankle-length black chiton and black leather sandals. He had a heavy brooch at his shoulder sculpted entirely from silver and rubies. He approached Persephone and extended his arm towards her, and she moved into his side, pushing back some of Hades's curly hair away from his face to kiss his cheek sweetly. Hades made a pleased grunt sound in acknowledgement, which Pan took to be an endearing sound. You could never be too positive with the god of the dead.

"What were you both talking about hiding from me?" Hades turned to Pan.

Pan's magic surged again, and his body came alive with electricity, rapidly shuffling between his two most prevalent forms. Hades said nothing as if he was entirely unaffected by such minor displays of power as he crossed the room to sit on his throne, eyeing Pan carefully.

"Should I be concerned? I would assume that you would be on the banks of the river, accompanying Eurydice for Orpheus's arrival." The god pressed again, and Pan started to feel sick. A wave of guilt washed over him as he turned towards the windows and tried to discern if Orpheus had arrived yet. Luckily, Persephone stepped in and saved Pan from having to respond.

"Husband." Persephone said it like it was both a statement and an admonishment. "Be kind. If Pan wants to watch Orpheus's arrival from here, it's not bothering anyone to let him do so."

"I don't see why…" Hades started to argue.

Pan watched as Persephone leveled Hades with one look, her brow furrowing and her eyes lighting up momentarily with some of her own dark fire. Pan gave an involuntary shudder.

Remind me to never, ever get on Sephy's bad side.

"…oh," Hades finished lamely, nodding repeatedly and waving his hand in Pan's direction as he stood up quickly. If Pan wasn't mistaken, he could've sworn that Hades was almost blushing.

"Whatever you say, darling." Hades nodded at his wife before turning his attention back to Pan. "Stay as long as you'd like, Pan." As quickly as he had come, Hades crossed the great room, kissed Persephone on the forehead, and disappeared in a pillar of smoke.

Persephone smiled, looking pleased with herself as she joined Pan at the windows overlooking the river.

"One day, you're going to have to teach me how you get people to do whatever you want." Pan shook his head in astonishment. It was impossible to reconcile the Hades he once knew before Persephone arrived. He had no idea how the goddess was able to wrangle one of the world's most powerful gods, but he wasn't complaining.

"Sexual favors, my dear Pan, sexual favors," Persephone laughed with a sly smirk.

She snapped her fingers, and two silk cushions appeared on the floor in front of one of the great windows with a fresh amphora of wine. She nodded for Pan to sit, and he fell onto the cushions with an exhausted sigh.

Persephone poured the wine, and Pan downed his entire glass in a single sip, holding his cup out for more before Persephone had even brought her own cup to her lips. She didn't even blink or react, simply refilling his cup at least twice more before Pan hiccuped and leaned his head against the cool windowpane.

"Do you want to talk about it?" Persephone asked softly, refusing to look out the window at the growing scene before them. The river banks were now crowded with people, as though every soul and shade in the Underworld had turned up for the reunion.

Pan could see Eurydice making her way through the fringes of the crowd, flanked by Makaria and Telodice. There was a rumbling noise building in the air that could only be identified as Thanatos... Orpheus was close.

"That's good that her friends are with her," Pan sighed, his melancholy slowly giving way to some of the anger that he had attempted to keep a lid on.

"Did she want you to go with her?" Persephone asked, her voice stoic and without judgment. Pan nodded, his voice cracking as his eyes filled with tears.

"She asked me to go with her this morning. I couldn't do it. I know that's horrible of me but I... I can't watch. I can't watch knowing what I know. Do you get t-that?" Pan sniffled as the wine soured in his stomach. For the first time in his life, Pan wondered if the wine mixed with his mood was going to make him sick.

Persephone put her hand on top of Pan's and squeezed it, her eyes sad. "I know it doesn't seem fair, but you have to respect Eurydice's choices."

"It's the wrong choice!" Pan cried in a sudden outburst, the tears breaking free. His shout echoed off the rafters and surrounded him in the manifestations of his own grief. Pan turned on his heel and slammed his hands against the window, watching with satisfaction as it cracked beneath his fists.

"Don't hurt yourself," Persephone chided, raising a hand as a lilac bush burst forth in between Pan and the glass to protect him. Pan sank back down to the cushions and buried his head in his hands, sobbing with a force that shook his shoulders.

"It's not fair, Persephone. She should know. She should know what he d-did!"

Persephone sighed, shaking her head in slow agreement. She poured another cup for Pan, watching as the wine turned into water, rightfully assuming that more wine was not what the moment needed—a rare and concerning moment when dealing with Pan.

"It was her decision, Pan," Persephone chided gently. "We don't have to agree with it, but it's what she wanted—"

Persephone was cut off as a roar of applause rose up from the banks of the Styx. Persephone and Pan turned to the window, watching as Hades appeared and said something to the crowds amassed near the river. Within a few moments, everyone started to disperse, and Pan was grateful that Hades had enforced a moment of semi-privacy for Eurydice.

They watched on in silence as Orpheus appeared on the far side of the river, practically leaping into Charon's boat. Pan turned away, unable to watch the actual moment of the reunion as his heart shattered inside of his body.

I don't know if it's possible for a body to contain so much grief. Pan wondered for the first time what it was like to have hurts that wine couldn't fix.

"It doesn't matter." Pan shook his head, staring blankly at the floor.

Persephone shook her head, "You know everyone has the choice to drink from Lethe, Pan. If you wanted to do it, too…"

"I could never forget her," Pan snapped, turning to Persephone with a sudden righteous anger flooding his veins. "I would *never* choose to forget her."

"Okay." Persephone held up a gentle, placating hand. "That is your decision. Eurydice wanted to forget, and you need to respect that."

"She doesn't remember!" Pan cried out again, resting his head on his knees. Another wave of muted applause rang out through the skies, and Pan moaned pitifully, knowing the lovers had reunited. "Eurydice doesn't remember that Orpheus betrayed her."

6

Eurydice thought she might pass out. All of the blood rushed out of her head and left her feeling quite faint as she tried to comprehend Orpheus standing in front of her.

Everything about him was exactly the same as she remembered him, but the details were fuzzy. It was as though she was seeing him through a dream. It was like looking at a memory come to life, some sort of carbon copy of an original that was blurred around the edges. He was standing before her in the exact same outfit she remembered him wearing on the day of their wedding. His golden hair was sticking up in all directions —as though he'd been running his hands nervously through it all day—and his tunic was rich and finely embroidered. Even his fingers were adorned with rings, shining with jewels, although that was something she didn't remember from the last time she'd seen him.

It must be more evidence of how rich a life he led in the mortal world, Eurydice thought to herself, completely hung up on a minuscule detail in the face of such an overwhelming sensation to have Orpheus standing in front of her.

Eurydice's heart was racing, and she suddenly sucked in a

breath, the realization dawning on her that she hadn't been breathing.

"Eurydice?" Orpheus's soft voice cut through the roar of her own blood pounding in her ears. "Are you okay?"

"What?" Eurydice choked out, her hands slick with sweat as she started rubbing them together. She was still trying to commit every minuscule inch of Orpheus to memory, studying him as though it was the last time she would ever see him instead of a reunion. She swayed on her feet as her heart slowly returned to a normal rhythm in her chest.

"Eurydice!" Orpheus sucked in a sharp, nervous breath, his hands going out to steady Eurydice.

His grip on her shoulders pulled Eurydice out of her overwhelming panic, the subtle heat of his hands awakening a thousand different recollections of nights past. The evenings and afternoons they'd spent exploring one another, desperate to soak up every minute they'd had together as if it was their last before they'd known how true that was.

Eurydice blinked several times, finally clearing some of the fog from her head, and her face broke out into a wide smile.

There he was, as sun-kissed as ever and smiling at her... Orpheus.

"Orpheus!" Eurydice half-shouted, grinning like a child with sweets as she threw her arms around his neck and launched herself at him. Orpheus didn't pause for even a moment, joining her in raucous laughter as he started swinging her around. For a few moments, the air was thick with the sounds of laughter and uncapped joy, the melody of a reunion for the ages drifting through the skies of the Underworld.

From somewhere off in the distance, cheers started to erupt from the crowds that Hades had dispersed—who clearly stayed as close as they could to the action. A chorus of well-wishes started echoing out from the skies around them, cheering the lovers on.

"Eurydice!" Orpheus repeated her name again, spinning

her in continuous circles, until after a few minutes, her feet finally touched the ground again.

Orpheus pulled back from her, cupping her face with his hands, his entire countenance as bright as the sun as he stared down at her face. They were both breathing heavily, trying to catch their racing, runaway pulses. Eurydice couldn't find a single reason why she had been so worried before.

This is Orpheus... My Orpheus, she reminded herself. *How I have missed my love!*

"I'm... I'm so happy to see you," Orpheus started, still shaking his head as if in mild disbelief. "I have to admit, I was nervous. I didn't even know if you'd be willing to see me."

Eurydice froze, the sudden joy and exhilaration she had been feeling moments before beginning to ebb away. That unfamiliar, cold, distant sensation started creeping up through her fingers and toes again.

What does that mean? Her thoughts started to run away from her as she desperately tried to make sense of the confusing barrage of feelings and sensations, unable to comprehend what her own heart was telling her.

Orpheus seemed to sense the confusion on her face, and his brow furrowed. He started to look Eurydice up and down as if he couldn't tell who she was. Eurydice began to panic.

"What do you mean?" Eurydice choked out, a cold sheen of sweat breaking out on her forehead. "I... I was excited to see you. I am excited to see you. You... You're my husband." Eurydice started to repeat the same words to herself over and over, the exact same incantation that she had been trying to convince herself of on her way to reunite with Orpheus.

Orpheus quickly buried his surprised expression and started nodding, rapidly confirming what Eurydice was saying. "Yes, of course, my love." His cocksure grin was back. "I'm excited to see you too. It's all that I've dreamed of for forty years."

"What did you mean by that then? What did you mean

when you said you weren't sure if I would want to see you? Why do people keep asking me that?" Eurydice was unable to keep her voice from sounding shrill. There it was again—the sensation that there was something innately wrong about this reunion, like she was trying on a pair of shoes that were the wrong size. Orpheus only forced his smile even wider and began speaking confidently, burying away his own surprise from a few moments before.

"Don't get worked up," Orpheus chided her softly, running his hands up and down her arms. "It's just been such a long time, Eurydice, that's all. People fall out of love all the time, especially mortals, you know. I didn't know if you'd wait for me after all this time. Time is the most fickle of masters. I'm positive that is what everyone else meant if they asked you about it too. We all weren't sure if you would still be excited to see me after forty years in the Underworld. I've been told being dead does funny things to people."

Some of the panic in Eurydice's chest receded, and she nodded her head slowly. Orpheus pulled her against his chest in a hug and held her there, his arms wrapped tightly around her body.

Eurydice took several deep breaths, allowing herself to be comforted by the scent of Orpheus and his strong presence. She let her thoughts drift to the warm afternoons they'd spent together in sunny meadows, coaxing her heart rate back down as Orpheus gently rocked her back and forth.

She let herself get lost in the sensation, opting for his placating words instead of the chaos that was bubbling right under the surface of her skin. It was an uncomfortable feeling, this notion that there were things unsaid between them, but she had no idea where to start.

Eurydice didn't know how much time had passed before Orpheus kissed her forehead, murmuring gentle words against her skin.

"Are you feeling better?"

"Yes," Eurydice sighed softly, allowing herself to surrender to the blissful feeling of being lead. There was one thing that she didn't always mind whenever she was with Orpheus—he'd always make decisions for her, and sometimes, like this exact moment, she didn't have any desire to pushback.

"Excellent. You probably were feeling overwhelmed. I'll be the first one to admit that it's...heavy seeing you again. I've missed you, Eurydice, but my goodness, is it something to see you again after all of these years."

Orpheus smiled down at her, and for a second, Eurydice thought he was going to kiss her, but he seemed to change his mind at the last moment. There was something in his eyes that Eurydice couldn't exactly pin down; it flickered for a brief second and was gone.

"Charon told me there's a small homestead for me somewhere in this valley," Orpheus grinned, "or off in Elysium, I think he said. I'll be honest, I was a little preoccupied so I may have missed most of his orientation speech."

Eurydice giggled at the idea of Charon monotoning his way through another 'here's what you need to know now that you're dead' monologue.

"I would assume Elysium, yes," Eurydice smiled, "but we can always ask Makaria. Some souls don't want a home in the Underworld. They prefer to remain more incorporeal, but others are much happier with a physical home, reminiscent of their time in the mortal world. I would assume you're one of the latter?"

"Of course. A man needs his land," Orpheus smiled, reaching down to grab Eurydice's hand and giving it a soft squeeze. "Let's go get your things, wherever they are, and then we can sort out where they've put me."

Eurydice paused for a second, a cold chill running through her.

"...grab my things?"

"Well, of course," Orpheus's smile widened. "You'll be coming to stay with me, wherever that is, won't you? It wouldn't do to have a wife sleeping apart from her husband." Orpheus tugged on Eurydice's hand and brought her closer to his body, his voice dropping lower. "Besides, we got so little time together in the mortal world once we were wed. I've technically never claimed my husband's rights."

He waggled his eyebrows in a way that was clearly supposed to be half-seductive and half-joking, but it only made Eurydice's stomach sink lower.

"Yes, of course." She forced a small grin on her face. "Of course I'll be staying with you." Eurydice forced herself not to think about surrendering her place in the forests of Asphodel, of saying goodbye to her refuge of trees and nymphs, and forgoing it all to live with Orpheus. The four stone walls of a mortal's home had always felt like a trap to Eurydice, and it was something she had told him many times leading up to their wedding when they were alive.

He probably just forgot, Eurydice began bargaining with herself, keeping a placating grin on her face. *You can always discuss it later. There's no need to start fighting right now, not so soon after we've been reunited. It's going to take time to get used to one another again. Yes, that's it. It's going to take some time.*

Orpheus seemed completely unaware of the inner turmoil Eurydice was sorting through.

"Excellent." Orpheus winked. "Lead the way."

Eurydice nodded, and they began walking through the valley of Asphodel, Eurydice lost in her thoughts as she tried to reconcile everything she was feeling with the solid, nearly ominous presence of Orpheus in the flesh beside her.

He immediately launched into a series of stories regarding his last few days in the mortal world, leading up to his death, and Eurydice pretended to listen to his depictions of grandeur, wondering all the while if he would ever stop to ask her a single question about how she'd spent her decades without him.

Reunions are meant to be this overwhelming…right?

7

Eurydice was struck by the awkward silence that befell her and Orpheus as they made their way through the valley of Asphodel. It wasn't comfortable. *Even after decades apart, it should at the very least be comfortable to reunite with one's spouse...right?* Eurydice's thoughts were spinning as she tried to focus on the sinking feeling in her stomach.

She spared a quick glance at Orpheus, trying to discern the expression on his face. He seemed content, if a little puzzled, which was likely how anyone felt arriving in the Underworld. It was not every day that a mortal died—although mortals died every day. The experience was incredibly personal. Eurydice knew that much from spending forty years in the Underworld. The memories of her life in Greece were all but background noise now, practically impossible to distinguish from a dream.

While he had undoubtedly aged throughout his lifespan, he'd reverted to the Orpheus that Eurydice recognized; if she could say she recognized him at all. He looked truly, from his head to his toes, like a favorite of Apollo. In the sunlight, he could even pass for Apollo's son. Orpheus was impossibly charming, with clear green eyes and curly blonde hair.

One thing that Eurydice would never be able to forget was

the constant barrage of comments she got from her fellow nymphs and dryads. They all fell in love with Orpheus at first glance. He had an ethereal beauty that was uncommon for human men, therefore ensnaring all the forest folk, but Eurydice viewed it differently. Orpheus was attractive, no person with vision could deny it, but she saw those pretty features every time she looked at a flower or a tree full of spring blooms. Orpheus's beauty wasn't uncommon; it was only uncommon in men.

If people looked beyond their own noses at the world around them more often, Orpheus's beauty wouldn't astound them so.

Eurydice almost physically recoiled at her own sharp thoughts, a sense of guilt beginning to stir with the nausea she hadn't been able to shake.

That's a horrible thing to say about your husband...

As if he could read her thoughts, Orpheus chose that moment to reach across the short distance between them and gently capture Eurydice's hand in his. She fumbled for a quick second, unaccustomed to the casual touch, before rather awkwardly interlacing her fingers with Orpheus's. Eurydice picked her head up and met Orpheus's gaze, her heart lifting to find a pleasant smile now etched across his features.

Maybe this isn't going as badly as I thought?

"I know this is a lot," Orpheus blurted suddenly, "but I think that's to be expected."

"Right," Eurydice agreed, forcing a wide smile on her face, "it's going to be a little bizarre after so much time."

Orpheus looked pleased with himself, sparing a glance around at the sloping valley walls. The forests of Asphodel were coming up on the horizon, with Eurydice leading the way to the small homestead that she had laid claim to over the past forty years.

"I don't even know how long it's been," Eurydice admitted with a sigh. "I mean, I know how much time has passed, but some days it doesn't feel real."

"What is it like?" Orpheus prodded gently, swinging their hands between them. A cold chill went down Eurydice's back as she tried to push back the mild feeling of revulsion at Orpheus's sweaty palm against hers, once again trying to convince herself that it was simply an adjustment.

It's going to take time getting used to having a man around you again, all the time.

"Being dead?" Eurydice clarified.

"Yes," Orpheus urged her to go on. "I know what it's like to be alive." He forced a little bit of laughter as if trying to make a joke that wasn't landing.

"You'll forget after a while." Eurydice shrugged. "What it feels like to be alive. It sort of...falls away, after everything. I hardly remember my life in Greece."

Orpheus stopped walking and stared at Eurydice, a horrified expression on his face. Eurydice's eyes widened, and another wave of panic crept up the back of her neck.

Did I say something wrong?

"What do you mean by that?" Orpheus insisted. "How can you forget what it was like to be alive? You don't remember your life?"

Eurydice was struck by the fact that Orpheus wasn't trying to clarify whether she remembered him at all. She shrugged.

"I remember it. If I think about it for a long time, then parts of it come back to me. The memories are there. It's as though I don't want to access them. It happens to everyone the longer they've been in the Underworld. Your mortal life is such a short timespan. You spend nearly eternity here, so...everything that was before fades away," Eurydice trailed off, not knowing if she was helping or making the conversation even more awkward than it already was.

Orpheus started walking towards the tree line again, but he didn't reach for Eurydice's hand again. He looked horrified by the news, as if this was brand-new information for him.

"I don't ever want to forget my life," Orpheus admitted, his voice sounding hollow. "I accomplished many things in Greece and to forget they ever happened… Well…" Orpheus made a smug, scoffing sound. "Then what was the point?"

"What was the point of your mortal life if you don't remember it?" Eurydice pressed, her brows furrowing together.

"Glory is supposed to be eternal," Orpheus remarked casually, not remotely self-aware of how much he was starting to sound like Apollo to Eurydice. "That's the only reason that anything should last forever."

"You do realize that by that logic, I shouldn't be with you right now, and we shouldn't even try to…rekindle whatever this is." Eurydice waved between them. "If nothing matters once you stop remembering it, if only your mortal glory matters to you, then it's pointless for me to move in with you and pretend as though we're a happily wed couple. I don't even remember our wedding day." Eurydice shocked herself with the admission, but a weight was lifted off her chest nonetheless. It didn't describe the extent to which she felt isolated from Orpheus, but it was a start.

Orpheus looked at Eurydice with a shocked and slightly infuriated look on his face, his lips pressing together in a thin line.

"Don't be ridiculous, Eurydice." He leaned forward and tried to kiss Eurydice, but she swerved at the last minute, resulting in Orpheus pressing a bumbling smack to the corner of her mouth. He recovered quickly, puffing out his chest and picking up his pace as they approached Eurydice's beloved forests.

"You're part of so many of my accomplishments in Greece," Orpheus stated warmly, instantaneously reducing Eurydice to one of the many impressive things in his canon. "I could never forget you."

Eurydice forced a smile, nodding along as if she was pleased by the compliment, although it burned through her chest like she'd eaten something with too much vinegar. Orpheus doted on her—he'd always had—but it was the little comments that betrayed his innermost thoughts—that Eurydice was akin to a possession to him—that always made Eurydice pause and question the relationship. As soon as Orpheus said it, a million little pieces of memories started coming back to her, reminding Eurydice that this was a dance they had done a thousand times.

This is always how he's made you feel...even when you were infatuated.

Still, there was nothing stopping her from seeing where things went, especially since she perished on their wedding day so soon. If Apollo had cursed Orpheus so, damning her as his bride, then certainly there was no greater punishment for Orpheus. If a god decided that Orpheus's ultimate suffering was to be without Eurydice...that meant something.

You are going to dig yourself into the dirt, thinking in circles like this. Try to enjoy your time together. Eurydice hyped herself up, forcing herself to get lost in the way that Orpheus smiled towards the setting sun.

They set an easy pace as they entered the forests, Eurydice feeling part of her anxiety ebb away now that she was amongst friends.

"I'm sorry I don't remember our wedding day." Eurydice sighed softly, hoping to extend an olive branch to Orpheus. He offered her a small smile in return, wrapping an arm around her shoulders and tugging her body closer to his as they walked. Eurydice leaned into the embrace, allowing herself the opportunity to at least feel physically close to Orpheus again.

"Well, it was rather traumatic," Orpheus joked, cracking an easy smile, "so I don't blame you. Do you want me to tell you about it?"

"Yes, please do." Eurydice nodded in agreement. If there was anything that Orpheus was good at, storytelling was up there with his musical abilities, although the two went hand in hand.

"You looked as gorgeous as you always do, which was to be expected, of course." Orpheus started with a wink in Eurydice's direction, and a gentle blush appeared on her cheeks, surprising her.

Perhaps there's still something between us after all. He's always been charming, that's not new.

"I had never seen you so concerned with your appearance," Orpheus pressed, his smile growing. "You were bent out of shape over it. You had at least three different nymphs attempt to do your hair, and you weren't happy with any of the results."

The fleeting pleasant feeling that Eurydice had disappeared as she picked through her brain for any memories of the wedding day. *That doesn't sound like me at all...*

"I guess a woman's wedding day is the one day she's allowed to be that preoccupied with her appearance," Eurydice acquiesced lamely.

Orpheus looked at the short tunic she was wearing and made a noncommittal sound. "I do hope that you'll plan on dressing a little bit more appropriately now that I'm here."

Eurydice stopped walking as they stepped into a small clearing, her humble home appearing through the trees. She turned to Orpheus with a confused expression on her face, the flush in her cheeks now deepening to one of embarrassment.

"What do you mean by that?"

"Well," Orpheus scoffed, his voice suddenly full of condescension, "you're dressed like a child, Eurydice. It's not fitting for either of us, especially considering how many eyes are going to be on us for a while. We're the hottest thing to happen in the Underworld since... I don't know. Regardless, it wouldn't hurt for you to clean up a little."

Eurydice took a physical step back at the nonchalant attitude Orpheus took when criticizing her appearance. Before she could even respond, he turned and got a look at the small stone home where she'd spent her long, happy years in Asphodel.

"Oh, gods," Orpheus cringed, "is this trivial shed where you've been living? I've seen more impressive stables. No matter." Orpheus waved his hand about as if he was shooing a fly and walked towards her house, Eurydice trailing behind him with a dumbstruck expression on her face. Orpheus walked right inside her front door as if he owned the house, the distaste on his face growing. "Grab what you need, Eurydice, and let's get out of here. You can move in with me as we discussed. Even if I eventually fell out of Apollo's favor, having a god's attention does grant you some privileges in the afterlife."

Orpheus took another long look around the tiny home, his dissatisfaction apparent. "I'll wait outside." He stepped out again without giving Eurydice the opportunity to say anything, and she slumped down into her favorite chair the moment she was alone.

She looked around the tiny space, filled with dried flowers and happy memories, and was stunned that Orpheus's comments hadn't even surprised her. A part of her knew the way he spoke to her and disregarded her home should infuriate her, but it didn't. It bounced off a high wall surrounding her feelings which Eurydice had long forgotten was there.

I guess I was used to him behaving like this, once...

8

Pan waited as long as he could before he sought out Eurydice.

It wasn't long.

It didn't sit right with him that Orpheus had already uprooted Eurydice from her home and demanded she move in with him; he'd heard the trees whispering about it. Eurydice had suffered in the Underworld until Makaria had shown her the forests, and Pan had put up a mighty fight with Hades himself in order to get access.

After Pan departed Hades's receiving hall in a fury, Pan sought refuge amongst the very same trees. He forced himself to take long, slow breaths as he settled underneath one of his favorite olive trees. It was a direct replica of his favorite olive tree outside of Athens—as above, so below. There was a particular spot on the tree trunk where some of the knots in the wood created the perfect alcove for Pan's wide shoulders and a wonderful spot for taking a long nap in the shade. Pan had a sneaking suspicion that Eurydice had actually grown this tree for him. It had appeared in the Underworld mysteriously close to his festival days, but she'd denied it.

Pan rolled his shoulders and closed his eyes, remembering

the telltale blush that colored Eurydice's cheeks when she tried to deny any responsibility for replicating his favorite tree in the Underworld. It was a small gesture—growing a tree was as easy as breathing for a nymph—but it spoke to something much bigger. Eurydice wanted Pan to feel comfortable in the Underworld; she wanted his presence around. He tried to keep his thoughts on those happier memories.

"I'm sorry I don't remember our wedding day." Eurydice's voice cut through the tree branches, and Pan was yanked from his stupor. Without thinking, he sat up straighter and angled his body towards the sound of Eurydice's voice, every part of him always subconsciously searching for her.

Pan listened in, easily picking up the sounds of Orpheus and Eurydice conversing with one another as they weaved through the trees.

Undoubtedly on their way to pack up Eurydice's things. The thought made Pan's stomach drop. The last thing he wanted to do was witness Eurydice packing up her things and leaving their sacred grove, the little pocket of nature they'd curated here in the Underworld. His curiosity got the best of him, which he always blamed on his lineage from Hermes, and he inched quietly towards the path. He kept himself hidden among the branches, utterly undetectable amongst the flora and fauna. It was one of the benefits of being a god of the wild.

"I've never seen you so concerned with your appearance. You were bent out of shape over it. You had at least three different nymphs attempt to do your hair, and you weren't happy with any of the results."

Orpheus's recollection of the wedding made Pan grow livid, the realization of what was happening slowly reigniting the rage he'd attempted to quiet.

He's rewriting their story together. Pan thought he was going to be sick. *This isn't how it happened at all!*

Pan nearly broke his cover, fighting off the temptation to leap out from his cover in the bushes and rip Orpheus limb from limb. His own power started rolling off him in waves, and Pan struggled to keep it contained in order to keep Eurydice from sensing him. The anger boiling under his skin erupted, and Pan's horns burst forth from their glamour, his hooves and tail emerging alongside them. It took only a few mere seconds, and Pan had shifted into his full expression as a satyr, feeling too furious and livid to maintain his human appearance.

"I guess a woman's wedding day is the one day she's allowed to be that preoccupied with her appearance." Eurydice's demure response shot Pan through the heart. He was shaking with the effort it took to keep himself concealed.

No, no, Eurydice... Pan cried out to any of the gods that might be listening. *That's not right at all. You couldn't have been less concerned with what you looked like. We got so drunk that morning, you were almost late for the ceremony. You were more worried about missing the start of the harvest.*

"I do hope that you'll plan on dressing a little bit more appropriately now that I'm here." Orpheus's cruel comment cut through Pan's recollection, and he surprised himself by just how much deeper his rage could get. Eurydice had always found freedom in dressing in shorter tunics, those favored by children or young men, and Pan couldn't think of anything that mattered less.

Who cares what she wears? Pan snorted before quickly covering his mouth in an attempt to keep his hiding spot from being discovered. *Besides, Orpheus is a damn fool. You want to deprive yourself of staring at Eurydice's legs all day?* Even though no one could read his thoughts, Pan blushed nonetheless as he peered through the leaves and dared get another glimpse of Eurydice.

She looked uncomfortable walking next to Orpheus, her steps unsure and her expression unsatisfied. Pan ached for her, and a deep need arose in him to make her smile. She was wearing her customary shorter tunic, and Pan nearly lost himself in visions of her lithe shape, dreaming of what she looked like when she allowed flowers and vines to twist up her ankles like jewelry.

"What do you mean by that?" Eurydice turned to Orpheus, the hurt written plainly across her face. Pan wanted Orpheus's blood.

"Well, you're dressed like a child, Eurydice. It's not fitting for either of us, especially considering how many eyes are going to be on us for a while. We're the hottest thing to happen in the Underworld since... I don't know. Regardless, it wouldn't hurt for you to clean up a little."

Orpheus sounded bored, as if there was anything he'd rather be doing than walking with the lost love of his life. Pan shifted his weight from one foot to the other, reaching the edge of his limit as he watched Orpheus criticize Eurydice. He forced himself to stop following Eurydice and Orpheus for a minute, closing his eyes and breathing slowly. If he listened to Orpheus for another second, there was a very real possibility that he was going to emerge from the forest like a wild, unhinged satyr and snap Orpheus's neck.

Pan's wild streak was as synonymous with his presence as his satyr form; he struggled with keeping his temper out of the common lore that surrounded him. It would only frighten his human worshippers if they knew how frequently Pan might be pushed to horrendous fury with an angry streak that could only be matched by Ares or Hephaestus. Unlike the other gods, Pan's anger was only ever triggered in defense of those he loved—the nymphs, the dryads, the forests themselves, and of course, Eurydice. If an overzealous farmer cleared out too many of Pan's trees, his vengeance would know no bounds. Now that Orpheus was hellbent on rewriting his story with Eurydice and guilting her in the process... Pan needed to get his heartbeat under control.

Once Pan was able to open his eyes and not see red, he slowly crept through the underbrush and caught up to Orpheus and Eurydice. They entered the small clearing where

Eurydice had been living, and Orpheus's critique pushed Pan to the edge in record time.

"Is this trivial shed where you've been living? I've seen more impressive stables. No matter. Grab what you need, Eurydice, and let's get out of here."

Pan picked up the pace and jogged around to the back of Eurydice's home, slipping through the backdoor. He heard one set of footsteps enter through the front, assuming that Orpheus was waiting behind in the clearing.

What sort of husband doesn't want to see where his wife has been living for forty years? Pan forced himself to take another slow breath, slowly poking his head into the main room of the dwelling.

Eurydice was furiously wiping at her eyes, which were red with unshed tears. Pan watched for a moment while she put her hair up, released it, then put it up again, as if she was undecided on how to wear her own hair. She looked uncomfortable in her home, Orpheus's comments clearly making her feel judged and nervous. There was a fleeting expression of anger that flickered in her eyes, and Pan could practically see the furious debate Eurydice was having with herself.

"Eurydice?" Pan whispered, peeking into the doorway. "Are you packing?"

Eurydice jolted and turned towards Pan, her eyes widening in surprise before breaking into a wide smile. Relief blanketed her expression, and her response to Pan's presence further twisted the knife in his chest.

"Pan," Eurydice exhaled heavily in comfort, "what are you doing here?" Eurydice crossed the space of the small dwelling and threw her hands around his neck, pulling him in for a tight hug. Pan couldn't help himself from grabbing her tightly, as if he could pour all the unspoken love he had for her into one embrace. Everything about holding Eurydice in his arms felt *right*, and when she pulled away, his heart broke all over again.

"I heard that you were moving closer to the other souls in Asphodel, wherever Orpheus will be living," Pan tucked a piece of Eurydice's hair behind her ear, "and I wanted to come see you off." Eurydice panicked slightly, her hand flying out to grip Pan's bicep.

"Will you not come see me anymore?" The terrified look in her eyes made Pan want to carve his own horns off if he could alleviate her distress.

"Of course I will." He put on a huge, warm smile for her benefit. "Don't be ridiculous, Eurydice. I'm limited to the forests of the Underworld, though. You know this. It's the only place Hades will allow me to return to freely, but I'll sneak anywhere to see you."

"As if you could keep me from the trees," Eurydice sighed happily. She turned around and took inventory of the room, tossing a few small keepsakes of flower stems and ribbons into a bag. "I wouldn't move out of here, honestly, but it's only fair to give this a chance."

Pan didn't know if she was talking about living with Orpheus or giving Orpheus himself a chance, but he bit his tongue. He knew he wouldn't be able to keep from telling her the truth if they started talking about her relationship with Orpheus, and Pan wasn't capable of giving her unbiased advice.

Eurydice moved around the room, her feet barely touching the ground as she practically floated through the bare earth home. Pan had helped her build it, adding vines and blooming flowers into the thatched roof so she'd always be surrounded by nature.

It'll physically hurt her to be away from the forest... Pan thought to himself as he watched Eurydice. *Does Orpheus even know that? Does he care?*

Eurydice stopped in front of a wall of ivy, which Pan had spent an entire afternoon helping her build indoors. The wooden grate which supported the vines was hand carved, with Pan refusing to use his magic but insisting on doing it himself.

"Will you take this?" Eurydice indicated towards the trellis. "I hate the thought of it sitting here without anyone to enjoy it. You worked so hard on it." Eurydice's eyes were sad as she stared at it. A surge of pride ran through Pan as he realized how much Eurydice loved something he made.

"How about this," Pan offered, stepping closer to her, "I'll move it for you. Find a place in your new home or garden for it, and I'll bring it there."

"Oh, will you?" Eurydice turned to him, her face lighting up. "I'd hate to leave it behind."

"Of course." Pan smiled at her, grabbing her hand and giving it a squeeze. "I'll bring you some clippings too so you can regrow the vines."

Eurydice's smile widened even further. "That would be amazing if you could—"

"Eurydice!" Orpheus shouted impatiently. Pan could hear him pacing out in the clearing. "How many things could you possibly have in there?"

Eurydice flushed with embarrassment, turning away from Pan. "I'm sorry about that," she whispered, only speaking to Pan. "I think he's still adjusting, you know? It's going to take some time for us to... I don't know... mesh."

"Don't worry about it." Pan waved it off. Everything in him was shouting to tell Eurydice to leave Orpheus behind and don't look back, but he knew she was confused and overwhelmed by the reunion. She didn't need another opinion telling her what to do with her relationships. Eurydice was a strong woman; she'd figure it out.

She doesn't know all her options, part of Pan's heart chimed in. *She doesn't know how you feel about her.* Pan throttled the notion and watched as Eurydice exhaled in relief at Pan's response, clearly pleased he wasn't judging her or Orpheus. Externally, at least.

"I should get going." Eurydice pointed towards the door, throwing her small bag over her shoulder. "I'll see you later, all right?"

"You always know where to find me." Pan winked, leaning against the wall and snapping his fingers, causing the trellis to vanish. "Let me know where you want it, and it'll reappear there."

"What would I do without you?" Eurydice giggled happily, hugging Pan tightly. She released him before he was able to return the gesture, turning on her heel and running out of the house without looking back. Pan forced himself to exit through the back door, unable to listen to Orpheus bark any more commands at Eurydice. He disappeared through the trees, praying the sweet smell of Eurydice's hair wouldn't ever leave his senses.

9

Pan sought out Persephone again, and they continued drinking, drowning Pan's sorrows in a never-ending amphora of wine. Pan appreciated many things about Persephone but her willingness to abandon the rest of her daily schedule for his pity party was one of his favorites.

By the time the soft, early rays of the sun were peeking through the high windows, Pan and Persephone were slumped over a pile of cushions, empty goblets scattered on the ground around them. Several nymphs had drifted in and out over the course of the night, which was typical to expect any time Pan was drinking, picking up their own goblets and delivering snacks to the now drunken duo.

Persephone slowly pushed herself up to a sitting position, pushing some of her mussed hair off her forehead. She narrowed her eyes as she blinked against the sunrise.

"Holy shit," Persephone hissed, "why is it so bright? This is the fucking Underworld."

"I don't k-know." Pan hiccuped, rolling over onto his back and kicking his legs out. "You're the one who is in charge here."

"I'm a figurehead."

"Bullshit," Pan scoffed, pressing his hands to his forehead and rubbing small circles around his temples. "I thought wine in the Underworld didn't come with a hangover." Pan looked at Persephone with an accusatory glance, but she rolled her eyes.

"That's something Hecate does to the wine."

"Remind me again why we didn't invite her?"

"I think we did, a couple hours ago." Persephone lay back down and snapped her fingers, turning the amphora of wine into water and downing several cups in rapid succession. Pan's melancholy slowly trickled through his veins, mixing with the throbbing ache of the hangover dancing between his ears.

Persephone and Pan sat in silence, trying to finish off as much water as they could in a meager attempt to rid themselves of their headaches.

"Hecate," Persephone shouted towards the ceiling. Pan immediately grimaced and covered his ears with his hands, groaning at the sudden noise.

"What the hell?" Pan snapped, and Persephone shrugged.

"Do you want help with your hangover or not?" Persephone raised an eyebrow, setting down her cup and crossing her arms over her chest. Pan opened his mouth to respond, but before he could get a word out, a dark red cloud appeared in the center of the great room. It started to swirl around in concentric circles, the crimson magic sparkling in the air, picking up speed until it became thick and opaque. There was a sudden burst, and Hecate stepped out of the pillar of smoke.

It was impossible to not look upon Hecate and be a little bit afraid. Pan had always assumed that was part of her charm. The goddess of witchcraft was a permanent resident of the Underworld, and while she often did her own thing, only Persephone was able to summon her just by yelling out Hecate's name into the ether.

May the gods bless if a man *ever tried to get Hecate's attention that way.* Pan shuddered at the thought.

Hecate started laughing as she took in the scene in front of her, grabbing the hem of her purple chiton as she stepped over several empty plates and cups. "I do think this is the first time I've ever seen Pan, of all people, hungover." Hecate conjured a mortar and pestle out of thin air and began pounding an unidentifiable mix of herbs while standing over the hungover deities.

"Excuse y-you," Pan hiccuped, pushing himself up to a sitting position. "I've been hungover before. It simply doesn't happen very often when you're a god of the wild. Only Dionysus himself is supernaturally protected against hangovers."

"I'll keep that in mind." Hecate grinned, leaning down and picking up two empty goblets off the floor. "Persephone, whatever did you do to this poor man?"

"Oh, don't blame me," Persephone scoffed, standing to her full height and wiping at a stain on her skirts. "And he only looks like a man right now."

"I didn't think you'd want hoof marks on your pretty floors," Pan deadpanned.

"Hades is the neat freak, not me. It's not like we can't conjure it away."

Hecate was shaking her head as she filled up two cups with the mystery mixture, looking around at the piles of cushions and dishes all over the great room.

"I've got something for that too if you need to clean up in here before Hades sees it."

Persephone grabbed at one of the cups that Hecate was extending towards them. Persephone downed it in one go, coughing slightly and tossing the empty cup over her shoulder once she was done. "I said that Hades was the neat freak, not that I was afraid of him."

"Leave me out of it," Pan grunted, "and thank you, goddess." He held up his cup in a salute before following Persephone in throwing it down in one sip, pleasantly surprised by the minty burn of whatever Hecate had concocted. It spread throughout his body and chased away the dull, pounding sensation of his hangover before he could get another word out.

"Goodness," Pan looked at the empty cup in amazement before turning his gaze to Hecate. "You could bottle this and sell it to gods and man alike. You'd make a fortune."

Hecate shook her head. "Witchcraft is never for sale, Pan. Be cautious of anyone pretending to tell you—or sell you— anything different."

"Understood." Pan dipped his head in reverence before sighing heavily and tying some of his hair back. He looked around the room and tried to piece together the events of the past night.

Persephone had stayed with him throughout the night. Pan couldn't keep his mind off the fact that Orpheus and Eurydice were most likely spending their night...*reuniting*...and Persephone got him drunker and drunker until he very literally couldn't keep his mind on anything. He was momentarily distracted from slipping down into an abyss of overthinking when the doors to the receiving hall were thrown open.

Everyone in the room jumped at the intrusion, freezing in place and looking around at the mess that they'd yet to tidy up as Hades stepped into the room.

"Shit." Pan blushed crimson and ducked behind Persephone, which he always considered the safest place when confronted with an angry Hades. Hades didn't take a single step into the room, merely raising an eyebrow and looking around at the chaos with a completely stoic expression.

"Well," Hecate smiled and clapped her hands together, "that seems like it's my cue to leave. Aeëtes is due back any minute now from a visit to his parents'. Pan, Persephone," she turned to them with a wink, "you know where to find me if you get in any more trouble."

Before Pan could even beg Hecate to stay and help keep

him from Hades's wrath for trashing the throne room, she disappeared on a cloud of red smoke.

"Hades." Persephone was grinning as if nothing was amiss. "Lover. How are you this fine morning?" She crossed the room with the grace of someone who had not been singing inappropriate sailor's rhymes at four in the morning while rose vines appeared in her hair and braided it for her as she walked.

Hades was dressed in formal attire—an elaborate, gold-trimmed himation pinned over his usual black chlamys. His brooch that morning was a large diamond, matching the circlet that sat on his brow, pinning some of his long, curly hair out of his face.

"We have an audience this morning, *beloved*," Hades grunted, looking past his wife and pinning his gaze on Pan. "It's probably good that you're here, Pan."

Pan paled and tried to stand up even straighter, nodding his head in what he hoped was a very polite, normal manner and not the demented, erratic way he felt.

There's no way that means anything good.

Hades took one step into the throne room, revealing the backlit silhouette of a man behind him. Pan's entire body tensed as the man walked forward, stepping into the light of the rising sun. He picked up his head, revealing his face to the small audience, and Pan's heavy heart was lit on fire with rage.

Orpheus stood at the entrance to the throne room, a smug, contrite expression on his face. Pan could hardly hear Persephone as she started yelling at both Hades and Orpheus. Memories started playing out in his head like a wicked tide he couldn't stop from crashing over him—memories of the last time he saw Orpheus in this hall, begging Hades for an opportunity to bring Eurydice back from the dead with him. The sick feeling in Pan's stomach, momentarily abated thanks to Hecate's magic, surged within him until Pan was dizzy on his feet.

He blinked rapidly and forced himself to turn away,

walking back towards the windows. He reached out and gripped the wall in support, trying to calm his racing heart as he looked out to the now empty banks of the Styx. Pan focused on his breathing, reminding himself that there was nothing he could do to Orpheus.

Think of how it would affect Eurydice… It would break her heart if anything happened to the poet. That's what you need to remember… Only a horrible friend would wish ill on their best friend's lover.

With Eurydice's heart at the forefront of his mind, only then was Pan able to push back the crippling ache in his bones. He turned around and faced the great room, turning where Hades and Persephone were now seated on their thrones. Persephone looked furious, unable or unwilling to keep the ire off her face as she squared off with Orpheus. Hades was as stoic as ever, the world's undeniable champion at keeping his cards close to his chest.

"Pan," Hades nodded once in acknowledgement. "Orpheus has requested a meeting with me here today to discuss his return to the Underworld."

Pan crossed his arms over his chest and refused to look at Orpheus.

"Hasn't he already come to this room and sought out a bargain with you once?" Pan quipped.

"I come seeking no bargains!" Orpheus hissed, pointing his finger at Pan.

"You haven't even been in the Underworld a full day yet," Pan growled, his voice dropping lower while his horns flickered and reappeared on his head, his fingers elongating into claws, "and you've already abandoned Eurydice. People can say whatever they want about you, but at least you're consistent."

"How dare you, beast," Orpheus cried, "and gods forbid I leave a grown woman alone for a few hours."

"She's a nymph, not a woman," Pan shouted. "Eurydice was always too much for you." Pan spun on his heel and make sure she doesn't remember your betrayal so she won't leave you."

"It doesn't matter!" Orpheus roared. "All that matters is you are not allowed to tell her."

Pan looked towards Hades and Persephone, who both looked at Orpheus with distaste and anger written all over their faces. After a few tense moments, Hades stood, dark smoke curling around his body as his bident manifested in his grip.

"The laws of the Underworld are as solid as the stone this kingdom has been built upon," Hades sighed heavily, his voice resounding off the obsidian walls. "If Eurydice chose to drink the waters from Lethe, my hands are tied. No one is allowed to remind someone of what they have chosen to forget."

"Thank you." Orpheus gave a grandiose bow. "You are the wisest of the gods, Hades."

Pan opened his mouth to protest, but Hades sneered at Orpheus and stepped off the dais.

"Do not thank me, Apollo's favored one. You would do well to remember that your immortal patron was vanquished. There is no support for you among the gods. The rules of Lethe were put in place to protect those who wished to forget horrors done to them, to protect victims and the innocent. They were not written into stone in order to protect perpetrators."

Hades's voice was gravel as he advanced upon Orpheus, forcing him to step backwards until his back was against the wall. Hades growled angrily and pinned Orpheus to the wall with a quick movement, his bident making a cracking sound as he shoved it past Orpheus's head.

"Listen to me," Hades snarled, his power crackling tangibly in the air. "I am bound by the laws of Lethe as much as anyone else in the Underworld. By law, no one will tell Eurydice what she has forgotten, including Pan." Hades spared a quick glance at Pan, whose hands tensed into fists at his side. "But know this, Orpheus. You have no sway with me. You will find no sympathy for you here. Consider me very *personally* invested in Eurydice's happiness, as a resident of my realm. Is that clear?"

Orpheus's eyes were wide as he nodded his head rapidly, terror etched into his features. "Y-yes, great Hades. I u-understand."

Hades dropped his bident and freed Orpheus, jerking his head in the direction towards the door. "Get out of my house. That's twice you've come to make requests of me, poet, and I won't take kindly to a third."

Orpheus sprinted out of the receiving room as quickly as his two legs could carry him, not bothering to say another word to Hades, Persephone, or Pan. Hades turned towards Pan, a rare display of sympathy etched across his features.

"I'm bound by my own laws, Pan." Hades walked back towards his own throne. "No one can tell Eurydice what she has chosen to forget."

Pan was lightheaded, staring down the empty hallway where Orpheus had disappeared to, suddenly desperate to get out of the Underworld. Persephone stood and held her hands out towards Pan, as if to comfort him, but he shook his head.

"I need to get out of here for a while," Pan muttered by way of goodbye, slipping out of the great doors and making his way to Greece as quickly as he could.

II

10

Eurydice hated Orpheus's home. It was too large for her taste, mimicking some of the estates he had lived in in Greece, and there was a dreadful lack of trees, which was her number one complaint about most locations.

Unlike some stories told by priests and parents, homesteads in the Underworld were not provided based on a sliding scale of morality. Wherever someone ended up in the afterlife was entirely dependent on their comfort. Some souls refused to even become corporeal; others spent their days in the same body they lived their mortal life in. Aside from the greater estates owned by the gods—with the exception of Hecate, who also preferred a smaller, cozier home—the lands of the Underworld were dotted with everything from coastal cottages to sprawling manors.

The first time Eurydice laid eyes on Orpheus's property, she viscerally fought to keep her initial reaction to herself. It was a near replica of the palace he'd passed away in, without the sprawling grounds. She forced herself to put on a wide smile and act pleased.

In the following few days, Orpheus and Eurydice fell into an awkward rhythm, something that disturbed Orpheus more than Eurydice. She was more used to her days consisting of slower paced activities, rendezvous with her friends, and spending time growing in one of her many gardens. Orpheus was having a more difficult time adjusting to the slower pace of the Underworld. He missed the endless parade of admirers he was accustomed to in the mortal world.

Eurydice was more comfortable in the silence between them, finding that any attempts at conversation always ended up with even more of an apparent divide. She'd only been living in his house for a few days, but she insisted on her own bedroom, another thing that she could tell was infuriating Orpheus. Jumping right back into a marriage she had no recollection of, sharing that sort of physical intimacy with Orpheus without her heart being in it, could only be disastrous.

Eurydice was out in the garden, the only part of the house she didn't despise. The late afternoon sun was pouring in over the tall walls, creating an effective barrier between Eurydice and the rest of the world. If she was going to be living in this more populated part of Asphodel, she appreciated the little bit of privacy the garden gave her.

The garden was tucked into an interior courtyard surrounded by a peristyle. There was a dirt trail running up the middle, flanked by beds of flowers on either side. The very center of the garden had a fountain, carved with a likeness of Apollo. Eurydice had half a mind to break off the top of the fountain and bury the statue. Apollo and Orpheus split ways from each other years before Orpheus died—and Apollo met his end years before Orpheus did—but Orpheus still had a bizarre obsession with the deity.

Eurydice ignored the numerous benches and opted to sit in the flower beds, relishing the feel of the cool grass and dirt on her skin. It was one of the first times since Orpheus's arrival that Eurydice felt genuine peace. Her gaze flickered towards the far wall of the garden and her beloved trellis. The vines, with a little bit of magical encouragement, were already fully intact and climbing up the stone. Eurydice thought of the hours Pan had spent hand-carving it for her, and her smile widened.

"Are you thinking about Orpheus?" A soft, dainty voice trickled through the air and snagged Eurydice's attention.

"Telodice?" Eurydice turned around without standing, watching in glee as Telodice appeared in the garden. A column of yellow smoke started evaporating from a patch of daisies, and one of the flowers stretched taller. A flurry of petals fell down from the skies as the flower morphed into the shape of a woman, and Telodice gracefully stepped out of the flower bed.

"Eurydice!" Telodice grinned, holding her arms out for her friend. Eurydice jumped to her feet and ran towards Telodice, practically launching herself into the nymph's arms. She hadn't seen Telodice since the day of Orpheus's arrival and was desperate to speak to one of her friends. Eurydice released Telodice and smiled.

"This place is beautiful!" Telodice looked around.

Eurydice nodded her head bashfully. "It's certainly something."

"Oh, come on." Telodice gawked, stepping around some of the ornate flower beds. "Who doesn't want to live in a house like this?"

"It's beautiful like you said," Eurydice agreed easily while avoiding the question. "What brings you here?" Eurydice followed Telodice and settled next to her on a marble bench.

"Well, it's been a week since you were reunited with Orpheus," Telodice waggled her eyebrows with a salacious expression, "so I figured it was safe to pop in for a visit."

Eurydice's eyes widened, and she wasn't able to hide the way her gaze flicked away from Telodice. A nervous feeling started building in her body, and her palms started to sweat.

I haven't even let Orpheus hug me for too long.

It was perfectly normal for her best friend to assume that

reuniting with her long-lost husband meant a week between the sheets, but Eurydice had nothing to report. Telodice leaned forward, sobering at Eurydice's reaction.

"Do you mean that you... You two certainly... Is there something you want to tell me?" Telodice put her hand on Eurydice's shoulder. Eurydice sighed heavily and turned away, pointlessly trying to hide her reaction from Telodice.

"Well, it's been a little awkward, you know?" Eurydice muttered, unable to meet Telodice's gaze. "I don't remember anything about him. I only know that we were a couple, so jumping back into a relationship like *nothing* happened is difficult."

Telodice looked stunned, her mouth dropping open. She turned to look at the entrance to the house as if she expected Orpheus to appear at the mention of his name.

"I mean, girl, who says you need to be in love with him to sleep with him?" Telodice chuckled awkwardly. It was written all over her face that Telodice had no idea what Eurydice was talking about. "That man is beautiful. It doesn't get more attractive than Apollo-blessed."

The first thing that popped into Eurydice's mind was Pan's face—the rugged wildness of his features, a slightly crooked nose that had been broken in drunken brawls, dark brown eyes...

Oh my gods. Eurydice's nervousness increased as realization dawned over her. *You cannot start thinking about your best friend when Telodice is trying to talk to you about Orpheus!*

"Yes..." Eurydice nodded slowly. "He is attractive, but I don't necessarily want to jump in bed with someone only because they're attractive."

Telodice nodded slowly as if she didn't fully understand what Eurydice was saying, a patronizing look on her face.

"That's true." Telodice looked around awkwardly. Her face lit up when she saw some of the flower beds, walking over to the gardens. "Tell me about these!" Telodice bent at the waist and smelled some of the blooms. "They're positively gorgeous."

Eurydice inwardly sighed in relief, grateful for the subject change, no matter how awkward it might be. Her heart lifted at the sight of her precious blooms. Eurydice's face flushed as she leaned down next to Telodice, a wider smile on her face. If there was one thing she could talk about, it was her garden.

"These are peonies and that is sage." Eurydice pointed out each delicate blossom, Telodice's face equally thrilled. For the next ten minutes, Eurydice was lost in the ancient pleasure of sharing her excitement over something with a loved one. It was one of the world's oldest sacred moments, for even Prometheus shared fire. Eventually, Eurydice led Telodice over to her favorite corner of the garden where Pan's trellis was safety tucked against the garden wall.

"Pan made this for you?" Telodice's eyes widened as she evaluated the delicate carvings and the intricate craftsmanship. "I didn't think Pan was capable of anything other than drunken destruction." Telodice scoffed, her head full of memories of the infamous god of the wild running through vineyards and forests drunk off wine and ambrosia.

"He's not always like that," Eurydice defended him sharply. "I mean, he's like that a lot," a smile crept across her face, "but he's fun. He reminds us all what it means to be wild, you know? Children of the forest…" Eurydice broke off when she realized Telodice was staring at her with a confused expression on her face. Her brow picked up as Eurydice carried on about Pan's attributes.

"Anyway," Eurydice coughed sharply, "these are crocus blooms. I'm hoping for a little more rain, and they'll bloom gorgeously."

Telodice dropped back into the conversation without another word, and Pan wasn't mentioned again. Eurydice was laughing at something Telodice said, her hair falling out of its braid and her cheeks covered with emerging freckles when Orpheus's voice echoed through the courtyard.

"Eurydice? Are you out here again?" A chill went down Eurydice's spine, and she noticed the speed at which her good mood vanished—as if a dark cloud had suddenly come up over her sunny afternoon. Telodice picked her head up and spun around, eager for a glimpse of the hero.

Orpheus was standing in the doorway to the main house, his toga gleaming in the bright afternoon sun. It was trimmed in gold, with elaborate patterns stitched into the border and decorated with pearls. Eurydice fought the temptation to roll her eyes.

I hate that ridiculous chiton. He looks like a child pretending to be Apollo in a school play.

Orpheus took one step into the garden, holding his hand up to see better. His bright yellow curls were practically cherubic, and Eurydice thought she heard Telodice audibly sigh. She looked at her friend, who had her hands clutched over her heart. Eurydice did roll her eyes a little bit at that.

Everything about Orpheus looked like he was truly Apollo-blessed, but his svelte stature cast a damning shadow over the garden path. Eurydice couldn't help but notice that he wasn't as strong as Pan... Pan was broad, thick, and covered in hair. Orpheus looked eternally like a young model for the sculptors—nearly hairless, tall, and lithe.

Oh, for fuck's sake! Eurydice shook herself out of her reverie, damning herself for thinking of Pan's body—her friend, of all people—when Orpheus stepped into the light.

"Eurydice!" Orpheus called out again, his voice notably tenser.

"Come and join us, my love!" Eurydice forced herself to sound cheery, cringing at the awkward high pitch that overtook her voice. She waved Orpheus over, but her heart fell when he shook his head. He tilted his head to the left, motioning for her to go to him.

"Can I speak to you privately, please, Eurydice?" Orpheus snapped.

Eurydice quickly spared a glance at Telodice, horrified to see the surprise and disgust on her face. Orpheus was being completely ignorant of the fact there was a guest standing in their garden and was snapping at Eurydice like she was a dog trained to heel.

"Now!"

"I'm coming, Orpheus," Eurydice shouted, quickly turning to Telodice. "Will you give me just a moment? He's been stressed recently. Forgive him. I think adjusting to the Underworld has been difficult."

Relief and understanding flooded Telodice's face, and she nodded rapidly. "Oh, of *course.*" Her voice was sickly sweet. "I understand that. It's difficult for everyone. I'll wait here. You go to him."

Eurydice gave Telodice a tight smile and started walking briskly towards her husband, growing more irate with each step.

It's wild how the world is so quick to forgive men for their tempers, but may the gods forbid a woman ever has a bad day.

Orpheus was tapping his foot repeatedly as Eurydice approached him and she attempted a placating expression.

"Are you not feeling well, husband?" Eurydice couldn't avoid the tense way she spit out the word 'husband'. Orpheus practically grunted at Eurydice, refusing to look at her as he studied Telodice in the garden.

"What is *she* doing here?" Orpheus's voice was full of contempt. It dripped with a hatred that shocked Eurydice. She had no idea why he would be upset at Telodice's visit.

"Telodice? She's my friend. I was showing her the garden. You've had an endless string of guests ever since I moved in. I didn't think it would be a problem for her to visit. She's not even inside."

Orpheus groaned dramatically, crossing her arms over his

chest. More bitterness took root in Eurydice's chest as Orpheus's expression twisted until it looked like this was the most annoying conversation he'd ever been a part of.

"I invited those guests, Eurydice, not you. I don't know who that nymph is. Her..." Orpheus stuttered for the right word. "Her energy is all over the house. It's messing with my process. I haven't been able to write a stanza since I arrived. You know everyone's expecting me to come out with new compositions."

Eurydice forced herself to swallow her pride, shame, and embarrassment starting to build at the base of her spine. "Do you not even want to meet my friends, Orpheus? I was showing her the garden."

Eurydice's eyes brightened as she implored her husband to see how happy the project made her, beginning to speak faster as she sought out a way to bring them closer together.

"There is a whole wall of crocuses in the back and some wonderful poppy blooms that I think you'll love! Why don't we take a walk through the garden now, together? That might inspire you. You can meet Telodice and..."

"Eurydice, *please,*" Orpheus groaned, rubbing his hand over his eyes. "I don't want to see the flowers," he snapped, the last of the kindness leeching from his tone. "I want you to send Telodice home. Now."

Eurydice's heart cracked in her chest. All of a sudden, she felt like a child again, scolded by her parents. The casual way that Orpheus tossed aside her passions and an opportunity to share something—share anything!—together, tossed her further down the spiral she'd found herself in. A deep, swirling pit of shame and embarrassment started manifesting throughout her body, giving her the chills.

Of course Orpheus wouldn't be interested in the flowers. He's a famous poet. He's Orpheus. You can't expect him to care about the little things that make you excited. Eurydice's internal monologue started to sound like Orpheus's tenor voice. *You've got to grow up sometime and be a wife, Eurydice. It's time to put childish things away.*

"You're right," Eurydice sighed. "I'm sorry, Orpheus. I'll tell Telodice to leave, and I'll join you inside if you're not feeling well."

"Don't do that," Orpheus groaned exasperatedly. "Now you look like a kicked dog." He sighed heavily, running a hand through his hair. Eurydice said nothing as he wrapped an arm around her waist and tugged Eurydice closer to his body.

"I'm sorry, my love, my wife, my morning star..." Orpheus sing-songed, pressing a series of quick kisses to her cheeks and nose. "I just want you all to myself sometimes. I've spent my entire life dreaming of you again, and sometimes I can't bear to share you."

Eurydice melted, some of Orpheus's words striking at the armor around her soul. *He's not perfect, but he's a good man, Eurydice, you know this.*

"It's okay. I forgive you." Eurydice gave Orpheus a soft smile. In return, Orpheus groped at Eurydice, squeezing her ass quickly before releasing her when she squeaked.

"Now, go let Telodice know that it's not a good time for guests. Then, come inside and meet me in the great room," Orpheus waggled his eyebrows, "and maybe you can *inspire* me a bit." The innuendo was clear, and Eurydice cringed internally. Orpheus disappeared inside the house before she could respond properly, leaving her standing alone on the balcony.

You'll find your footing together eventually. It's going to take time. You don't even remember being married, and you've spent forty years doing whatever you want, single and careful. There will be an adjustment period. Eurydice tried to convince herself the awkwardness between her and Orpheus and his attitude were merely symptoms of a sudden reunion after years apart — and not indicative of something more.

Telodice was waiting patiently on a garden bench, standing

up and grinning when Eurydice approached her. She smirked, shimmying a little with a playful expression.

"Let me guess, do you two lovebirds need me to get lost?"

"Oh, um, yes," Eurydice stuttered. "Orpheus isn't feeling very well and is worried about something he needs to compose, so…"

"You don't need to tell me twice!" Telodice laughed, throwing her hands up in the air. "You don't need to give me any excuses either. If you need to go get bent over the back of a couch, then do it, Eurydice!" Telodice laughed harder, and Eurydice fought the urge to gag.

"I'm sorry Orpheus wasn't very welcoming—"

"Don't even worry about it!" Telodice scoffed, a small whirlwind of petals picking up around her feet as her magic started to envelop her. "It's Orpheus," Telodice gushed. "He's so *perfect*, Eurydice. You do whatever you need to!"

Telodice vanished on the wind before Eurydice had time to respond, leaving her standing in the garden. She glanced over at the trellis with its crocus blooms, and her anguish started to boil into something more potent.

11

Eurydice crossed the garden, storming back into the house. Her sandals slapped against the polished marble floors, the sound mocking Eurydice with every step she took. Everything in the house repelled her, from its overly ornate trappings to the disgusting size of it all.

Orpheus was in the great room, waiting for her, with his chiton lazily undone at the shoulder. He was leaning against a divan of purple silk, and his relaxed posture was the only thing keeping him clothed. If he stood, his chiton would inevitably fall off. There was a barely corporeal shade standing behind the sofa, fanning Orpheus with a large leaf.

The massive atrium was covered in tapestries that told the story of Orpheus's adventures in Greece and every one infuriated Eurydice further. It was a reminder of the life she hadn't gotten in the mortal world—and while she had no complaints about her time in the Underworld, what loving husband decorated their marital home with accolades from their period of separation? A separation that Orpheus claimed was full of torment.

"Orpheus!" Eurydice hissed, startling the shade. The specter dropped the frond and disappeared. The sight of

Orpheus lounging like royalty caused all of Eurydice's frustrations to come boiling over to the surface. She had spent a week making excuses for Orpheus and trying to give him credit for adjusting to the Underworld, but his dismissal of her interests and refusal to meet Telodice was now setting her on edge.

"What is this?" Orpheus scowled, cracking one eye open. "I told you I wasn't feeling well, Eurydice. I'm worried about writing a new song for another party this evening..." Orpheus's hand dropped to his thigh, and he trailed it slowly back towards his navel, revealing most of his leg to her. "I thought you were going to come inspire me?"

"Can you genuinely think that I want to drop to my knees in front of you right now?" Eurydice hissed, thorns bursting through her skin as her anger manifested. Orpheus's eyes widened, and he sat up straighter, his hands scrambling to tie his chiton closed.

"What the hell, Eurydice? Where is this coming from?"

"Where is this *coming from?*" Eurydice growled. Vines burst through the marble tiles around her feet, winding their way up her legs. "You have been acting like an ass since you arrived, and I won't sign up for a life of this, Orpheus. I fucking won't. Do you hear me?"

Orpheus's expression darkened as his hands clenched into fists at his side. He jumped to his feet and took a few paces towards Eurydice before stopping himself short.

"I don't even know what you're talking about. You're the one who doesn't want anything to do with me! You won't even touch me, and now you're complaining we're not getting along? Who does that?"

"Excuse me for not wanting to spread my legs for you!" Eurydice stabbed a finger in Orpheus's chest. The thorns breaking her skin snagged on Orpheus's tunic and ripped it. "You've been boorish and rude to me since you arrived. I don't even remember who you are! This is hard for me." Eurydice forced the words out. It was a dangerous game to admit any vulnerabilities to Orpheus, but after only a week, she had reached a breaking point.

"How dare you say you don't know me!" Orpheus thundered, stomping his foot. He turned around and grabbed the nearest vase he could find, throwing it against the wall. Eurydice shrieked and covered her face with her arms as it exploded, sending shards of pottery all over the room. "Everyone knows me! Everyone knows of my grief *for you*. Even the rocks and the ghosts cried for you when you died!"

"But I did not!" Eurydice snapped. "This story—our precious, infamous story—is known by everyone, but I've already lost my memory of it. Do you understand how off-putting that is?" Orpheus's brow furrowed as he stared at Eurydice, the expression on his face turning into something that Eurydice couldn't place. He shook his head slowly, standing up to his full height and looking around the opulent room they were in.

Orpheus took a few steps towards the far wall, his gaze turning to one of the many tapestries that hung there. Eurydice followed his gaze, feeling queasy as she settled on the same one he was looking at. It was clearly a depiction of both Orpheus and Eurydice, but she couldn't remember it at all. They were huddled together in a clearing in the woods, with trees and rocks crying around the couple, as Orpheus wept over Eurydice's pale body. It made Eurydice's stomach turn.

"Do you see?" Orpheus didn't look at her, his eyes fixed on the tapestry. "Our love story is one for the ages. There is hardly a story in all of Greece that is more popular than ours." Eurydice's anger bubbled anew in her veins, and she found herself rubbing her temples, tempted to start tearing her hair out.

"This is what I'm talking about, Orpheus," she growled. "This is fucking confusing and off-putting to see. Who wants a larger-than-life depiction of their death hanging in their home? There're depictions of my dead body in every hallway and room in this damn house! Because it glorifies you and your fucking struggle. Well, I'm struggling now, Orpheus. And you're only making it worse." Eurydice's voice cracked at the end as she turned away from the grotesque imagery, wrapping her arms around herself and hugging tightly.

I wish Pan was here right now. Eurydice found herself wishing for one of his hugs, to feel the sensation of how safe she felt in his arms. He had always been one of her most steadfast companions and... Now, here she was, fighting with her husband and dreaming of her best friend.

No wonder your relationship isn't working. You're certainly not helping dreaming about your best friend during an argument.

"Eurydice..." Orpheus was right behind her now, and she felt his hand on her shoulder. She said nothing and allowed him to gently turn her around to face him. "I had no idea."

He did look rather miserable, as though this was a sudden realization to him. Eurydice sighed, feeling the weight of a thousand lifetimes instead of only one. How could you explain this to someone else?

"I'll have the art all changed throughout the house. I swear it. Will that make it better?"

"Oh, fuck the gods," Eurydice cursed, "it's not only about the artwork, Orpheus! Are you kidding me?"

Orpheus's face morphed again, immediately turning back to anger. His brow furrowed as his expression darkened, and a pang of fear trickled through Eurydice as she realized how quickly he switched moods on her.

"What the fuck do you want me to do then? How do you expect me to know what to do?" Orpheus growled, his grip on her arm tightened as he started to shake her. "You told me that the artwork bothered you. I can see that now. I'll take it all down. Now, that's what you want?"

"Let go of me," Eurydice hissed. The thorns stretched across her skin grew taller, pricking Orpheus's palm. He cursed and released her quickly, shying away from her.

"What do you want then?" Orpheus snapped, still staring at Eurydice like someone might look at an intruder they discovered halfway through robbing their home.

"The artwork is only a symptom of a bigger problem." Eurydice sighed, some of her anger turning into exhaustion. "I don't know how to explain that to you. You didn't even understand why it might be bizarre for someone to be surrounded by artwork, tapestries, and statues of their own death! It's all you write about, for god's sake. On top of that, you've been practically awful to me ever since you arrived. You didn't want to see Telodice; you haven't had a conversation with me about anything other than your own inspiration and fucking songwriting, and you want me to jump back into bed with you as if nothing happened."

Orpheus stopped for a moment, the air thick and oppressive between them. Eurydice was breathing hard, wondering if this was the right time to walk out of Orpheus's house once and for all, their legendary marriage be damned.

"I can see how none of this has been fair to you," Orpheus admitted quietly. Eurydice nearly fell to the ground in shock. The thorns and vines on her skin disappeared, and her mouth dropped open in surprise. The last thing she expected was Orpheus admitting that their relationship had had a power imbalance since the day he arrived in the Underworld.

Orpheus cleared his throat awkwardly and continued. "I put a lot of expectations on you after being obsessed with you for forty years. I remember all of our time together and you don't. I didn't stop to think about how differently seeing me again would affect you."

That's the problem, isn't it? Eurydice's thoughts were quick and biting, and they sounded remarkably like Pan. *You didn't think at all about your wife's fucking feelings.*

Eurydice said nothing and only nodded slowly, encouraging Orpheus to keep talking.

"I don't want to lose you, Eurydice. You're everything that

makes me who I am. I'm nothing without you, and I know that. I think that's why I've been so keen for our relationship to...go right back to the way it was. I don't know who Orpheus is without Eurydice."

Eurydice offered him a tight smile. "That's very kind of you to say, Orpheus, of course.., but it's not going to go back to the way it was. I don't remember hardly anything from our time together. You spent the last forty years thinking of us, constantly being reminded of us. I know that. You need to understand that isn't how I've been spending my time. This whole thing is like jumping into freezing water. I'm out of breath, trying to stay afloat."

"If you would just indulge me, I know that you would..."

"You don't know anything about me," Eurydice cut Orpheus off, holding up a hand. "I know that you think you do, but I've become another person over the past four decades. If this is going to work between us, you need to commit to getting to know me as I am now. This version of Eurydice," she pointed to herself, "not that version." Eurydice indicated to the tapestry on the wall. "Do you think you can do that?"

Orpheus said nothing for a few long minutes. He slowly looked around the room, taking in all the finery that had been woven together from his lifetime in the mortal world. Eurydice's heart was pounding in her chest, unsure of what she even wanted Orpheus's reaction to be.

Do I want him to say yes? Do I want to simply walk out of here as a single maiden again? Eurydice's thoughts frightened her when she realized part of her was hoping that Orpheus would agree it was better if they went in their own directions.

Finally, Orpheus broke the silence. He smiled warmly at Eurydice, even giving her a short bow.

"I understand, Eurydice, and I'll do everything in my power to woo you again. To help you remember. To be a husband that you're proud of. Would you do me the honor of attending a party with me tonight?"

"As your wife?" Eurydice raised a brow, skeptical of Orpheus's rapid mood swings.

"As my date," Orpheus beamed, clearly proud of himself, even though Eurydice needed to rake him over the coals to get him to understand.

You owe it to him and yourself to see this through, Eurydice reminded herself, forcing a small smile on her face.

"I'd be honored to attend tonight as your date, Orpheus."

"Wonderful!" Orpheus clapped his hands together before nearly jogging out of the room. "Wear something pretty tonight, my darling!" he called back over his shoulder, and Eurydice felt nauseous.

12

Eurydice brushed her hands down the edge of her chiton, smoothing out some of the pleats in the fabric. It wasn't a common choice for a party, and typically it wasn't a woman's fashion either, but Eurydice loved how it made her feel when she wore it. The drape of the fabric made her feel more powerful, which was something she gravitated towards when thinking about attending a party with Orpheus. She wanted to be a little more optimistic about the event, but she didn't care much for the friends that Orpheus had made in the Underworld. He rubbed elbows with the rest of the Underworld's 'elite', including Perseus, who was loathed by the chthonic gods and deities alike.

The dinner they were headed to that evening was held at none other than Perseus's home, another massive monstrosity that made Eurydice wonder why Hades even allowed it in his lands.

She was lost in her thoughts and attempting to boost her own morale for the evening when there was a subtle knock at the bedroom door. Orpheus and Eurydice had been living in separate bedrooms since she moved into the property, even though Eurydice knew that Orpheus was pushing for her to join him in his bed.

"Coming," Eurydice called out, cringing at the forced joy she heard in her tone. She crossed the bedroom and opened the door, finding Orpheus standing on the other side. He was dressed in an elaborate tunic with a brooch the size of a child's fist at his shoulder. It was a gilded lyre, studded with gemstones, and Eurydice couldn't help but mentally turn up her nose at it. She always preferred flowers or natural adornments to hard, cold jewels and metals.

"Is that what you're wearing?" Orpheus blurted out, his face morphing into a sneer as he studied Eurydice's outfit. Eurydice started grinding her teeth together.

"Yes, it is. Is that a problem for you? You can always go alone if you want to."

"No, no," Orpheus grunted. "Everyone is going to expect to see you by my side." Eurydice sighed heavily, the hesitation in her veins growing as she toyed with the idea of staying home instead.

"Do you even want me to come with you? Or do you want to be seen with me because otherwise people will ask questions?"

"That's not fair…"

"What did we just talk about this afternoon, Orpheus? This is what I want to wear. Do you want to go with me, as your date, or do you just want the infamous muse of Orpheus on your arm?"

Orpheus held his hands up in surrender. "You look lovely, Eurydice. Please." He offered her his arm. "I simply don't want anyone else to give you a hard time. You're not even dressed in a woman's garment."

Eurydice took a step back, raising an eyebrow and leaving Orpheus with his arm extended towards her in the air awkwardly. She flipped some of her hair over her shoulder, knowing how the fabric draped over her curves—even for a man's garment. Eurydice tightened the fabric at her shoulder, adjusting the neckline so her cleavage deepened.

"Do you really think anyone will mistake me for a man?"

"N-no," Orpheus stuttered. His eyes were transfixed on Eurydice's figure, and instead of feeling even more alluring or beautiful, Eurydice fought the temptation to roll her eyes at Orpheus's simplicity of character.

"Do you see what I'm talking about?" Eurydice deadpanned, adjusting the fabric and bringing up the neckline. "We can't even have a conversation without it turning into an argument." Eurydice bit her lip, turning her gaze out the window. She could see the forests of Asphodel in the distance. The trees were calling to her. "Maybe it's not the best idea for me to come with you tonight."

Orpheus looked frightened, stepping closer to Eurydice and inviting himself into the bedroom. "Please, come with me. I'm sorry. Really, I'm simply nervous. I don't know how to talk to you, it seems," Orpheus grinned sheepishly.

Eurydice couldn't help but feel her heart warm at the sight. Orpheus was excellent at always saying the right thing. He found a way to make it sound endearing that he had such horrible communication skills with his own wife.

"I'm not going to change," Eurydice challenged. She wasn't going to be dimmed by Orpheus's perception of her; that was a person that she had no desire to be. "If you want to be with me, if you want to try and make this work, you need to be with *me*. Not the version of me that you have created through song and stanza these past forty years."

Orpheus blushed, ducking his head slightly in embarrassment.

"I understand, Eurydice." He offered his arm to her one more time. "Would you do me the honor of coming to dinner with me this evening? My experience will always be better if I have you alongside me."

Eurydice tilted her head and studied him, reminding herself of her commitment to try to make this marriage work. *It's going to take some trial and error, isn't it?*

"I would love to." Eurydice slid her arm through Orpheus's and allowed him to escort her out of their home. The walk to dinner was a short one, several of the more grandiose mortal shades lived close to one another in the Underworld.

Eurydice could hear the party before she saw it, sounds of drunken revelry spilling out from the walled garden behind Perseus's massive estate. It was even grander than the home Eurydice was forced to live in, and the very sight of it made her want to scowl. The marble steps leading up to the front door were covered in drunken bodies, women and men alike, sipping from shared jugs and in various stages of undress. Orpheus didn't even react as he helped Eurydice navigate through the chaos, making Eurydice take note of his nonchalant reaction. *I suppose that's rather telling of the life he's been used to living.*

The scene inside Perseus's house was even worse. There were bodies crammed from wall to wall, and everything smelled like alcohol and sweat. Orpheus tugged on Eurydice's hand and dragged her to the dining hall, where the hallway opened up to a huge room that was open to the outdoors.

A long banquet table was set up, overflowing with an endless array of food and drink. There were no less than three suckling pigs over open fires and Eurydice counted a few nymphs there too.

Eurydice was no stranger to wild parties. She was a deity of the forest. Pan was her best friend, for the gods' sake. No one threw a party like the creatures of the wild with Dionysus as their leader. The difference was palpable, however, and Eurydice knew this was the kind of party were everyone was ready to take advantage of one another, something that was vastly different from the dinners she was used to attending.

"Orpheus!" A loud voice called out over the cacophony of

the hall. Eurydice turned her head and nearly spit in his face when she saw Perseus.

"My friend!" Orpheus laughed loudly, releasing Eurydice and opening his arms to embrace Perseus. The men embraced warmly, and Eurydice's stomach turned.

"I can see you have finally brought your pretty muse around." Perseus's expression was lecherous as he shamelessly ogled Eurydice. "Although it is an interesting choice of dress she's wearing. Do you intend to find a woman to take home for yourself dressed as a man, Eurydice?" Both Orpheus and Perseus broke out in exuberant laughter at that. Eurydice's stomach dropped as she watched Orpheus nearly double over with the strength of his laughter.

Why the fuck are we together?

"Who gives a fuck if I do take a woman home?" Eurydice tilted her chin up and looked down on Perseus. "It's not like we haven't all heard the rumors about you and Polydectes."

"All I ask," Orpheus grabbed a goblet of wine from a passing servant, "is that if you take a woman home, make sure I get to come too."

Perseus and Orpheus started laughing all over again, turning away from Eurydice and moving towards another group of drunken men. Eurydice didn't care to follow and didn't care to meet any more of Orpheus's friends.

This entire thing was a mistake, Eurydice thought to herself, slipping away into the crowd and finding a quiet corner of the room to hide in.

I wish Pan were here.

For the next hour, Eurydice mingled with a few of the nymphs and dryads that were in attendance, watching Orpheus from afar. He got drunker and drunker, mingling with men who shamelessly harassed and ogled other partygoers. Eurydice was getting ready to slip out of the back and meet up with Orpheus later when she noticed him making his way to a raised dais at the far end of the room. She knew what was coming as soon as he stepped up above the crowd, plucking a lyre from somewhere within the mass of bodies.

"Attention!" Perseus shouted, cupping his hands around his mouth and getting everyone to quiet down. "The illustrious Orpheus has decided to give us a song, ladies and gentlemen! Let's give him a hand."

The party exploded as people started cheering, holding their hands up in the air and exalting Orpheus as if he was one of their gods. It was the first time that Eurydice got to see firsthand what sort of fame Orpheus had gotten used to while he was alive. It was daunting; an entire dining hall full of drunks dropped everything, including some of their wine cups, to hear Orpheus.

When Orpheus looked out over the crowd, his expression softened. There was a glimmer of something in his eyes that Eurydice could see all the way from the corner of the room. It sparked a little bit of remembrance in her, reminding her of a simpler time.

That was the Orpheus she remembered, the one who sang to her under the trees and wrote poetry on scraps of paper.

Orpheus held up his hand, and the applause quieted. Everyone went silent. His eyes scanned the room until they landed on Eurydice. He smiled warmly, his attention entirely focused on her. Eurydice's heartbeat picked up, and a blush appeared on her cheeks. She wrapped her hands around herself as her stomach flipped. There was something heady and powerful about having all of Orpheus's attention in a crowded room; the way he looked at her made her feel like the only woman in the world.

Orpheus adjusted the lyre and pushed back some of his hair, taking in a deep breath and preparing to sing. When the first few notes came out of his mouth, Eurydice nearly fell in love all over again. He sounded the way that spring felt to

Eurydice. His singing reminded her of fresh flowers and fields drenched in sunlight. It was hypnotic.

"I would much prefer to see the lovely way she walks... and the radiant glance of her face...than the war chariots of the Lydians or their foot soldiers in a race..." Orpheus's words hung in the air, and Eurydice's heart softened. He continued to sing, and the entire crowd was raptured, not a single attendee walking away from the impromptu stage. No one even dared to breathe.

Orpheus finished, and the room exploded in applause once more. He held his hand out towards Eurydice, and she suddenly felt the weight of hundreds of pairs of eyes on her. Her heart jumped up into her throat; her blush deepened. Eurydice, through no fault of her own, was pulled toward the beautiful and wild things; she was a nymph, after all. When Orpheus sang, he was both beautiful and wild, and it was all that pulled her to him in the first place, all those years ago. She felt reckless and wild when he motioned for her to come up on the stage beside him, beckoning her, claiming her in front of the masses of people.

"Please, direct your warmth and applause to the love of my life, Eurydice. Without her, I would not exist. These songs would not exist. Give her your hands as she comes up on stage to join me."

Eurydice said nothing but smiled gracefully as she moved through the crowds, people parting to make a path for her towards the dais. Orpheus's hand was warm and soft as Eurydice slipped hers in his. He helped her step onto the dais and made room for her to stand beside him. Eurydice opened her mouth to address the room, planning on thanking them for the warm reception, but Orpheus seemed to sense her intention.

He quickly intercepted Eurydice, cupping her jaw with his hand and tilting her head towards him. Eurydice stiffened immediately, still unaccustomed to Orpheus's touch unless she initiated it. Luckily, he didn't kiss her on the mouth, but pressed a firm kiss to her cheek. The warm feeling in her chest disappeared, followed by a sinking feeling in her stomach.

I had no idea that a kiss could feel so much like a rebuke.

The crowd erupted anew at the sight of the affection between one of the Underworld's most famous couples. Eurydice realized what Orpheus was doing with shocking clarity. She was only welcomed up on the stage next to him as a showpiece, as a decoration. He only saw her as a way to boost his own fame, and he kissed her to keep her quiet and give the audience something to talk about.

In front of such a crowd, Eurydice said nothing, but the tumultuous buzzing in her head wouldn't stop. Her opinion about Orpheus changed every hour, and his behavior did too. Only minutes ago, she was won over once again with the memories of how it felt when he sang for her and her alone, but those days were long gone. Could she learn to love a man like this? Was it possible to reconcile this Orpheus with the one that she had very scant memories of?

Eurydice was lost again in the labyrinth of her thoughts, wishing there was someone who could tell her exactly what she was feeling so she didn't need to decode her own emotions.

Orpheus said something else to the crowd that Eurydice didn't catch, and then he launched into song again. Eurydice had no choice but to take another step back and watch Orpheus while she was now stuck up on the stage behind him like a tapestry.

"Your enticing laughter that indeed has stirred up the heart in my chest...For whenever I look at you even briefly, I can no longer say a single thing..." Orpheus crooned out over the audience, driving the watching crowd into a frenzy.

Eurydice spotted Perseus in the crowd, looking incredibly smug as he watched the stage and surveyed his own party.

He must be feeling very smug about this, Eurydice thought to herself. *His reputation will surely skyrocket now that he got Orpheus performing with me standing beside him.*

Eurydice sensed the thorns under her skin fidgeting and threatening to make an appearance.

Even the flowers in the wild were not objects only to be stared upon for their beauty. They fed the insects and strengthened the soil.

I am no mere flower, Orpheus, and I am not your object.

13

Eurydice lost track of the time as Orpheus serenaded the raucous party. She let her mind wander, completely disassociating from the chaos around her, blocking out each of Orpheus's lyrics. They all plucked at her heart strings, and she wasn't ready to reconcile how he made her feel as opposed to his actions. They were at odds with one another, and she wasn't going to try and decipher them in the middle of a party.

When Orpheus paused in between songs to grab some water, Eurydice took the opportunity to feign that she was going to look for the lady's room. She quickly stepped off the stage and disappeared into the crowd, barely listening as Orpheus dedicated another song to her and started up his set again.

Eurydice returned to her previous hiding place in the corner, grabbing a cup of wine for herself and watching the rest of the party unfold. A few people had begun to turn away from Orpheus and were sneaking off to dark corners or helping themselves to the banquet. Eurydice was debating a quick exit when there was a sudden pulse of power from beside her, the pressure in the atmosphere dropping drastically. Eurydice was too familiar with immortals not to recognize the telltale sign of their arrival, but the rest of the party didn't seem to have any idea what was going on. The ripple of magic echoed from beside her, making her shiver.

Eurydice turned around and bit back a little gasp of surprise, realizing none other than Hermes and Dionysus had arrived at Perseus's drunken house party.

"By the gods," Eurydice exhaled heavily. "This can't be *that* good of a party."

Hermes was smirking, leaning against the wall with a golden circlet adorning his blonde curls. He was wearing a short toga with shining sandals, with matching wings and straps that criss-crossed up to the knee.

"My darling muse," Hermes smiled, perpetually looking like he was keeping a secret, "every party gets better when we show up."

Dionysus's laughter boomed in agreement. "Besides," Dionysus's expression intensified, "my wine means my rules, and I don't trust a single one of these fools."

"Isn't it all your wine?" Eurydice asked gently.

"Exactly the point he's making, lovely," Hermes cooed. "Dionysus doesn't like it when men get too handsy and blame him for it."

"I don't like it when anyone gets too handsy and blames me for it," Dionysus added, crossing his arms over his broad chest. "Revelry and consent are not mutually exclusive."

Eurydice said nothing, still slightly in awe that she was face to face with Hermes and Dionysus. She was used to being around immortals, especially the Underworld gods, and Pan was a deity too, but there was a great difference in power between immortals and some of the major gods of the pantheon.

"He has a bit of a thing for castrating people." Hermes

waved his hand in the air like he was shooing a fly. "It's rather endearing, actually."

Dionysus only grumbled something in response, too low for Eurydice to hear, but Hermes started laughing in response. She knew it was rude, but she couldn't stop staring at Dionysus. *Was it rude, though?* Eurydice's thoughts started running wild. The gods thrive on attention and devotion.

Dionysus was nearly double Hermes's size, with a broad chest and wide shoulders. His chiton was a deep, dark purple, and his hair was black and streaked with gray. It hung down to his shoulders in elaborate curls. He didn't have a circlet or any other obvious identifier of his divinity, but his entire demeanor radiated immortality. His skin was ruddy and tanned from orgies and parties out in the sun and days spent in the grape fields, with warm lines by his eyes and mouth, which betrayed how much Dionysus laughed. As intimidating as he was, there was a warmth around him that Eurydice found herself drawn to. She knew Dionysus and Pan were very close, and that paternal feeling was rubbing off on her too.

"Are you not having a good time, friend of Pan?" Dionysus seemed to read Eurydice's thoughts, leaning toward her and lowering his voice. Hermes's brows shot up.

"You're not having a good time, are you?" Hermes echoed, as if this was a sudden realization for him. Eurydice sighed heavily and turned away from the gods, her eyes going to Orpheus on the stage. She must have been silent for a second too long because Dionysus and Hermes both nodded in understanding.

"Of course I'm having a good time." Eurydice almost visibly cringed at her feeble attempt to deny Hermes's accusation.

"I would know," Dionysus stared at Eurydice, "and you are not the picture of a party attendee who's enjoying themselves."

"Well," Eurydice balked under Dionysus's unwavering

glare, "it's been...difficult. Adjusting to being in a relationship again. That's all."

"Should we petition Eros on your behalf?" Hermes smirked, his brow raising slightly. There was nothing mocking in his words, but something in his tone made Eurydice blush with embarrassment. Hermes was Pan's father, after all, and he had a way of being incredibly protective over his son. Even, apparently, protecting his son from his own friends.

"It's normal, I'm sure. We've been through a lot that most couples will never even begin to understand."

Eurydice was cut off by a sudden barrage of exuberant screaming, getting everyone's attention. Perseus and Orpheus were in the center of a small crowd, aggressively chugging jugs of wine that were being poured directly into their mouths by lovely serving girls. Eurydice's stomach dropped at the sight, and the sick feeling of nausea returned.

"Bastards," Dionysus growled. "They didn't even let that wine breathe."

"I don't think this is the crowd to appreciate a good vintage," Hermes chuckled as he watched Dionysus's angry expression. "You are so pretty when you're mad though."

"Save it for Hercules," Dionysus grunted. Hermes turned his attention back to Eurydice.

"No one would blame you if you left him," Hermes suddenly blurted, jumping straight to the heart of the matter.

"What?!" Eurydice blanched, the color draining from her face as a few thorns exploded on her shoulders. "I mean... I couldn't... What would everyone say?"

"What would everyone say?" Hermes's brow raised. "My sweet, beautiful flower child, do you think I've gone about living my life by being concerned about what people think?"

"Well, you're a god."

"You're a nymph," Dionysus countered quickly. Eurydice looked around the party nervously, her eyes falling on Orpheus once again. He caught her gaze, as if he sensed her looking at him from across the crowded room and smiled. There was something about it that stirred Eurydice's memory, like she was looking at a glimpse of Orpheus from years past. A warm feeling took feeble root in her chest, and Eurydice's heart picked up.

Hermes and Dionysus saw the look on Eurydice's face, and they nodded in understanding.

"You care for him," Hermes stated simply, his eyes evaluating Eurydice.

"I do," Eurydice acquiesced.

"You can care for someone and know that you are still not right for one another." Dionysus sipped at a cup of wine, keeping a careful eye on the party proceeding around them.

"Hush, drink your wine." Hermes tsked in Dionysus's direction. "You're only going to confuse the girl."

"As if you don't have your own reasons for being here." Dionysus's eyes got wider as he obliged Hermes and took another deep draught from the cup he was holding.

"Is there... Is there a reason that you came here to talk to me?" Eurydice put her hand on her hip, suddenly wary why the two gods had come to Orpheus's party and were talking to her in the corner.

"You're my son's best friend." Hermes shrugged. "Do I need a reason to check up on you?"

"You never have before..." Eurydice started to argue with Hermes when Dionysus's face suddenly turned red.

A deep, almost guttural sound came out of his mouth as he dropped his cup, sending wine splattering over the pristine marble tiles of Orpheus's dining room. Eurydice gasped sharply and tried to see what had gotten Dionysus's attention, quickly turning towards the noise. A small crowd was fighting near the end of the banquet table, and Orpheus and Perseus were on their way to the dispute. Hermes and Dionysus started moving, and Eurydice followed out of curiosity. A woman was angrily pushing against another man's chest while he spat angrily. A second woman had her arm around the first woman's waist, joining in shouting accusatorially at the drunken man.

"What is the meaning of this?" Dionysus was spitting angrily, his voice echoing off the rafters. A thin, shining silver circlet appeared on his brow as he grew taller while his divinity took over. The simple purple garment Dionysus had been wearing suddenly revealed itself to have a matching elaborate silver trim as etched sandals appeared on his feet. A wicked looking scythe appeared in his hand while his eyes flashed black and violet.

"Whoa-a," Perseus hiccuped, holding his hands up in a placating gesture. "I'm sure this is all a misunderstanding, Dionysus. We're honored that you would grace us with your presence." Perseus made a feeble attempt at a bow, tripping over his own ankles. Dionysus was still livid, holding a white-knuckle grip on his blade. He couldn't take his eyes off the man who'd been berating the tipsy female.

"You see," Hermes suddenly appeared next to Eurydice, his voice low in her ear, "most mortal men don't realize that Dionysus is the god of wine, but that means that no one abuses it. He castrated Zeus over his many violations of consent."

"You're kidding." Eurydice blanched as she turned towards Hermes, dropping her voice down to meet his hushed tone. The argument was carrying on beside them, and out of the corner of her eye, Eurydice could see Dionysus stepping in front of the women to defend them.

"Do I look like I would joke about something like that?" Hermes placed his hand on his chest dramatically. "Don't answer that. It's true. There are two things that Dionysus holds dear, my lovely garden flower. And those are the proper techniques for sealing a barrel of vintage wine and the importance of informed consent."

"Huh. I wouldn't have guessed." Eurydice found herself looking for Orpheus in the crowd again, unamused to see him sitting down at the banquet table behind Perseus with a serving girl in his lap.

"Men aren't that keen to go around spreading the news that they were castrated by Dionysus, so that part of his reputation... Oh." Hermes gasped salaciously, realizing what Eurydice was staring at. "Well, he's certainly a keeper." The sarcasm in Hermes's tone was evident.

"We're going through an adjustment period." Eurydice rattled off the excuse without even thinking.

"So you've said." Hermes hummed something inconsequential. They both watched the chaos escalate as Dionysus thundered out a loud string of curses. He dropped his scythe on the floor and clapped his hands twice. A massive boom echoed off the rafters as vines exploded through the walls. The sentient branches started weaving around the ankles of the partygoers, causing mass chaos as attendees started to scream and flee. The vines caught several of the angry, drunk male guests around their legs and suspended them in the air.

"Oh my," Hermes grinned, a mischievous gleam appearing in his eye, "this is what I was hoping to see this evening. Dionysus always looks ravishing when he goes all 'berserker farmer.' Hercules will be frustrated he missed this."

Eurydice didn't know how to respond to Hermes as she tried to process the scene in front of her. The dining hall had descended into chaos until the only people left were the men held in Dionysus's thrall. He had the blade of his scythe pressed to one man's thigh, asking if he enjoyed the helpless feeling that came from being so incapacitated.

"He certainly knows how to make a point," Eurydice murmured, not feeling particularly upset for any of the ill-fated dinner guests.

"Eurydice!" Orpheus's sharp voice called out through the vines that were covering the dining hall, and soon, he emerged from underneath the banquet table. "My love!" he cried in relief, opening his arms as he stumbled towards her. "I was worried that you were injured. Are you okay? Let's get out of here, quickly." Orpheus was talking too quickly, clearly coming off whatever high or drunken stupor he'd been in.

"I'm all right, Orpheus. It's fine." Eurydice put her hands on his shoulders and rubbed them soothingly. "Don't panic. We can go home."

"My love," Orpheus repeated cupped her cheek, stroking his thumb gently over her skin, "let's go home. I just want to be with you."

Eurydice's heart gave a jump, and it betrayed her slightly. Was that really all it took? She watched Orpheus be the life of the party for a few hours, so now she had a stomach full of butterflies because he wanted to leave with her?

"Excuse me," Hermes butted in, his lips pressed in a thin line, "I'd like to speak to Eurydice for a moment."

Orpheus's jaw dropped at the sight of the god next to his wife and nodded dumbly.

Hermes tugged on Eurydice's elbow and pulled her away to the corner of the room again. His judgmental expression vanished as he looked down at Eurydice, chewing his lip as if he was debating whether or not to tell her something.

"If you ever need anything, call me. I'll answer. Pan speaks highly of you." Eurydice was taken aback by the offer. It wasn't every day that a god offered you the extreme favor of being able to call on them.

"I don't see why that would be necessary," Eurydice found herself pretending to assure Hermes that everything in her life was going swimmingly, "but I appreciate the great honor you've shown on me by extending such an offer." She bowed her head, but Hermes only let out a loud, guffawing noise.

"Ha! Keep those elaborate pleasantries for the rest of the pantheon." Wings appeared on Hermes's feet as he prepared to depart.

"Oh, and one more thing?" Hermes raised a brow and leaned in a little closer towards Eurydice. "Those lyrics that Orpheus was singing to you, sweet muse? He stole those from Sappho."

Hermes disappeared in a cloud of golden magic, leaving Eurydice in the wreckage of the banquet hall.

14

Hermes was never more grateful for his own swift footedness than for that very night. It had been slightly dastardly, letting Eurydice know that her beloved Orpheus hadn't actually written those loving lyrics about her, but he couldn't be too bothered to care. Pan was his son, after all, and although he had never acquired a strong sense of paternal instincts, it had certainly never been part of his reputation—he hated seeing Pan upset.

The creatures and inhabitants of the forest, associates of Dionysus and all the revelry that Greece produced, should never look so haunted. It was hardly a secret that Pan was in love with Eurydice, except to Eurydice. So what if he happened to poke a few more poles in Orpheus's shining reputation? He should actually try if he wanted to win his wife's affections back, not steal from other poets. Orpheus wouldn't even have a chance with Eurydice if she remembered the trials he put her through.

If Orpheus wanted to play dirty, then Hermes would play dirtier.

Hermes knew exactly where to find Pan—lurking in the forests. He had been spending most of his time there recently, except for when he snuck out to go visit Eurydice in the Underworld. Hermes had never been prouder of his son when Pan came to him with his plan to skirt around Underworld rules and visit Eurydice as often as he wished after her death. He was the son of a trickster, after all.

Pan was half asleep when Hermes crashed into the wooded clearing. There was an empty amphora next to him, and his lips were stained with wine. His magic was ebbing and flowing around him, unrestrained in his subconscious, reacting to his dreams. Flowers and entire shrubs grew up from the earth around Pan and wilted away back to nothing in seconds while the air around him was tinged with an emerald glow. His features were restless even in sleep. Pan jumped to his feet at the thunderous sound of a god crashing to the earth, his horns appearing on his head in a bright flash of magic.

"Who is it?" Pan bleated out into the clearing before his eyes could comprehend who was in front of him. As soon as he saw Hermes, his posture deflated, and he exhaled heavily. "What the fuck? Did you feel like giving me a heart attack?"

Hermes gracefully sat down on an upturned tree stump, crossing his ankle over the knee like a mortal woman of high society. He grinned from ear to ear, his golden magic reaching out and interacting with Pan's in the moonlight.

"I thought you would be happy to see your father."

Pan snorted. "You are a co-conspirator at best."

"Isn't that what every little boy wants growing up?" Hermes winked, and Pan scoffed, but there was no genuine frustration in his reaction.

"Well?" Pan stretched his arms above his head with a yawn, his bones popping as he did so. For the first time in his immortal life, Pan was feeling the weight of his existence and of his foolish heart. He could've sworn his joints ached and muscles tore a little more easily these days, now that Eurydice was truly forever out of his grasp.

"I thought you would want to know that I saw Eurydice

tonight." Hermes raised an eyebrow, and Pan's body went rigid. He turned all his attention to Hermes, his cheeks flushing red. He nearly jumped over to his father, grabbing his shoulders.

"Is she all right? Do you think she was having a good time? I'm assuming she was at a party? What was she wearing? Does Orpheus know she prefers black wine to white wine?" Pan rattled off an obsessive number of questions before Hermes managed to stop him.

"I didn't leave her in peril, if that's your main question. Yes, she was at a party at Perseus's house tonight. Orpheus was performing there."

"Fucker." Pan released Hermes and took a few steps back. He ran his hand through his curly hair, pushing some of it off his forehead. "Did she look like she was enjoying herself?"

Hermes let out a short chuckle. "Ha! I've seen more lively people at funerals."

"That doesn't help me. You go to funerals of people you didn't like to celebrate," Pan deadpanned. "Was it like that or do you think she was enjoying herself?"

"She was not having a good time." Hermes shook his head. "Eurydice was hiding in a corner half the night while Orpheus dedicated a song to her with lyrics he stole from Sappho."

"That fucking pig," Pan hissed. His face turned redder with his anger while his hands drew up into fists. Pan started pacing through the clearing, his magic rolling off him in erratic waves. He pivoted between his human and satyr form, kicking up dirt with his frantic movements. "Eurydice should know what he did to her."

"I agree," Hermes hummed in agreement. "But you know the rules of the Underworld."

"Hades is a fair ruler! He cares for the young, for women, for victims. You would think he'd use a little judgement to bend the rules in this case!"

"Pan!" Hermes snapped, his eyes going wide. "You know as

well as I do that Hades is the most honorable god in the whole damn pantheon of them. If the rules the gods preside by ever become up for interpretation, it won't always be Hades doing the interpreting. Then what do you think would happen?"

"I know," Pan slumped down and buried his head in his hands, muffling his voice. "I despise Orpheus. I hate that man. I know it's immature of me to despise him solely on the fact that he won Eurydice's love…"

Hermes made a tsk sound. "Well, judging off her expression all night and the way that Orpheus paid the serving girls more attention than Eurydice, it seems to me there is trouble in paradise."

"What did you say?" Pan jumped to his feet while a series of rose brushes sprung up around him. "He was disrespecting her like that all night?"

"I don't think Orpheus would call it disrespect." Hermes crossed his arms over his chest. "He'd probably say he was simply showing appreciation to Perseus's hosting skills. There were a few moments throughout the night where Eurydice really did seem to be in love with him, but they were fleeting. I got the sense she was trying to hold onto those moments, but Orpheus wasn't making it easy."

Pan didn't respond, picking his head up and propping it on his knees.

"If I were you…" Hermes continued, a familiar glimmer appearing in his eye. "I'd reckon that Orpheus is going to pass out from the amount of wine he drank tonight within minutes of getting home." Hermes looked up at the sky. "It's a full moon tonight. I'd make a wager, if I were a betting man, that Eurydice is out enjoying her garden tonight. Alone."

There was a pregnant pause as Pan looked at his father quizzically.

"Are you suggesting that I go to Orpheus's home and visit his wife under the cover of night?"

Hermes's grin stretched into a smile. He waggled his

eyebrows as he held his hands out wide. "I am simply suggesting that a dear friend of yours had a bad night out and where to find them. Also..." The wings appeared on Hermes's sandals, and he began floating, ready to depart, "Moonlight is romantic."

Hermes disappeared in the blink of an eye in a cloud of golden magic before Pan even had the chance to respond. It was something that he was known for, and Pan had long grown used to his father's antics.

Is this the right thing to do? Pan's thoughts raced through his head. *It's hardly ethical. I want to give her the space she needs if she wants to try this relationship with Orpheus and give it a chance...but that doesn't mean I can't go to her as a friend, right? Yes, I can go to her as a friend. Forget what Hermes said about the moonlight being romantic... It's a friendly visit. That's all.*

Pan convinced himself in a record amount of time that visiting Eurydice was a good idea, as if his heart ever thought it could possibly be a bad one. He took a few deep breaths and walked over to the largest oak tree surrounding the clearing, letting his power ebb and flow through the root system beneath it. Pan's eyes fluttered closed as he slowly started to evaporate into a dark emerald cloud. All the plants that had sprung up due his influence in the clearing disappeared, leaving no trace that Pan had ever been there. He traveled through the roots and trunks of the trees, deep into the soil, breathing in the earthy scent. It grounded him, the feel of the dirt and the presence of the earth, and Pan was feeling much more settled by the time he arrived in the Underworld.

He was on the outskirts of Orpheus's property, and he had the same reaction to it that Eurydice did. It was garish and devoid of life, an utterly massive complex of stone and riches that was devoid of anything organic. The marble was shining in the bright moonlight, practically beckoning Pan to hop the garden wall. He could sense the thriving garden in the courtyard, and he identified Eurydice's influence and signature all over it. Her power and magic with everything green called to him like Pan himself was a vine, dying of thirst and stretching out towards water. Whenever he was in Eurydice's orbit, he felt like a flower turning towards the sun as it moved through the sky, and he had no problem being in her gravitational pull forever.

Pan closed his eyes and traveled through the air, only glimpses of a green hue in the sky giving him away. He landed in the walled garden without a sound, and sure enough, there was Eurydice.

The sight of her took his breath away. Pan's chest seized with a physical longing, a pain so sharp that it threatened to stop his heart. He'd welcome death if it was brought about to him through Eurydice's presence alone. He'd kiss Thanatos's feet himself if it was Eurydice's beauty that took him out.

Eurydice was sitting on one of the marble benches, overlooking one of the many fountains in the garden. The cool air was rich with the scent of roses and lilies, which he knew to be Eurydice's favorites. Her hair was free from any braids or ornaments, hanging loosely down her back. It went all the way to her waist, shining in the moonlight like bright copper. If weapons were made of copper and iron, the hue of Eurydice's hair would be the arrow that shot Pan straight through the heart.

She was dressed in a simple, short tunic, revealing her long legs and skin that glowed like stone, as if she was lit from within.

Pan's thoughts were overrun with his devotion and love for her, wondering what it would look like to have those legs wrapped around his own... His more animalistic side practically grunted in agreement, taking over Pan's thoughts with ones of lust and obsession. He wanted to find out what noises Eurydice made when his tongue was between her thighs, what magic he could coax out of her when she was feral with pleasure.

That was one of the things Pan hated most about Orpheus. He never seemed to welcome the wild side of Eurydice; he always wanted her to be 'presentable.' Pan wanted her to rip up the earth with her magic and grow a forest from the ruins of Orpheus's estate. He wanted her to run naked through the trees until the moon herself talked back. A wild Eurydice was a happy Eurydice, and Pan didn't know how to get that through Orpheus's head. He didn't know if he even wanted to.

Pan shook his head to clear it when he realized he'd been staring for far too long. He prepared to step out from the cover of the bushes when he paused. Eurydice had turned her attention to the trellis at the far end of the garden. Pan caught the tears in her eyes.

She was staring at the gift he had given her. Pan's heart threatened to beat out of his chest. Part of him wondered if Orpheus knew who'd given it to Eurydice. Orpheus probably didn't realize it was there.

Pan watched as a single tear tracked down Eurydice's cheek, creating a tragically beautiful sight that was only worthy of such a mythical figure as Eurydice. But Pan didn't care about legends or reputations; he cared that Eurydice was upset.

Pan stepped out gently from behind the walls, raising his voice only as much as he dared.

"Eurydice?"

Eurydice turned on her heel with a gasp. She quickly wiped away the tears on her cheeks while her face split into a wide smile. Eurydice's smile nearly sent Pan to his knees; he'd never get used to it and prayed he never would.

"What are you doing here?" Eurydice ran down the garden path, joining Pan underneath the vine's shadows on the trellis.

"Is it a bad time?" Pan had an adoring smile on his face, looking up at the night sky, insinuating that he was clearly aware he showed up in the middle of the night.

"No, never." Eurydice shook her head rapidly and placed

her hand on his arm. Heat streaked up Pan's arm where she touched him. "Were you in the area?"

"Ha." Pan rolled his eyes. "No, I don't think I'd ever be in this area of the Underworld if you weren't here."

"I can't say that I'm partial to it either," Eurydice admitted. She glanced back to the massive house behind her. "I miss the forest."

"I can only imagine," Pan agreed. "It's making me itchy right now being apart from it. Although, the garden is lovely. Your work, I'm assuming?" Eurydice's smile widened until it stretched across her entire face; she looked like a child surprised with extra sweets.

"Yes! Can I show you?"

"Your husband won't mind?" Pan teased, and Eurydice only rolled her eyes, practically skipping down the garden path.

"He's going to be sleeping off that hangover for at least a day. It's for the best, though. I didn't need another night of him pawing at me until he finally gets the hint that I don't want to climb into bed with him."

Pan stopped walking, all of his muscles tensing. His body immediately went on high alert.

"Gets the hint?" Pan practically growled. His magic flared, and he slipped into his satyr form again, scratching at the heavy stubble on his jaw. Eurydice turned around when she realized Pan had stopped following her.

"Oh, yeah," she mumbled awkwardly, "it's fine though, Pan. Don't get upset."

"It is not fine," Pan grumbled. He reached out towards Eurydice and touched her arm, dragging his fingers over her skin until he reached her hand and grabbed it. "Eurydice, please," his voice was pleading, "tell me now. He hasn't hurt you, has he? If he has..." The grass underneath Pan's feet started to die in response to his fury. Pan didn't care if all the gods in the pantheon came after him. Fuck the Underworld and fuck the rules. If Eurydice was being hurt by Orpheus, he'd march right inside and cut the singer's throat in his sleep without a second of remorse.

"No! Oh goodness, Pan, no." Eurydice disputed him, and some of Pan's anger receded. They continued walking through the garden, Eurydice sighing heavily. "It's taking some time for us to...find our footing. I don't remember my life with him, you know? He does remember. Orpheus wants to pick right up as if nothing has changed between us, but I can't do it. Sometimes that annoys him."

"It annoys him?" Pan's lip curled. "I can't imagine that anything about reuniting with your wife after a forty-year separation would be annoying. He should relish the chance to win your heart all over again, Eurydice."

"It doesn't work that way." Eurydice laughed as though Pan had no idea what he was talking about. "We've been in love for a long time, you know? That's how love is after a while."

Pan stopped walking and watched Eurydice bend down to smell some night-blooming flowers. He was dumbstruck by her figure in the moonlight, the way she cared for every growing thing in the garden. Pan had been in love with Eurydice for a hundred years. He didn't think he'd ever stop.

"No, Eurydice," Pan whispered quietly, "that's not how it is. It changes over time—love is always different after years—but it only gets stronger."

"I don't think that's always true." Eurydice gave him a playful look, as though she wasn't ripping his heart out.

"Then that's not love."

Pan couldn't help himself before he said it, and Eurydice didn't respond. She made a small, noncommittal noise and started drifting down the small path again, heading towards another row of fountains.

Eurydice and Pan didn't say anything else to one another, simply enjoying the silence and each other's company for the rest of the night. They communicated without words, merely nods and small touches, and Pan had helped Eurydice grow a small grove of trees at the far edge of the garden before sunrise.

Eurydice excused herself to go to bed just before the break of dawn. Pan couldn't bear to leave until a few hours later, waiting in the garden until he was sure she had fallen asleep.

15

When Eurydice finally blinked her eyes open, her bedroom was glowing with late afternoon light. It was a misconception that nymphs and dryads were daytime creatures. Eurydice found pleasure in being both a day and a night person. When she woke up with a smile on her face, all she could think of was her moonlight walk with Pan. As the memories came flooding back, she ran to the window, thrilled to see their trees blossoming in the sun.

"Beautiful," Eurydice exhaled heavily, feeling lighter than she had in weeks. She turned around and quickly started doing her hair, brushing it out and throwing it up in a braid. While she was finishing getting dressed, her other memories from the night before came rushing back. It hit her like a bolt of lightning, shocking her system and draining it of the warmth she'd been feeling.

"Orpheus..." she groaned, sitting back down on her bed and chewing her lip anxiously. What had he been thinking last night? He had been kind to her and exalted her in front of everyone in attendance at Perseus's party. But drinking excessively? Getting friendly with the serving girls? And Hermes's accusation... Although it couldn't have been an accusation if

Hermes said it. Hermes was the god of many things, including a trickster, but the god of messengers wouldn't lie about something like that either.

The great Orpheus, stealing lyrics, Eurydice hissed mentally. She looked around the small, barren bedroom. She preferred it to the opulent rooms of the manor, but she knew that Orpheus intended it as a slight. He'd hoped that she would be lured into the master bedroom by the embroidered bedclothes and elaborate furniture, but Eurydice would just as soon sleep outside. Still, the spare mattress and small table in the bedroom were a testament to how Orpheus had hoped to drive her into his arms. He said one thing and did another. It had only been a couple of weeks and surely, as her husband, he deserved a little bit more time than that to fall back in sync with his wife?

"With any luck, he's still asleep," Eurydice muttered to herself, brightening her own spirits with the thought of checking on last night's progress.

Eurydice practically floated through the house without a word. Orpheus had his own staff of adoring fans who were willing to do anything he requested around the house, and more than once, Eurydice found herself wondering what 'anything' truly entailed. This afternoon, however, she was given a blessed reprieve when there was no one to be found in the house. It was quiet enough that she could hear the birds in the garden, causing her to pick up her pace.

Eurydice stepped into the sun, practically sighing in relief as the sun warmed her skin. The garden was in bloom like never before, with every flower bed exploding over its confines. Eurydice clapped her hands with joy at the sight of how much gardening she now needed to do. Anyone else would likely be put off at the sight of such an overgrown mess, but to Eurydice, it was paradise. It proved that her and Pan's efforts from the night before had been accepted by Rhea.

Eurydice started whistling a happy tune, causing several

swallows to swoop down and start bathing in the fountain. She sat down on the ground in front of the flower bed closest to the door and got to work.

The hours passed until the sun was setting again, Eurydice spending the rest of the daylight in the garden. The space was bathed in pink and orange light as Eurydice took another walk through the elaborate garden, double-checking all her handiwork. She stopped at the small grove of trees, which were already in full bloom, thanks to a little bit of Pan's magic the night before. Orpheus preferred to keep the kitchen stocked with meats and bread; Eurydice was delighted to see that Pan had planted her a collection of apricots, peaches, nectarines, and cherries. She couldn't even remember telling Pan that she got annoyed with Orpheus's preferences for mealtime, but maybe he simply remembered that fruits were her favorite.

The trees were enchanted; Eurydice could tell when she placed her hand on the trunks, and they were blessed with a rapid cycle of growth. She imagined she'd be eating fruit by dinner time and would have a fresh harvest at the same time tomorrow.

"What a lovely gift," Eurydice smiled to herself. She sat underneath one of the widest trees, deciding to wait until the fruit ripened and watch the sunset. She had slept through most of the day, but the burst of gardening tired her out again. The waning light of the sun made her sleepy, and her eyes were about to flutter closed when there was a sudden strong breeze that rippled through the garden.

Eurydice knew the presence of immortality when she sensed it. There was a pleasant, white light that appeared in the center of the garden. It flashed bright as the sun for a brief moment, and Makaria stepped out of it.

"Makaria!" Eurydice brightened, wondering what she had done to deserve visits from Pan and Makaria in the span of a single day.

"Oh, lovely nymph." Makaria grinned, holding out her

arms for Eurydice as she crossed the garden to join her. "Did you do all of this? I love what you've done with the place. I must say," Makaria got a devilish grin on her face, "I had to do plenty of decorating myself when I moved in with Thanatos."

"Oh, yes, of course," Eurydice laughed awkwardly and hugged Makaria. "Well, I've only really touched the garden. That is the only part I'm interested in."

Makaria sat down underneath the tree, her watchful eye picking up the shift in Eurydice's demeanor.

"Do you not like the house?" Makaria tilted her head. She'd become very familiar with Eurydice's tells.

"Well, houses aren't really my thing, you know? I'd prefer to sleep in the garden anyway." Eurydice motioned to the stunning grounds around her.

Makaria looked right at home among the stunning blooms. Her long, white hair was shining in the setting sun, and she was wrapped in a tunic that looked like oil—black at first sight, but it shifted colors when she moved. Eurydice couldn't help but wonder what Makaria had been doing before she decided to pop in for a visit. The life of someone who was known as 'blessed death' must be interesting.

"Regardless, you've done a marvelous job with the space." Makaria smiled warmly. She had always been a very kind, if not aloof, presence in Eurydice's life. It was something Eurydice had always appreciated about the goddess. She knew there was a lot surrounding Makaria's own story of understanding and belonging in the Underworld, and one day she hoped to hear it.

"You're being too kind." Eurydice was pleased; she cared much more about compliments regarding her gardening than her appearance. It made her flush infinitely more so than thoughts or comments on what she was wearing.

"Now, I have to ask." Makaria's hand dropped casually to the handle of her scythe, and she traced the leather wrapped around it. It was worn in several places where her fingers must have consistently gripped it; the thought made Eurydice shiver internally. "How are you enjoying living here? Besides not being in the forest, of course. How is Orpheus?"

Eurydice should have anticipated that this question was coming, but something about it set her off guard again. She appreciated how many gods were checking in with her regarding her arrival in the Underworld, but at the same time, it was a little exhausting defending Orpheus constantly and explaining herself. Makaria must have sensed this as her face turned a little more quizzical.

"You don't have to answer if you don't want to," Makaria supplied, her hair rippling like water in the sunset's low light.

"No, I don't mind," Eurydice lied easily. "Everything is going well. As well as to be expected, at least. There is an adjustment period, but I'm happy to be with my husband again." Eurydice nearly split her face in two with the strength of her smile, hoping that it was convincing enough for lying to a god. If Makaria noticed, she didn't say a thing. Her face became impassably neutral, without a single tell or even a slightly raised brow. The atmosphere between the two changed slightly, and Eurydice's stomach sank with guilt.

This is what it means to be married, Eurydice tried to console herself with her thoughts. *It's important to defend your husband. Orpheus and I can work out our issues without everyone else's interference.*

"An adjustment period is to be...expected." Makaria's tone was somehow both neutral and cautious, which was a carefully curated skill that only the gods and immortals seemed to possess. "I would simply hate for you to go a single day without finding joy in your life, Eurydice. You've suffered enough. Besides, you're fucking dead anyway," Makaria laughed, "so you might as well make sure you're enjoying it. If you were alive, I'd tell you that life is too short to be unhappy, but you've got all the time in the world to make decisions for yourself. I'm here if you ever need anything."

Eurydice's heart started beating faster, and she started to fight against a lightheaded sensation. She was a private person, and this was officially one inquisition too many. She knew it wasn't fair to judge her friends this way, but really, how much input on her life was she supposed to consider? There were too many factors bouncing around in her head, and it was starting to feel like she had a constant hive of bees between her ears. Before she opened her mouth to respond, Orpheus's voice called out from the other end of the garden.

"Eurydice? Are you out here?" Orpheus shouted in alarm. "What in the name of the gods has happened to the garden? It's disgusting. These unkempt weeds are everywhere."

Eurydice's heart sank. The garden was not overgrown, and she would know. It was finally full of life, with blooms and bushes and birds. How could she find a way to make Orpheus see the world the same way she did? She recovered quickly as she realized Makaria had unsheathed her blade, a venomous look on her face. From where Orpheus was in the garden, he couldn't see Eurydice and Makaria. He was unaware that someone was listening to the way he spoke to Eurydice and what he had to say about her efforts.

"Orpheus," Eurydice shouted quickly, waving her hands, "we're over here. Makaria is visiting." Eurydice stressed the goddess's name, hoping that it would put Orpheus on his best behavior. It did just that. When he responded, Orpheus sounded as polite and optimistic as ever.

"Oh, the lovely goddess! What a surprise." He sounded like a politician as he emerged from the garden path, walking eagerly over to the grove of fruit trees.

Orpheus had spent the entire day sleeping off his hangover, yet he was gleaming like his own golden lyre. His chiton was pressed and featured a purple trim with an expensive brooch at his shoulder. Eurydice tried to not roll her eyes at the sight.

He's outside in a garden right now. Who walks through a garden with jeweled sandals? Be fucking barefoot like the rest of us. Eurydice barely avoided another guilt spiral when she realized how sharply she critiqued her husband in her mind; that wasn't giving him a fair shot, was it?

"It's lovely to see you here, Makaria," Orpheus held his arms out in a welcoming gesture.

"It's 'goddess,' thank you," Makaria replied with a curt nod. Eurydice watched as the muscles in Orpheus's jaw twitched. She could tell he wasn't used to being corrected in such a manner and didn't appreciate Makaria's sharp insistence he not use her first name.

"Goddess," Orpheus replied through clenched teeth with a tight smile. He turned his attention to Eurydice. "These trees are certainly new, aren't they? And already bursting with fruit!" Orpheus walked closer and went up on his tiptoes, plucking a nectarine from one of the low hanging branches. When it didn't pop right off the stem, Orpheus grunted, snapping the entire branch in half to get at the sweet fruit. Eurydice visibly flinched at the sharp crack of the tree limb falling apart.

"Yes." Eurydice was quick to flash another reassuring smile. She was well aware of Makaria's attempt to light Orpheus on fire with her stare. "These grew last night. They're enchanted," Eurydice's voice picked up in excitement, "so you know that they'll bloom..."

"Of course!" Orpheus slapped his forehead as if just remembering something obvious. He tossed the nectarine up int he air and caught it. "It must have been the music." He smiled at Eurydice. "Your sweet presence just coaxes the best things out of me, my love. And then the music makes the trees grow. That's what all the songs say about us, you know. You give me the power to make the rocks weep and the trees grow." Orpheus held out a piece of the nectarine to Eurydice. She leaned forward to take it with her fingers, but Orpheus pulled it back quickly, a playful grin on his face. He shook his head and held it out again, clearly indicating he wanted to feed her.

Eurydice flushed with embarrassment. She was as wild as

the forest, but she didn't appreciate such a display of forced affection. It made her feel cheap. Nonetheless, she obliged, as Makaria was sitting with them and clearly judging Orpheus. Eurydice was keen to prove that everything between them was fine, even if just for the reason to convince herself that everything was going fine.

Eurydice leaned forward and allowed Orpheus to feed her a small wedge of the fruit. The sweet, citrusy tang of the nectarine was completely obliterated by the foul, wine-soaked taste of Orpheus's fingers as he haphazardly shoved the piece between her lips. Eurydice nearly recoiled, turned off by the old sweat that still clung to Orpheus's skin from the night before. He didn't allow Eurydice to delicately pluck the fruit from his fingers, instead, practically choking her with his eagerness.

Eurydice sputtered a short cough, reeling backward as she swallowed the nectarine. She slapped her chest twice, trying to rid herself of the gagging sensation. It was entirely unpleasant and felt incredibly violating in its own way. Eurydice didn't want to dwell on the fact that such a small gesture and physicality between them made her feel so sick, but she suspected that was because of Orpheus's sense of entitlement to her that he flexed any time that he seemed to get the chance.

"Careful, my love." Orpheus seemed annoyed. "I suppose these fruits are a bit more bitter than intended. We'll have to make some sweeter music together and see what happens." Orpheus's comment would've come across as playful between almost any other couple, but he only made it sound predatory. Eurydice could see Makaria gripping and releasing her blade repetitively out of the corner of her eye.

No one said anything for a few long minutes. Orpheus kicked at some of the rocks on the ground, whistling a half-assed tune while he looked up at all the blossoms on the fruit trees. Eurydice fought against the urge to start crying. She wanted to run. She wanted to be alone. No, she needed to be alone. Everything in her peaceful life had been taken from her, and while good intentioned, there were too many forces trying to understand what was happening between Orpheus and Eurydice. Eurydice needed to figure it out for herself first.

"Well," Orpheus finally cleared his throat, "I'll get going, I suppose, and I can leave you two to your conversation..."

"No, no," Makaria interrupted Orpheus sharply and stood up. Her soft, shining clouds of magic began swirling around her feet as she began to disappear. "I'm the one intruding. Please, enjoy your evening." Makaria vanished entirely until only her disembodied voice echoed throughout the garden. "And Eurydice? If you need anything, you know where to find me."

The emphasis on 'you' was clear; Makaria's favor was being offered to Eurydice, not Orpheus. As soon as the goddess's presence vanished entirely from the garden, Orpheus's face soured.

"I don't like that goddess," he snarled. "Eurydice, I don't want her visiting you here anymore."

"She's a goddess, Orpheus," Eurydice sputtered in surprise. "Do you think I control her movements?"

"No, I suppose not," Orpheus sighed dramatically, as though a visit from one of the Underworld's most beloved deities was thoroughly inconveniencing for him. "Why don't you come in for dinner, Eurydice?" His tone softened. "I'm sorry about Perseus's party last night." Orpheus's cheeks pinked with a little bit of shame. "It wasn't very becoming of me to act the way I did."

Eurydice was taken back by his apology, but it was welcome nonetheless. The smallest seeds of hope in her chest anchored their roots a little bit deeper. Orpheus extended his hand out to her, and she took it, accepting his aid as he helped her to her feet.

He offered Eurydice his arm, which she gracefully accepted, and he escorted her through the gardens and back towards the main house. The silence between them was somewhat peaceful, for once, and didn't feel awkward.

Eurydice was getting whiplash from Orpheus's moods, but she would take any pleasantness with him that she could.

As they were about to step into the house, Eurydice paused. She turned around and looked lovingly at her new grove of fruit trees before turning back to Orpheus.

"One thing, Orpheus," she paused, and he nodded for her to continue, "I grew those trees. *I* did. You didn't even play any music here last night." Eurydice's words started coming out in a rush as she tried to get her entire statement out before she lost the confidence. "Those trees are from my efforts, with...you know, some help with the creatures of the forest." She was careful to exclude Pan's name although she didn't know why. "I don't appreciate you taking the credit for my responsibilities like that."

Orpheus stared at Eurydice for a moment, and she expected him to roll his eyes at her or disregard her. Instead, he leaned in towards her and pressed a chaste kiss on her cheek.

"Of course, my love. But you know, we are married. What's yours is mine."

Orpheus dropped Eurydice's arm and walked inside, hollering for the closest serving girl to start preparing the banquet hall for their dinner. Eurydice turned towards the garden and wondered if she could clear the outer wall if she had a running start.

16

Eurydice followed Orpheus inside, going through the long, elaborate hallway that led towards the banquet hall. When she stepped inside, she noticed how similar to Perseus's dining room it was. The room had the same layout, with a raised dais and an elaborate, long table in the center. There were massive braziers in each of the four corners of the room, already lit and burning with the thick, cloying scent of a heavy, artificial incense. It made Eurydice's eyes water as she rapidly blinked through some of the smoke.

The walls were covered from floor to ceiling in elaborate friezes and murals, all of which were pertaining to the stories of Orpheus's mortal life.

Eurydice heard Orpheus talking to some of the house staff in the far corner of the room, so she took the opportunity to get a little closer and examine the artworks. As she studied them, she couldn't quite put her finger on what it was about them that seemed odd. There were depictions of Orpheus on the Argo, many images of him singing or playing the lyre, even a very elaborate painting of the moment where Apollo turned his back on Orpheus.

Then Eurydice realized what it was about all the artwork

that was different. None of them featured her. When she had fought with Orpheus earlier in the week, she distinctly told him about how disconcerting it was to be surrounded by depictions of her own death. Now, all the work in the dining hall was still very flattering to Orpheus, but Eurydice and any tales of their time together had been removed. Eurydice leaned a little closer to the wall, gently reaching out and running her finger through some of the oils. She let out a quiet gasp when she pulled her hand away and the paint was still wet.

He had these all redone recently. Eurydice was surprised by the gesture. Orpheus was being very hot and cold with her, but having all the artwork in the house repainted was certainly the boldest step he'd taken in trying to win over her affections.

"Eurydice?" Orpheus's voice was suddenly right behind her.

"Oh! Gods!" Eurydice spun around, pressing her hand to her heart in surprise. She smeared a little bit of paint across the bodice of her draped gown. "Shit," she cursed, looking down at the mess and then towards the painting, "I'm so sorry. I didn't know that they were still wet, and I..."

"Don't worry about it, my love." Orpheus smiled gently. He reached out and ran his finger through the painting, deliberately smearing his own carefully portrayed face. Orpheus streaked paint down the front of his own tunic, only looking up at Eurydice to smile.

"See? Now we match."

Eurydice's heart flipped inside her chest; the seeds of hope that had feebly taken root in her mind that very afternoon dug in a little deeper.

"The painting though... Orpheus, I feel terrible. I didn't know that it was still wet."

Orpheus gently grabbed a hold of Eurydice's hand and led her towards the banquet table. It had been elaborately set for two, with lit candles, a fresh amphora of wine, and a myriad of meats and cheeses.

"It's only a decoration." Orpheus shrugged, nearly completely out of character from what Eurydice had come to suspect from him. He pulled out her chair for her, and Eurydice sat, unable to keep some of the pleasant surprise off her face. "I had them redone after you told me how you felt about all the artwork in the house."

"That was very kind of you, Orpheus." Eurydice beamed at him as he took his seat. Her body was flooded with relief. This was the Orpheus that she could be married to. This was someone that would've captured her affections when she was living in the mortal world. She wouldn't be concerned about being seen with this man; this was someone who she could be with, and no one would question the legends.

"It was the very least I could do." Orpheus shrugged modestly. "Quite honestly, I was rightfully very embarrassed as soon as you pointed it out to me." Orpheus served Eurydice a plate, and she nearly fell out of her chair. There was a very small voice in the back of her head trying to remind her that Orpheus was only displaying the barest amount of manners, nothing exceptional, but she ignored it.

Orpheus and Eurydice fell into an easy conversation. It shouldn't have been remarkable, but it registered to Eurydice like she was suddenly existing in a whole new world. Who was this person who nearly broke her nose feeding her a piece of fruit in the garden, not even an hour ago?

Perhaps Orpheus was nervous with Makaria around. Eurydice's thoughts quickly defended him. *He might not be the only person who is a little overwhelmed at the sudden attention of the entire Underworld on his relationship.*

Eurydice popped a bit of bread and cheese into her mouth. "What happened when Apollo revoked his favor?" She asked the question quietly, wondering if it was too inappropriate to ask. "You don't have to retell the story if you don't want to, of course."

"No, no, I don't mind." Orpheus wiped a little bit of wine

from his lip. "You're my wife, Eurydice. There's nothing from my life that is off limits for you. It's a fair question, anyway, seeing as it was that day that Apollo decided to send that snake to our wedding."

"That was Apollo?" Eurydice's eyes widened. She didn't remember much, and she definitely didn't remember the reason that a snake bit her on her wedding day was because of Apollo. Orpheus blanched as if he'd done something wrong, freezing with a bite of food halfway to his mouth.

"Oh, shit. Yes. That was because of Apollo. I'm so sorry, I thought you remembered that."

Eurydice waved her hand to encourage him to continue. "I don't remember much. It's okay. Now I do really need to hear the story though." She finished with a lame chuckle. Orpheus picked up her hand and placed a small kiss to the back of her palm.

"You're entitled to every story I have. Every bit of me is because of you, Eurydice, and I won't forget that."

Eurydice blushed furiously, and Orpheus continued with his story.

He spared no detail in spinning the entire bawdy tale. Apollo had grown angry with some drunk satyrs approaching the Feast of Dionysus, and he rigged a bet that resulted in the death of one of the satyrs.

"A satyr?!" Eurydice gasped, dropping her goblet. Wine splattered everywhere, staining the bottom of her tunic. She cussed and jumped up from the table while several servants rushed over to help clean it up.

"Don't worry about it. Let them help. Thank you." Orpheus nodded towards the staff. Eurydice said nothing as she sat back down at the table, suddenly in a mild state of shock. Orpheus continued with his story.

"Pan was there," Orpheus mentioned Pan's name without any consequence, but Eurydice's heart jumped. "He was furious. Rightfully so. I knew the gods were deceitful and tricky, even downright conspiratorial when it came to their own political plotting and whatnot. I never imagined Apollo to be that cruel, however. That satyr didn't need to die, and he didn't need to die the way he did either. I rejected Apollo on the spot, and he revoked his favor."

Eurydice was staring open-mouthed at Orpheus. "You rejected Apollo?"

"I did," Orpheus murmured casually, as if this wasn't a world changing revelation for Eurydice. "Are you upset?" Orpheus studied the terrified and surprised look on her face. "Because what I did, rejecting Apollo—it led directly to your death," Orpheus whispered the words as though it was a great secret he'd been carrying all his life.

"I... No..." Eurydice shook her head. She grabbed Orpheus's hands and squeezed them. "How could I be mad? Orpheus, I'd never heard you tell this story before. Everyone assumed Apollo rejected you first, likely for some ridiculous reason because, you know, it's Apollo. But you abandoning him? A mortal returning the favor of a god? And because he was involved in the murder of a creature of the forest, no less!"

It was a bizarre sensation, but Eurydice was overjoyed. There were pieces of her memory that started trickling back, of pleasant evenings and long nights spent with Orpheus. She would marry a man who abandoned the gods to defend the deities of the wild, without a doubt. A pleasant weight settled in Eurydice's stomach, resolving some of the doubt she had been feeling since Orpheus's arrival in the Underworld. She'd finally heard a story about Orpheus that made her realize—no, it made her remember—why their love had once been, and could be again, the stuff of legends.

Orpheus said nothing, simply chewing his food quietly for a few minutes. When he finally spoke, his voice was solemn.

"It was a cruel thing to see. No matter how many things I've seen happen at the hands of the gods, it was...barbaric. How could I sing about something like that? How could I worship someone who was so excited to destroy life? Music celebrates life, even in memoriam. It doesn't destroy it. I had to walk away, but it meant Apollo's revenge killed you in the end. I didn't know how to live with it."

Orpheus paused. There was a look on his face that Eurydice couldn't quite place, as though there was more he wanted to tell her but couldn't. Eurydice leaned closer to him, crossing the small distance between them, and linked their fingers together.

"It's okay, Orpheus. You don't need to tell me anything else if you don't want to."

"No, no," Orpheus shook his head, grabbing another bite of food and feeding it to Eurydice. This time, she accepted it gracefully and relished the sweet bite of honied bread.

The rest of the dinner passed simply. Orpheus never talked directly about Apollo again but rather entertained Eurydice with stories of some of his more benign adventures in the mortal realm. Eurydice found herself enjoying Orpheus's company with every passing story, some of her fears and concerns over their relationship slipping away. His hand kept moving around to touch her, whether he was holding her hand or tracing his fingers on her thigh. Eurydice was surprised to find that in combination with his warm smile and the sudden shift in his attitude, the barely there touches were starting to make her shift in her seat.

After the household staff had removed most of the serving platters and empty dishes, Orpheus stood up and offered his hand to Eurydice.

"Would you like to retire with me, my wife?" His smile was open, but his eyes roved over Eurydice hungrily. Her stomach flipped as she realized what Orpheus was implying; he didn't think they'd be sleeping at all if she followed him to his bedchambers. Their dinner together had been wonderful, and Eurydice was starting to remember what it felt like to love Orpheus for the first time since she arrived in the

Underworld. But she wasn't nearly ready to have sex with him.

"I would," Eurydice slowly placed her hand in his, and her voice dropped lower, "but I feel like I need to warn you that if I come with you, nothing else is going to happen between us tonight." There was a pause, and Orpheus said nothing, simply staring at Eurydice as though he was confused.

Eurydice cleared her throat. "Physically, I mean." Orpheus dropped her hand and let out a short, exasperated breath.

"I'm not an idiot, Eurydice, I know what you meant."

Eurydice fought the urge to shiver; her skin erupted with the sensation of being covered in bugs. All the warmth drained from her body as she watched in confused horror as Orpheus morphed back into the cold, inconsiderate person she'd become used to.

"I want to keep our evening going…" Eurydice struggled to find the right words. She didn't feel confused any longer; she was furious. That was the emotion that threatened to overtake her and was robbing her of her speech. After all of this, this back and forth with Orpheus, he was going to pretend to be genuine with her only for the opportunity to finally seduce her into his bed?

"Is that what this was all about?" Eurydice snapped, pointing to the remnants of their dinner, strewn out on the table, only a few dirty dishes left. "You just wanted to fuck me?"

Orpheus let out an exasperated groan, sounding annoyed like he couldn't find what he was looking for at the merchant's. He was still acting incredibly blasé, as if he was being inconvenienced.

"Well, excuse me," Orpheus grunted, "but I didn't think you'd take it well if I cheated on you either."

Eurydice stared at him without being able to say anything. Her mind rapidly flipped back and forth between being completely blank and overwhelmed with rage. Her blood started to boil, and thorns started popping out all down her arms and spine. Wild vines started growing out of her scalp, twisting around her hair and braiding it like she was about to go into battle. Even the breeze picked up around their ankles, all the elements of the wild reacting to the furious nymph in their midst.

"What in the name of the gods is fucking wrong with you, Orpheus?" Eurydice shrieked, jabbing her finger into his chest. "That is one of the most insane things... I mean... Honestly, all I can say is what the fuck!"

"Oh, please." Orpheus rolled his eyes. "I tried to seduce you. It's hardly a crime. You should be flattered."

"Flattered?!" Eurydice growled. "You intentionally were engaging and charming. You were kind to me all night not because you wanted to work on our relationship, but only because you were desperate to fuck me!"

Orpheus chuckled. It was a dark and self-satisfied sound that made Eurydice want to snap his neck. It sent chills down her spine. She didn't remember much of their time together, but she knew she had never heard Orpheus make that sound.

"You don't know much about men, Eurydice. I promise you, husbands are only ever trying to get a fuck out of their wives. Or they're cheating. I chose the former, so I really don't see the issue." Orpheus turned around and started walking away from Eurydice, down the empty hall towards his behemoth bedchambers.

"Are you seriously walking away from me right now?" Eurydice shrieked, some of the vines growing all the way down to her ankles and seeking out the floorboards. They chased down the hallway after Orpheus.

"I will talk to you tomorrow. I'm a little too buzzed for this. I'm either going to fuck or go to bed, and you've clearly indicated that the former is not an option."

Eurydice's breath was coming in uneven gasps. She was feeling naive and furious. The vines receded as quickly as they grew, disappearing from the hallway. Eurydice said nothing as she slowly watched Orpheus's retreating form, trying to determine if there was anything left for her to save.

Eurydice walked straight out into the garden, making it all the way to the fruit tree grove before she buried her head in her hands and screamed.

Who am I anymore? Who the fuck is Orpheus? What are we doing together?

Eurydice waited until her breathing had calmed down and sighed. She let her head fall back and looked up at the sky, looking for the moon out of habit. It was a full moon night, which meant the creatures of the forest were somewhere under the trees, enjoying Selene and Pan's attentions.

I wonder if Pan is celebrating in the Underworld? The thought popped into Eurydice's mind, and then she couldn't let it go. She didn't know who she was any more in Orpheus's house, but she always knew who she was in the forest.

Without a parting thought or a second glance, Eurydice slipped out the garden gate and took off as fast as her feet could carry her towards the trees.

17

Eurydice started running as fast as her legs could carry her; her feet practically flying over the ground as she sped off towards the forests. The trees were calling to her, ringing out in the clear night sky, beckoning for their daughter to return to them. As she ran, Eurydice ripped off the expensive brooch that was tied to her shoulder, pulling off the jewelry Orpheus had given her. It scattered on the ground like remnants of a lifetime she didn't remember and no longer cared to. Her only focus was on getting her feet away from the overly lined and paved streets from Orpheus's neighborhood and towards the wilderness of the Underworld.

As she got closer, the houses started becoming further and further apart. Selene's song grew longer, and the moon shined brighter above Eurydice. It was a long shot that Pan would be celebrating in the Underworld this full moon, but he regularly took time to visit the forests of Asphodel since Eurydice's death. There was a chance he was there. It was the only thing she needed. Eurydice was abandoning her marriage and the legacy of her relationship with Orpheus for the mere chance that Pan was somewhere in the Underworld.

Eurydice didn't know how long it had been since she

started running, but she didn't care. It was like a heady aphrodisiac, being able to run as fast as she could, and it made her feel like a young maiden again. The wind whipped past her hair, and there was a pleasant burn in her legs from the sudden exertion; she reveled in it.

The ground seemed to move of its own accord under Eurydice's feet, pushing her further, getting her to the forest. She didn't question it when the Underworld's magic rose up to greet her, spinning the dirt beneath her feet to get her to her destination faster. She let her head fall back, her red hair shining in the light like a torch, and howled. It was an ancient sound, deep from within the core of her, her wildness calling back to her. That part of Eurydice had been abandoned these past few weeks, and it was furious at her for it. Eurydice was a creature of the open sky, the dirt, the leaves, the tallest trees. To pretend anything else would be a farce; she was no poet's wife. She was no muse. She was nature incarnate, and all of Gaia's ancient rage now simmered in her bones that she had been pushing back against her truest self all for the opinions of a man.

When the forest appeared on the horizon, Eurydice howled again before she started laughing freely. She didn't even think about how unhinged she might appear; she was only thinking about how good it felt to be unchained.

As she skipped past the trees and made her way towards one of her favorite clearings, she could hear the sounds of a full moon feast. It was a familiar scene but one that she never grew tired of. Every nymph, dryad, and creature of the forest was gathered around a long, low table made of a tree trunk. Some of the creatures were sitting at the table, dining on meats and fruits and drinking heavily from overflowing amphoras of wine.

Other party guests were in various stages of undress, touching, groping, fucking, and dancing under the shining light of the moon. In the very center of the clearing, there was a massive bonfire, stretching up to the skies. It was taller than a human man, and the smoke was heavily perfumed; cinnamon and myrrh were constantly being thrown into the flames to create a heavy incense that hung in the air long after the smoke cleared.

Decorations made from flowers hung from the trees, stretching out from branch to branch. Petals were strewn about on the fresh grass floor, adding to the incense burning away in the fire. The clearing was alive, and Eurydice could've sworn that even the gardens of Olympus themselves wouldn't look as beautiful. Although she was not alone in the sentiment that many elements of the Underworld were far superior to their Olympian counterparts.

"Eurydice?" An excited voice called out from the melee of bodies. "I didn't think you would join us this evening!" Telodice appeared as naked as the day she was born, her golden hair tastefully arranged over her breasts. She looked like liquid in motion in the fire light, her body shining with fragranced oil that smelled like lilies.

"My friend," Eurydice practically breathed in relief, "I couldn't do it anymore." Eurydice started talking faster and faster. "I couldn't stay with Orpheus for one more second. That vile house, so far removed from the woods..."

"Whoa, Eurydice!" Telodice grabbed Eurydice's arm and pulled her towards the edge of the clearing, where it was only marginally quieter. "What are you talking about? Are you leaving Orpheus? That man loves you. I'm sure you can work it out. Whatever it is."

"He's not like us, Telodice," Eurydice grabbed her friend's shoulders and shook her gently. Eurydice's eyes were wild; her expression was crazed as her heart beat rapidly in her chest. "Do you understand? Can you try to understand? He wants to keep me like some garden flower, but he doesn't realize flowers are alive..."

Telodice looked startled, suddenly very worried about her

friend. She said nothing as Eurydice went on, waxing lyric about the call of the wild and her need for freedom. Luckily, Telodice was a nymph, too, and at the end of the day, she would always understand the importance of being connected to nature.

"Stop now, Eurydice. Breathe." Telodice finally placed her finger gently over Eurydice's mouth to get her to stop talking. She smirked playfully, nodding towards the party that was descending further and further into Dionysian debauchery behind them. She grabbed Eurydice's hand and tugged her towards the beautiful chaos.

"Don't worry about that right now. You know what they say—party by moonlight, make decisions by sunlight." Telodice winked and ran right back towards a group of dryads on the edge of the clearing, sliding into one's lap without a second thought. Eurydice breathed a sigh of relief. This was the kind of wildness she craved.

Her heart faltered for a brief moment when the realization settled in that Pan was indeed not in the Underworld; he had chosen somewhere in Greece to spend the full moon. Eurydice walked towards the banquet table and poured herself a goblet of wine. She downed the entire glass without taking a breath and helped herself to a second. She let the wine trail down her chin and drip onto her short tunic, staining her skin and the fabric. Eurydice's head fell back, and she laughed again, pouring a third glass.

This was so much better than any of the dinner parties that Perseus or Orpheus would ever throw. Here, there was no one who would criticize her for spilling wine all down her body; Eurydice embraced it.

She waited until the wine started to pulse through her veins, making her pleasantly buzzed but with her wits about her. There was one way that she knew to channel Pan, to call out to him. He was a deity, after all, and every god had a way for worshippers to contact their gods.

Eurydice walked towards the edge of the clearing and began rummaging around in the grass. It only took her a few minutes to salvage what she needed—a dandelion, two mushrooms, and the bones of a hare. As she turned around and headed towards the fire, her tunic snagged on a low tree branch and ripped a tear through the fine fabric. Eurydice barely noticed, letting the tunic hang haphazardly from her shoulder.

She squeezed in between two dryads making out at the banquet table and grabbed an amphora. The wine never ran out, which was a benefit for all the creatures of the forest who were blessed by Dionysus and Pan. Eurydice carefully approached the fire, closing her eyes as she dug her feet into the sandy soil that surrounded the blaze.

Eurydice started chanting, a low, rhythmic sound that could hardly be heard above the raucous party happening all around her. She tuned it out, focusing all her senses on the heavy smoke of the incense and the beat of the drums. It was a steady cadence that mimicked her racing heart, making Eurydice feel like the drums were keeping her alive. She started to sweat from her close proximity to the fire, the cloying scent and wine mixing in her veins until she wasn't sure what was reality anymore. As soon as she crossed that threshold into the unknown, when her mind began to slip, she tossed everything she was holding into the fire.

The small bones crackled instantly from the heat as the dandelions and mushrooms charred; the wine caused the flames to stretch even higher in the night sky as they burned off the alcohol. As the wilderness accepted her offering, Eurydice's voice became clearer.

"Pan, god of the wilderness, purveyor of the forests, father of the trees. Pan Aegocerus, Pan Lyterius, Pan Maenalius..." Eurydice started to sway back and forth as she called out each of his epithets.

Pan was not a god of temples and ceremony; he was a god

of edifices and altars, the cruder the better. Pan was a wild thing, rustic and unpredictable, and while his devotion to Eurydice had never been questioned, she knew that a traditional prayer would never get the satyr's attention. The only way to do it was to toss offerings into a burning fire and call out his many names—the wilder the setting, the better. The offerings could be any number of things, but they always had to include wine, at the very least.

Eurydice was lost to the rhythm of the drums, which picked up their tempo. She didn't know if it was all in her head or if the drummers realized that she was moving to the beat, but she didn't care. She swayed more drastically, her shoulders moving back and forth while her hips shimmied in an alternating rhythm. As if she had no control over her body, Eurydice started to pick up her feet. Before she knew it, she started to dance.

Eurydice began moving in a circle, embracing the warmth and smell of the flames. She moved like wind and water over the earth, weaving her hands together and tossing them up towards the sky in offering to Selene. Her hair was as bright as bronze in the glow of the raging fire, whipping around her face as though it had a mind of its own. Eurydice picked up her pace to match the escalating drums, closing her eyes as she began to spin in circles while she kept moving around the fire. All of her senses started to blur together until her consciousness slipped further and further away, leaving her with only the mind of a nymph. She was only preoccupied with what was in front of her, dancing and offering herself up to the wilderness in tribute. There was nothing else that mattered to her in that moment, besides her rhythmic movements around the flames.

Eurydice didn't notice that she had garnered the attention of the entire party, which had all but completely turned into an orgy. Several other nymphs and dryads got up and began to dance around the flames, following Eurydice's every movement. She was a painfully beautiful creature when she danced, every twist of her body carefully crafted, simultaneously effortlessly and unbelievably technical in every way. Eurydice was the physical embodiment of everything that was beautiful and wild about nature, as if Gaia carved Eurydice from her own breast.

The screams and shouts of the party continued to get louder and louder, and the drumbeat had reached an impossibly fast tempo. Eurydice didn't stop. She spun and spun, beginning to howl to the moon, revealing the most feral parts of herself that had been locked away for far too long. Even before Orpheus had arrived in the Underworld, Eurydice had lost this part of herself. Her only cognizant thought as she danced was the realization that there were parts of her that had been chained up since she met Orpheus—not even since their reunion.

Eurydice's body came alive in another burst of movement, and the strength of it shocked her. She kept dancing as the wine in her veins turned to arousal. There was a steady pulse between her legs that Eurydice hadn't felt in a long time. She had assumed that infallible lust and animalistic craving to touch and fuck had long ebbed away from her. At one point, she assumed it might have been a factor of simply getting older, even if she was immortal.

But another surge of arousal warmed Eurydice's body all over, hotter than even the fire could manage, and her eyes flew open with a gasp.

There, standing in front her, in the middle of the chaos and the reckless party happening in the woods...was Pan.

Eurydice didn't think; she acted. Without a moment's hesitation, Eurydice leaned forward, grabbed Pan by the face, and kissed him.

18

Pan had heard many whispers and legends about the end of the world over the years. Every deity had their own way of telling the story or preventing their demise during the apocalypse. Pan had spent too much time in the Underworld to ever question the Fates or the strength of the titans in Tartarus, so he never thought about it too much. Until the moment that Eurydice kissed him.

In a matter of seconds, Pan realized that the world could end at any time and only now would he die happy. For an immortal and a god who was infamous for always being in a good mood, even if he was a bit of a trickster—although you could hardly blame him when you considered his parentage—Pan was suddenly obsessed with the concept of mortality.

All it took was the feel of Eurydice's mouth against his, her fingers combing through his beard, and Pan was consumed with how much time he had left. No matter when the world ended, it wouldn't be enough time, especially if Eurydice kept kissing him like that.

He reacted entirely on instinct, his more beastly side taking over. He wrapped his arms around Eurydice's waist, pulling her body flush against his. All the blood in Pan's brain rushed south so quickly, he was practically lightheaded. He tightened his hold on Eurydice's body, feeling the warmth of her skin through her ripped tunic, hotter than the flames they were standing in front of. She was as soft as rose petals, and Pan's desire flooded his veins until he thought he might collapse if she walked away from him. One of his hands slid up Eurydice's back and into her hair, gripping it tightly and pulling on it as Pan took dominance over the kiss. He poured a hundred of years of longing into the embrace, holding onto Eurydice as though she was his oxygen.

Someone in the melee picked up a lyre, and the sudden sound of it shocked Pan; it doused over him like ice water.

"Eurydice," Pan gasped. He didn't let go of her but pulled away, gently cupping her cheek and staring her dead in the eyes. "What's happening right now?"

"What do you mean?" Eurydice looked a little surprised. "I was kissing you, until you stopped for no damn reason."

Eurydice leaned in to kiss him again, and Pan shook his head, avoiding her although it pained him.

"What about Orpheus?" Pan couldn't believe that he was stopping, not when he had the love of his life in his arms and begging to kiss him, but he couldn't partake in something that Eurydice was going to regret later. He barely survived her getting married to Orpheus; he wouldn't ever survive knowing that he was something Eurydice regretted.

Eurydice paled, turning her face away from Pan so he couldn't see her face.

"I don't want to talk about him right now." Pan could see the pain etched in her features, which lit another fire under his ass. He wrapped his arms tighter around her waist, gently trailing a thumb down her cheek.

"Did he hurt you?" Pan's voice was tense—coaxing in the way he approached Eurydice, but ready to behead Orpheus at the slightest provocation. As soon as he had anything that would justify the violence, he'd act on it.

"No, no, nothing like that." Eurydice shook her head, but Pan didn't believe her. "I mean... He did hurt me, but not the way you're thinking. I don't want to talk about him right now, Pan, please. Don't make me."

Pan couldn't possibly sort through all the emotions he was feeling at that precise moment. He needed to know what had driven Eurydice into his arms, even if it killed him and he stopped whatever this was in its tracks.

"I don't want to make you do anything you don't want to," Pan sighed, "but you've got to tell me. You were committed to making your relationship with Orpheus work. What happened?"

The drums increased, and there was a cacophony of joyful shouts and screams from the crowd around them. It was potentially the worst time and place to be having a discussion about Eurydice's relationship, but Pan didn't have a choice.

Eurydice shook her head. "I don't want to fucking talk about Orpheus. Everyone wants me to always talk about Orpheus. I don't give a fuck anymore, Pan. Do you understand me? Don't fucking be like everyone else and just let me be!" Eurydice's voice broke with emotion, tears slipping down her cheeks. It shattered any of the resolve that was left in Pan's body, which wasn't very much to begin with.

"That works for me. I could go the rest of my life without hearing his damn name ever again," Pan grunted, cupping Eurydice's cheek and kissing her again.

It was intoxicating; it was the sweetest wine and the most sublime high he'd ever experienced, all rolled up into one. Pan tugged them further away from the bonfire until they were at the edge of the clearing, some of the trees providing them partial privacy from the Dionysian madness surrounding them.

He kissed Eurydice with everything he had inside of him, his passion pouring into every lick and bite. Eurydice was wild against his body, jumping up into his arms and pinning Pan against the trunk of a tree. She wrapped her legs around his waist, and Pan nearly collapsed. He could practically feel her heat so close to his cock, only mere scraps of clothing between them. All he'd have to do was tug a little bit of fabric to the side, and he'd be inside of her.

A small part of Pan's brain started screaming at him, reminding him that this was not how he wanted everything to go with Eurydice.

She can't regret this.

Pan pulled away with a sharp gasp, Eurydice biting onto his lower lip and tugging it as he recoiled.

"Fuck, Eurydice." Pan tightened his grip on her, breathing heavily. "What do you want?"

"Stop asking me questions," Eurydice nearly started crying again, wrapping her arms around Pan's neck. "I don't know what I want. I don't want to even know right now. I need to just...embrace the fucking chaos!"

Pan knew what she was talking about. They were children of the wild, after all. To suddenly have her afterlife mapped out for her, to go from living in the forest to suddenly becoming the proper wife of a famous poet, would've been like clipping a bird's wings. Eurydice would figure out what she wanted in life because she always did. If she needed to embrace the possibilities of not knowing, he'd give that to her. But he couldn't give her all of him; he wouldn't survive if she determined later on that what she wanted didn't include Pan.

"Then just tell me what you want right now," Pan breathed, pressing a long line of tender kisses down her neck. It was intimate and caressing, something that he'd never bothered to do with any of his hook-ups before.

"I want you to fuck me," Eurydice exhaled all the words at once. She let her eyes flutter closed, and her head fell back while she started grinding her hips gently against Pan. He cursed under his breath, desperately praying to not come practically untouched under his clothes like a young satyr.

"I can't," Pan moaned, sounding like he was in physical pain. He started lowering Eurydice down to the soft earth beneath them while she made a noise of protest. Pan laid her on the ground and sat up on his knees, gently putting his hands on Eurydice's ankles.

"I can't fuck you," he whispered, leaning down and kissing Eurydice's bare knee. He trailed his tongue up her thigh, and her whole body shuddered. "But I can make you come, Eurydice. Do you want that?"

"Yes, fuck," Eurydice whimpered, screwing her eyes even more tightly closed and wriggling in place. "Please, Pan, do whatever you want to me. Only you." The words came out like a prayer, and Pan thought his heart would explode. In any other circumstance, he would've fallen to the ground and rejoiced.

She's drunk and she's upset, Pan reminded himself. *She doesn't mean it.*

If Pan only had one night with Eurydice, however, he knew he'd never forget it, no matter how many years he lived. He was hellbent on making sure that Eurydice never forgot it either.

Pan lay down on his stomach, wrapping his hands around Eurydice's legs and pulling her closer to him. She smelled like smoke, musk, and roses, and Pan had never smelled anything as heady and intoxicating as she was. Her body was practically vibrating off the ground, enticing Pan further.

"Come on, my wild thing," Pan purred. He trailed his lips across her thigh again, getting closer and closer to her core, dragging the stubble of his rough beard across her skin. Her skin was as delicate as petals, and Pan relished in the red beard burn that followed in his wake.

He grabbed the torn remnants of Eurydice's chiton and ripped them further, causing them to fall away. When all of her was revealed to Pan, his brain completely cut out. Eurydice looked like she was carved by the gods, only for him, curvy and soft all over. Pan leaned down and sucked a bruise at the junction of her thigh and hip, making Eurydice cry out.

"I'm going to send you back to that fucking poet with my beard burn on your thighs, Eurydice."

She only moaned in response, her hands surging forward and grabbing hold of Pan's horns. She gripped them tight, maneuvering Pan until he was in front of her weeping pussy.

"Do you like the sound of that?" Pan teased. Her grip on his horns tightened in response. Pan had to shift his hips and bend his back to give his aching erection some relief, pressed between his body and the dirt.

"I think you do," Pan chuckled dirtily to himself. "I think you like the idea of going back to that conceited motherfucker with my marks on your skin. Every time you walk, you'll feel me between your legs."

Pan placed one hand on her thigh and trailed one finger gently through Eurydice's core, carefully circling her clit without putting any pressure on it. Eurydice made a sound that was suspiciously close to a wail, her back bending and coming straight off the ground. Pan knew that she was wound so tightly, she was already dripping on his fingers, and she wouldn't last long. But he wanted to make it count.

Pan kept circling his finger, taking his sweet time exploring Eurydice and relishing her soft, dripping flesh. She was sweating and shifting her hips wildly, practically bucking her thighs to get his mouth on her. Pan relished it, enjoyed every millisecond as if it was an eternity. He studied her body for every reaction, paying attention to which spots made her sing.

"Orpheus might be the musician, but you're going to sing an even sweeter song for me, Eurydice, okay?"

"Pan," Eurydice panted, picking her head up. Her face was flushed, and her hair was sticking to her forehead with sweat. "I will do whatever the fuck you want, but please, just fucking put your mouth on me." She stared at him with a gaze so intense, it burned even brighter than the bonfire behind them and turned Pan's willpower to ash.

Pan pushed Eurydice's thigh a little wider, spreading her open for him so she was completely exposed. The sounds of the party had descended into utter debauchery behind him, their own coupling drowned out by the sounds of dryads and nymphs fucking each other with abandon in every corner of the clearing. The air around them now smelled heavily of smoke and sex, and it was the wild, debauched part of worship that mortals would never be able to comprehend. It was the wilderness at its wildest, its most primal; it was devotion to Dionysus and Pan himself, bared naked to bring glory to the gods with their basest instincts.

Pan looked at Eurydice, practically glowing, and her pussy spread wide for him, and growled in satisfaction.

"I need you to say my name when you come, Eurydice," Pan grunted. He stuck his tongue out and licked one thick, hot swipe up her center before pulling back. Eurydice's legs started shaking, and she let out another gasping cry. He had barely touched her but the anticipation and atmosphere around them was pushing all of Eurydice's suppressed urges to the surface.

"Say my name when you come," Pan repeated, "and I'll give this pretty little pussy exactly what it needs. Is that a deal?"

"Fuck, g-god, yes," Eurydice moaned. She gave another tug on his horns, pulling him closer to her core. "I'll do whatever you want but stop fucking teasing me."

Pan grinned, his pupils nearly entirely dilated. He had a dangerous smirk on his face; this was the god of fertility in action.

"As my wild thing commands." Pan bent his head to Eurydice's center, and without another moment's hesitation, he feasted like a starving man. He wrapped his lips around her clit and sucked hard, simultaneously slipping two fingers in her pussy; he had teased her long enough and was now hellbent on wringing every sensation possible out of her body.

Eurydice started moaning and couldn't stop, each sound louder and more unhinged than the last. Pan curled his fingers upwards and started fucking her mercilessly, grinning against her core in satisfaction when Eurydice screamed so loudly, her voice went out.

Pan hit the spot over and over again, relishing the burning feeling in his scalp as Eurydice yanked on his horns with all of her remaining strength. Her thighs shook on either side of his head, and he relished her juices dripping down his chin. He could feel his own precome drenching his thighs at that point; somehow, he was harder than he had ever been in his life. He came closer and closer to his own climax and worked harder to manipulate Eurydice's body in ways that she had never felt before.

He never let up on her clit, alternating between gentle sucking and tiny licks that brought her to the edge and back repeatedly. His fingers continued to curl inside of her, hitting that sweet spot until her body was nearly wrung out underneath him, and she hadn't even climaxed yet. She was a panting, incoherent mess, letting out a string of babbling words that Pan couldn't even comprehend. It didn't matter. He could die happy with Eurydice's wrecked body underneath him and smothered between her thighs. Eurydice was practically ripping his horns from his head, but he couldn't remember any other purpose for them, so he languished in the feeling.

"Pan, p-please," Eurydice gasped. "I-I have t-to... I can't..."

"Oh, poor wild thing," Pan murmured gently, placing kisses on her pubic bone, "do you forget the ways of the wild, my love? Do you forget what it's like to be worshipped?" Pan twisted his fingers again and watched in satisfaction as Eurydice's eyes rolled back in her head. "That repugnant show-off wants to reduce you to his arm candy," Pan scoffed, lowering his head. "How ironic that he doesn't know how to make his *muse* sing."

Pan slipped a third finger inside of Eurydice and flicked his tongue against her clit. Eurydice screamed, and Pan knew the exact moment Eurydice shattered. She started bucking her hips and riding his face, tightening her grip on his horns and pulling him toward her to meet her short thrusts.

Pan held onto her thigh and kept fucking her with his fingers, keeping his mouth open and licking up every drop of Eurydice he could touch.

"I-I'm... I'm..." Eurydice could barely get the sentence out, but Pan knew she was close. He couldn't speak, smothered in her heat, and he didn't care if he ever said another word aloud again. He wrapped his lips around Eurydice's clit and sucked hard, curling his fingers at the exact same moment with a precision that only a god of fertility and debauchery would possess.

"Pan!" Eurydice came with his name on her lips, convulsions rolling over her entire body. Rose petals and vines exploded out of her hair, and her release drenched Pan's beard, even dripping down onto his chest. The sight and sound of Eurydice coming sent Pan over the edge, his heavy, aching cock releasing into the soil. He came with a shout, delving back in to lick up every trace of Eurydice's climax. She shuddered sporadically through the aftershocks, until they were both on the ground, panting and exhausted.

Pan picked himself up and dragged his body on top of Eurydice's before collapsing next to her and pulling her into his side.

"Pan..." Eurydice started, but he kissed her to quiet her thoughts.

"Don't say anything," Pan murmured. The party was still raging around them, offerings to Dionysus and Pan abounding. A bed of baby's breath sprung up underneath their bodies, cradling their sweat-soaked flesh and caressing Eurydice's tingling and overstimulated skin.

"My wild thing," Pan whispered to himself, watching as Eurydice fell into a deep sleep. "My eternal love." Pan refused to sleep for the rest of the night. He wouldn't miss a single moment of the sensation of having a sleeping, satisfied Eurydice in his arms.

Especially if it was only for one night.

19

When Pan blinked his eyes slowly open, he immediately started cursing. He was mortified to realize he had fallen asleep, which was the last thing he wanted to do. Eurydice had been sleeping in his arms, and he didn't want to miss a single moment of that bliss. He sat up and quickly looked around, his melancholy going bone-deep when he saw Eurydice was no longer next to him. Pan was sitting on the edge of the clearing, between some trees where he'd hauled Eurydice the previous night to achieve only a modicum of privacy. All around him, the ground was covered with fresh baby's breath. It was as thick as wool, woven like a heavy carpet across the ground. Pan blushed furiously when he noticed a fully grown oak tree had sprung up from the ground near his feet.

"Oh god," Pan grunted, running his hand through his thick curls. He slowly stood up and stretched out his arms, relishing the soreness in his shoulders from clutching Eurydice to him all night long.

I can't believe she left. Pan's heart was collapsing inside of his chest. He knew that last night wasn't going to go anywhere...but he at least expected to see Eurydice's face in the morning to soften the blow. Creatures of the forest weren't often prudish when it came to sex; everyone ended up getting into bed with their friends at one point or another. It happened eventually when you gathered with each other to celebrate the god of wine and the god of fertility. The nymphs and dryads, belonging to Pan, had adopted a culture of 'what happens at the banquet, stays at the banquet.'

Sex wasn't anything to be ashamed of; it was the most natural part of themselves. The fact that Eurydice had left Pan the morning after cut deeper knowing that whatever she was thinking when she woke up, it superseded that long-held mentality of Dionysian devotees.

If I made her feel ashamed or uncomfortable... The thought sat in Pan's stomach like sour wine.

"That is the most depressing look I've ever seen on anyone's face, ever."

"Fuck!" Pan nearly jumped out of his skin when Hermes's voice suddenly cut through the empty clearing. "Are you always hellbent on greeting people in the most chaotic way possible?" Pan crossed his arms over his chest and mustered his best attempt at a glare aimed at his father.

Hermes was looking cherubic as always, his golden hair forming a nearly perfect crown around his head. He was dressed casually, without his staff or winged sandals, the impish grin always present on his face.

"Chaos is what I do, my child, and don't act like it doesn't run in your blood too," Hermes scoffed playfully.

"Knock it off with the 'my child' nonsense. You may be my father, but we're both as old as Greece itself at this point."

"You should never remind a lady of her age." Hermes clutched at his chest dramatically.

"I don't see Hercules around," Pan quipped back, and Hermes nearly fell over with laughter.

"Ha! I have taught you a thing or two." Hermes suddenly looked wistful. "He is pretty though, isn't he?"

"Yes," Pan rolled his eyes, "your husband is very pretty, father dearest. Did you come here for a reason or just to torment me specifically?"

"Touchy, touchy!" Hermes's brows raised. "What's got your horns in a twist? I heard you were celebrating the full moon in Greece last night, and then you suddenly whisked away to the Underworld without a word."

"I'm allowed to celebrate the full moon wherever I choose. It's my celebrations after all, next to Dionysus."

Hermes held up his hands in mock surrender. "I never said that you weren't allowed to." Hermes's face contorted into a softer expression. "I can tell that something happened. You're being pricklier than usual, and you're half goat."

"Fuck off," Pan grunted, rubbing his hands over his face in exasperation. "I don't want to talk about it right now."

"The only thing that has ever gotten you this worked up is... Oh my god!" Hermes sucked in a sharp breath. "Eurydice! Did something happen?" Hermes crossed the small clearing to get closer to his son, gossiping like one of the Fates.

Pan dropped dramatically back down into the field of baby's breath, resting his chin on his knees. A few of the flowers started to wilt in a perfect circle around him.

"Gods," Hermes whistled in a low tone. "You are upset." Hermes studied the flowers that were rapidly decaying around Pan's presence. "I'm assuming you saw her with Orpheus, or..."

"Don't mention that shit musician's name in my presence," Pan growled. A wave of angry, powerful green power rippled over Pan as his satyr form broke free. His beard lengthened, and the hair over his body turned coarser, even his horns stretched out further as he shifted.

"I can see that." Hermes raised a brow. "So nothing happened at all with that darling muse?"

Pan said nothing for a few moments, not knowing how much he wanted to divulge to Hermes. He trusted Hermes unlike most deities, not only because Hermes was his father, but because he knew the gossip around Hermes's reputation was just that—gossip. He could keep a secret for millennia if it was required of him. Finally, the heaviness on Pan's heart outweighed his hesitations.

"She called for me last night," Pan muttered, looking anywhere but at Hermes's face.

"Oh." Hermes did an excellent job at keeping the emotion out of his voice. "She called to you during...during a full moon celebration?"

Pan looked up at Hermes, mortified when a few tears sprung free. He nodded.

"Did you..." Hermes turned around and stared at the oak tree that had sprung up out of the ground, fresh dirt still upturned around it. He spun back around and looked at Pan, his face surprised and delighted. "You did! Or didn't you? I've been forced to hear plenty of rumors of how you make the forest grow..." Hermes's trailed off, scrunching up his face in displeasure.

"Oh my god!" Pan flushed, covering his ears. "I do not want to discuss this with you."

"Okay, that's mutual," Hermes assured him, waiting until Pan removed his hands from his ears. "Why do you look so upset then? If you two... Oh." Hermes quickly put together the scene before him. "She went back to him?"

Pan didn't say anything, resting his chin atop his knees again. He was torn between the raging loss and heart-wrenching sadness within him to come so close to Olympian levels of bliss and have it ripped away from him again. He leaned into the numbness that was threatening to consume him, clutching onto memories and the scent of Eurydice that still clung to him.

"That fucker," Hermes growled. "I can't stand that she doesn't know what happened." Hermes's winged sandals appeared on his feet as a golden aura of power fluttered over his skin. Pan appreciated the outward show of magic, knowing that it was his father's powers reacting in displeasure to the heartache that Pan was suffering through.

"I know," Pan sighed heavily. The tears were falling freely down his face now, and he did nothing to stop them or brush them away. "She's not even happy with him now. He treats her like shit, but she feels pressure to stay with him because they're *'Orpheus and Eurydice'*." Pan grunted the names with displeasure.

"She told you this last night?" Hermes pressed. Pan couldn't decipher the expression that popped up on Hermes's face.

"No, she didn't say much last night."

"Did she say she wanted to fuck you? Explicitly?" Hermes growled, his temper suddenly flaring. "If she was drinking and if you..."

Pan was on his feet in a flash, throwing his body weight at Hermes. They crashed into the oak tree with Pan's forearm against Hermes's throat.

"I would never," Pan hissed, "and I'll kill anyone who tries to hurt her."

Hermes's face beamed with pride as Pan caught his breath and released his father.

"Just checking. So she's told you she's upset?"

"Yes," Pan sighed, pinching the bridge of his nose and beginning to pace. "I don't know what to do. Part of her has to remember what happened because she's unhappy with Orpheus and doesn't know why."

"Well, the answer is he's a prick," Hermes scoffed. "She doesn't need to remember his betrayal to not want to be with him."

"Correct, but she thinks they have this great love affair that was tragically cut short. She's staying in that relationship based on a precedence that isn't there. It's practically cruel to watch, but Hades is determined to let Eurydice suffer."

Pan's melancholy morphed into something darker, a righteous defensiveness of the woman he'd loved for a hundred years.

"Now, now," Hermes scratched his chin, "Hades is a rule follower, and that's for a good reason. He wouldn't want anyone to suffer. Especially in his realm."

"He's doing a shit job of it," Pan growled, beginning to pace back and forth. He grew more agitated, and Hermes didn't know what to do with it; he watched helplessly as Pan worked himself up into a frenzy. When he finally dropped to his knees, Pan released an anguished scream that ripped through the trees.

Hermes ducked as the trees shook, watching in horror and awe as all the vegetation as far as he could see shriveled up and died. The landscape around them simply disappeared, withering away to nothing. The lush, green forest turned into a twisted mess of thorns and weeds. Hermes was one of the few deities who understood just how fucked the world was if Pan was this devastated; there wouldn't be a living green thing left alive when he was done. Demeter would have a fucking conniption, and they'd all had enough of her tantrums.

Hermes's heart ached for his son, and he walked slowly towards Pan on his knees, weeping softly in his hands. Hermes sent a ripple of power out through the ether, requesting the presence of one of the Underworld's gods.

Hermes got down on Pan's level and opened his arms, clutching his son to his chest like a babe. Pan's silent cries erupted into a barrage of sobs, and his hands held tight onto his father. Hermes sat there patiently while Pan cried, his mind made up. A soft breeze drifted over the dried and dead ground. Hypnos slowly appeared on the winds, his figure half obscured by white clouds. He tilted his head curiously and yawned, studying the scene in front of him.

Pan didn't even notice the god's presence. Hermes nodded, a silent conversation happening between the two gods. Hypnos nodded once and stepped forward, gently placing his hand on

Pan's back. As soon as he touched him, Pan's sobs quieted, and he fell into a deep, heavy sleep.

Hypnos disappeared without a word while Hermes muttered his thanks to the wind. He laid his son down on the earth, which sprung up to meet him. Hermes breathed a sigh of relief as another fresh mound of grass and flowers grew around Pan, cradling the god while he slept.

"At least your dreams must be pleasant," Hermes whispered, pressing a gentle kiss to his son's brow. "When you wake, it'll be to a different world."

Hermes vanished in a cloud of rippling, golden power, sprinting across the Underworld to his destination. Orpheus had caused too much suffering, and Hermes wasn't going to let it go on any longer.

Hermes moved in total silence. His footfalls were devoid of noise, even the wings on his circlet and sandals were quiet. The god of thieves had a legacy to protect and creeping through Hades's halls was difficult enough, even with a thief's magic.

The long, winding hallway was covered in thick carpets and had arching ceilings. The walls were made with glittering obsidian and flecked with jewels. There were tables and heavy chests lining the sides of the hallway, covered in shining weaponry, gold and silver, and even more jewels and treasures of priceless value. Whenever Hermes was inside Hades and Persephone's home, he was filled with the undeniable urge to start pushing things over, like a cat knocking things off a tabletop.

Hermes's thoughts were then interrupted by a very loud crashing sound, followed by the sound of breaking glass. Hermes clapped a hand over his own mouth to keep himself from reacting out loud, spinning on his heel to see the cause of the chaos.

"Hercules!" Hermes hissed, whisper-yelling down the hallway. "I told you to be careful!" Hercules was bent over the remnants of a shattered vase, an embarrassed look on his face with his cheeks flushed pink. Hercules, Hermes's consort and the greatest warrior Greece had ever known, was horribly clumsy at times when he wasn't very literally counterbalancing his own weight with a sword.

"I told you not to bring me!" Hercules whispered back, delicately stepping over the broken shards of glass. "I don't know why I'm necessary for a reconnaissance mission, Hermes." Hercules tiptoed over to his husband with a pout.

"Because..." Hermes exhaled in relief when he realized they hadn't been caught, "if we run into Cerberus, he likes you more."

"Cerberus guards the gates of hell. He's not inside Hades and Persephone's household."

"Of course he is," Hermes scoffed and continued walking down the hallway. "Persephone demanded that Cerberus be allowed to sleep in their bed."

"Do I want to know how you know that?" Hercules flushed a little deeper, and Hermes shivered pleasantly. There was nothing he loved more than the big demigod when he got pouty and jealous.

"I'm the god of thieves, my love." Hermes winked. "It's my job to know the comings and goings of guard dogs."

Hercules said nothing but crossed his arms over his chest, clearly skeptical. Hermes went up on his tiptoes and quickly kissed Hercules on the chin, relishing in the hazy look it gave Hercules.

"Let's hurry up, and we can go home." Hermes waggled his eyebrows, his seduction apparent. Hercules held his hand out towards the heavy double doors at the end of the hallway, indicating for Hermes to get on with it. Hermes stole another kiss from Hercules and squeezed his hand.

"Wait here and watch daddy go to work." Hermes chuckled

to himself, dissipating into a soft cloud of golden magic. He slid effortlessly towards the doors to Hades's office and slipped through the crack in between them, reappearing on the other side.

"Not even a little ward or some magic to stop me?" Hermes whispered to himself as he headed straight towards the apothecary cabinet behind the oak table Hades used as a desk. Hades's office looked like every other room in the house, which was elaborately decorated and stockpiled with riches that would make mortals and immortals alike weep. There were hundreds of tiny shelves nestled across the walls, each small alcove holding anything from a sparrow's skeleton to a ruby the size of an infant's fist. You never knew with Hades.

However, Hermes was looking for one thing in particular—something that would help him skirt around Hades's rules and hopefully bring Pan some peace. It might result in a little chaos first, but it would—he hoped—inevitably ensure that at least Eurydice was making fully informed decisions.

Hermes's hands glowed as he started tracing his finger over the wooden shelving, feeling the little cracks and pops in the atmosphere from the magical signatures of all the tiny keepsakes. Hecate may have been the goddess of witchcraft, but if she ever needed an ingredient she couldn't find, she asked Hades if he had it.

After a couple desperate minutes of searching, Hermes giggled to himself when he landed on a tiny, sealed jar. It was made with a typical red clay, nothing fancy, with a wax seal over the top of it. Arguably, it looked like the plainest thing on the shelf. Anyone who didn't know what they were looking at would inevitably leave it behind, assuming it had no value.

"Hello, my pretty!" Hermes cooed, snatching the jar off the shelve and reading the label. There was a small piece of parchment tied around the lip of the jar with string that had nearly rotted away. Hermes read the tiny, neat handwriting.

"*Krasi tis alitheias.*" Hermes's smiled widened. "Oh, you lovely thing, you."

Hercules hissed through the door. "I don't know what you're talking to, but it better not have a pulse!"

Hermes had to bite his lip to keep himself from laughing too loudly; he could never get enough of a jealous Hercules. He could never really get enough of Hercules at all, which was partially why he found a reason to bring Hercules everywhere he went.

Hermes slipped the tiny jar into a small drawstring bag, looping it across his body before tiptoeing as quickly as he could out of the office. Hermes swung the doors open and grinned at the shocked expression on Hercules's face.

"What's that look for? We can go... Oh." Hermes's eyes widened as soon as he realized Cerberus was sitting at Hercules's feet, and a very angry Hades was standing in the hallway.

Hades had very clearly been pulled from bed, only wearing a bedsheet haphazardly tied into a loincloth around his waist. It was one of the few times that Hermes had ever seen him without a single piece of jewelry, except for the gilded string he wore wrapped around his ring finger. Hades's face was twisted in anger, but Hermes could tell it was giving way to meager frustration. The lord of the Underworld must have assumed there were actual thieves in his office. Knowing Hades, he would have been less bothered about any missing material items and more livid that something in his home had potentially jeopardized Persephone's safety.

"Hermes," Hades growled. His voice was low and groggy with sleep, and he pushed his shoulder-length black hair out of his face. "I should have known. Do you want to even try to lie and tell me why you're here?"

"Shit," Hercules cursed, getting both Hermes's and Hades's attention. Hercules gave them an awkward smile and immediately turned around to start petting Cerberus again.

"Well," Hermes cleared his throat, "there's a very good reason for this, my liege."

"Hades rolled his eyes. "There always is, if you're the god of thieves."

"Quite right." Hermes's lips pulled into a thin line. "I suppose you want the truth?"

"The truth is probably what will keep me from stringing you up by your sandals outside the gates of hell for a few days. It won't hurt you, but I imagine your pride will suffer to have you as my lawn ornament."

Hermes cringed. He screwed his eyes shut and took a deep breath, exhaling slowly. He leveled his gaze at Hades, pushing his heart out on his sleeve.

"It's for Pan."

Hades's countenance changed instantaneously. The furrow between his brows softened, and the frustration on his face ebbed away. He opened his mouth and closed it several times, as if he couldn't decide what he wanted to say. Hermes's heart started beating faster. Hercules must have sensed the tension, and he stood behind Hermes, placing a heavy, warm hand on his back for comfort. Hermes leaned into it, grateful for the touch. Finally, Hades turned around and started walking away without a word. Hermes stood shocked for a few seconds before he called out after the god.

"You don't want to know?"

Hades reached the opposite end of the hallway and turned around, a mischievous smirk on his face.

"Plausible deniability," Hades grunted. "I can't stop you from breaking the rules if I don't technically know it's happening."

Hades patted his thigh twice, and Cerberus bounded over to join him before they made a quick exit. Hermes looked over at Hercules, somewhat shocked.

"I didn't expect that reaction out of Hades," Hermes admitted. Hercules only shrugged, slipping his hand into Hermes's and walking them out the front door of Hades's home.

"I did." Hercules looked up at a tapestry depicting Hades and Persephone. "He's terrifying...but he's fair."

Hermes nodded in agreement, and the pair slipped back out into the night, the tiny jar labeled 'truth wine' in Hermes's pocket.

20

Eurydice had been staring out the window of Orpheus's kitchen, her eyes fixed on the tree tops of her fruit grove. It haunted her—the way she watched Pan help her grow it, and how Orpheus once again tried to take credit for it. She tried to focus on those small interactions instead of reckoning with the events of the night prior. Eurydice didn't remember much from the full moon ceremonies, but she remembered calling out to Pan. She retained every single second of their time together, the feeling of his body against hers. Pan set her body on fire, and he looked at her like he was willing to burn alive as collateral.

The scariest thing of all was the warm, fluttering feeling that had taken hold of Eurydice's chest ever since. She was no stranger to casual sex; nymphs typically viewed sex as casual as eating and breathing. Eurydice was horrified to realize when she woke up to Pan's sleeping frame that morning that it wasn't a simple infatuation she held for him. One night together, nestled underneath the open sky and surrounded by Dionysian rituals, and a deeper, more eternal feeling had shaken Eurydice to her core.

There was no gentle progression of feelings through time

spent together. No, this was as if everlasting, romantic love for Pan had been hibernating in her heart and woke up starving. She had to rip herself away from Pan's sleeping body that morning, hating herself for every step she took farther away from him. It was the only thing she could do to even get to a place where she could think straight. Eurydice knew that she didn't remember all the time she'd spent with Orpheus, but not a single memory came even close to the way she felt about Pan.

Everything about Pan was right. Ironically, it felt like a melody. This was something that Eurydice could dance to, an ebb and flow of trust and attraction that had been built over centuries of time spent together. It seemed that all Eurydice's heart needed to get on board was the juxtaposition of Orpheus's increasingly unhinged behavior and one night with Pan.

No, not even one night, Eurydice's thoughts interrupted themselves. *It was one head job. That's all it takes for you to turn your attentions to someone else. Oh, the gods below and in Olympus. Am I horrible person?*

Eurydice had dismissed the staff from the kitchen that morning, wanting to wallow in peace in the one room of the house that Orpheus would never willingly go into. She looked out at the fruit grove and down at her empty plate, debating going to pluck something off the heavy branches to eat.

"I'm an awful cook, but I'm happy to pour you a drink if you'd like."

Eurydice squeaked and jumped up from her seat at the table, spinning around with her plate in her hand, holding it like a weapon.

"Hermes," Eurydice let out a relieved sigh. "I didn't think I'd see you here this morning, of all places." Eurydice blushed slightly and replaced the plate.

I can't say that the first person I wanted to see this morning was Pan's father. Eurydice knew their relationship was different than mortal sons and their fathers, but it still wasn't a good reminder of everything she walked away from.

Hermes was dressed casually, stripped of anything that would identify him as a god. His entire presence exuded immortality and power, but his notable winged accessories and staff were missing. He leaned against the door frame, crossing his arms across his chest. He looked rather pensive as opposed to flirtatious, which was not how Eurydice was used to seeing Hermes.

"God of tricksters, the unseen, messages..." Hermes chuckled, "the god of everything no one else wants to do, apparently. I can come up with a reason to be just about anywhere."

Eurydice shook her head, some of her anxiety thawing in Hermes's presence. His energy was similar to Pan's in some way, and it soothed her. It took her mind off the fact that she was in Orpheus's house.

"What's your excuse for being here this morning?"

"Friendship." Hermes winked.

"That's Philotes."

"Psh," Hermes scoffed in reply, "he's a minor deity at best. I'm major Pantheon, my love. Consider it an upgrade."

Eurydice laughed in spite of herself, nodding towards the empty seat at the kitchen table. "Well, god of friendship, do you want to take a seat? I'm assuming Orpheus is sleeping off another hangover."

Hermes gave a short bow in reply and sat down graciously, pulling a tiny, ancient looking jar out of a satchel. Eurydice hadn't even noticed that he was carrying anything before. The tiny bag had been hidden between Hermes's body and the door frame. She raised a brow.

"Should I be concerned?"

"You wound me!" Hermes cackled dramatically, going to tug on the small string that fastened the jar's lid. "I was just going to say that I have some kykeon if you want it."

"Psychedelic kykeon? If so, I'll have to pass."

"Um, no," Hermes flushed, "not a psychedelic. It's the barley variety." There was something in Hermes's countenance that Eurydice couldn't identify, but she trusted him enough to know he wasn't lying. Eurydice said nothing but nodded, pushing an empty cup towards him. Eurydice expected a cloud of dust to come out of such an ancient looking jar. The string practically disintegrated and fell away when Hermes touched it, the linen lid revealing a wax seal over the top.

"What kind of kykeon is this, again?" Eurydice stared at the artifact, sensing some sort of weak magical hum coming from it. Hermes looked like he was a kid who got caught looking for sweets.

"Damn," he cussed under his breath. "I always forget that you've got enough immortal in you to sense a magical object when you see one."

"So it is a fucked up kind of kykeon!" Eurydice shrieked, her brow furrowing when she stared at the god. Kykeon came in plenty of different varieties. It was a fermented drink that plenty of peasants preferred to wine, but only occasionally did it function as a hallucinogenic.

"It's not fucked up." Hermes held up a finger. "It is not a psychedelic. I wouldn't lie about that."

"Then what is it?"

"I... I can't tell you," Hermes sighed in defeat, letting out a frustrated grunt as he leaned back in his chair.

"You can't tell me? Why do you want me to drink it?" Eurydice leaned a little closer, suddenly growing more intrigued as to what it might be that Hermes wanted to serve her.

"I can't tell you that either," Hermes grunted, looking increasingly upset. "But do you trust me?" The question was loaded, and the atmosphere grew more tense between Eurydice and Hermes.

"Yes," Eurydice nodded slowly, "but only because I know if you do anything to me, Pan will be furious."

"He'd kill me for it," Hermes agreed easily. Eurydice's heart skipped a beat.

Would Pan really kill a god, one of Greece's most powerful gods, for me? Even if that god was his father? Before Eurydice had another second to contemplate everything that Hermes's answer implied, she found herself reaching for the tiny jar.

"Will it hurt me irrevocably? Or put any of my loved ones in danger?" Eurydice grabbed the jar and brought it up to her nose, giving it a smell. She expected it to smell rancid, but it only reminded her of baby's breath and poppies. It was a light, floral scent.

Hermes looked at Eurydice with a hopeful expression; she noticed how keen he was, for whatever reason, that she consume the contents of that magical jar. He leaned forward, his broad torso stretching across the table, and held out his hand for Eurydice to shake.

"I promise," Hermes swore, "that the contents of this jar will not hurt you or your loved ones irrevocably. I cannot promise that it will be comfortable. I cannot promise that it will not change the world in which you think you are a part of. I will promise it is necessary."

His words were spoken with a solemn serenity. Eurydice had never seen that look in Hermes's eyes before; he was deadly serious. He may have been a trickster, but it was apparent that Hermes was putting his honor on the line. Eurydice looked down at the unassuming jar in her hands, the dust rubbing off on her fingers and the clay warming in her palms. Eurydice swallowed thickly and met Hermes's intense gaze. The air between them grew thick and Eurydice found herself nodding.

"Then I accept."

Hermes nodded, sitting back in his chair and patiently waiting for Eurydice to drink the jar's contents. She flicked a little bit of dust off the lip of the jar, took a deep breath, summoned her courage, and brought it to her lips. She held it with both hands and tipped her head back, consuming the jar's entire contents in a few messy sips. It was syrupy and thick, but it tasted as floral as it smelled.

It dripped down Eurydice's chin, staining the front of her clothes. Some part of the jar's magic consumed her, and she was overcome with the urgency to keep drinking, greedily gulping it down. She nearly fell off her chair, gasping for breath when the jar was finally empty. She dropped it, and it fell to the kitchen floor and shattered across the tile, sending pieces of wet clay scattering all over the kitchen.

Eurydice collapsed back into her seat, her eyes fluttering closed as a sudden heaviness overtook her limbs. She didn't possess the strength, it seemed, to keep her own eyes open. She faintly heard Hermes calling to her. There was more shouting. Two voices. Three? She tried to open her eyes, but it was impossible; her body felt like stone. She was faintly aware of her body sliding towards the ground and arms catching her to prevent her fall.

She could've sworn someone was shouting her name, but all the words sounded like they were underwater. Eurydice was hit with a sudden feeling of nausea, and her head threatened to explode under pressure—then everything went black.

The air smelled like sulfur. It was cloying and thick, as though it was fighting with the atmosphere to strangle the oxygen right out of the air. It made Eurydice feel sick, but she trudged on. One step after another. She couldn't remember anything anymore; the only thing that rang out in her mind was a warning. Someone had warned her this might happen. They said walking out of hell was not for the faint of heart. Her memories might come and go. There was a chance that she would forget her own name.

There was no way to measure time; the portal between worlds existed in a universe all its own. The only point was to keep walking. One foot after another. Do not stop. Do not slow your pace. Do not increase your pace. Heel to toe. Do not stop. Eventually, the bridge would be crossed, and when she saw the full light of day, her memories would be returned to her.

The stranger had warned her a final time before she started on this journey with no end and no beginning—say nothing and follow Orpheus. Orpheus loved her. Orpheus would keep walking. They would not stop... Keep going until the sun appeared.

The rough stone cut the soles of her feet and burned her skin. Eurydice was caught in a state that was somewhere between walking and sleeping, dead or alive. The atmosphere burned her eyes. She stumbled and held her hands out to catch her fall, biting her own tongue to keep from crying out and betraying the vow of silence. Eurydice hauled herself to her feet, dropping her hands to her knees and forcing herself to take a few deep breaths before continuing.

Finally... finally... Eurydice thought that the shades of darkness surrounding her started to lighten. Ever so slightly. The pitch black started to ebb to gray in some places, the corners of her vision were a little brighter than they had been a few paces ago. An impossible sway of hope started building in her chest. Was this torture over? How long had she been walking? How long had she lived in the space between worlds, with no sky, no flowers, no trees?

It doesn't matter, *she reminded herself.* You did this for Orpheus. You will reunite amongst the green trees and embrace the sweet earth you love again...and Orpheus. You will see Orpheus.

Eurydice's heart swelled with love, and it gave her what she needed to keep pushing. One foot after another. She started to be able to decode some of the landscape around her, the rock-strewn path covered in stones. She was able to dodge them now, sparing her feet, and started to pick up her pace. Finally, she was surrounded by the low light of dawn. The world around her was bathed in shades of grey and blue. The light of the sun was so, so close. She could sense it. Every part of her body was attuned to it—being a nymph—and she ached for the sun and for

Orpheus. He had braved the Underworld itself to come after her, and the songs he had sung her!

She felt lighter thinking about it. There was nothing she wouldn't do for him; if there was anything she could do to make Orpheus feel as adored as he made her feel... Alas, that was why she was the muse, and he was the artist. There were times when he was hard to reach. More than once it had been obvious that his art was taking priority over Eurydice. But that was the cost of artistry, no?

Eurydice put those thoughts aside as the world around her started to glow. Far off in the distance, no bigger than a pin prick, she saw it—a tiny, warm ball of light.

The sun! Eurydice practically shrieked in her mind, keeping her lips tight together. She couldn't make a sound.

She started running at a full sprint, pushing herself until her limbs were on fire. Eurydice could only think of Orpheus's arms, of collapsing into his chest after so long. Her feet were torn to shreds. She wept as the air whipped at her face, but she kept running. The ball of light grew larger and larger until Eurydice could begin to see some of the outlines of distant trees. Soon! She would be in the warm sunlight, running with Orpheus through the grass, brushing her fingers through those golden curls while he wrote verses praising her beauty above all else's. What it would be like in a few mere moments to kiss—

"Eurydice?" Orpheus's voice cut through the still darkness like a knife. It ripped through Eurydice's exalted visions and stabbed her directly in the heart. She tripped and went flying, barely avoiding smashing her head on a massive boulder lining the path. Eurydice scrambled to her feet, her pulse racing, trying to make sense of what happened.

There was Orpheus, standing at the mouth of the massive cave system they were in. His blonde hair was dripping with sweat, and he had a dismayed expression on his face.

"Orpheus!" Eurydice gasped. "What have you done?" Eurydice was so horribly confused. "I was right behind you! How could you not believe me?" Her voice increased in pitch as the sensations in her body started to ebb away; her fingers and toes were already going numb.

Eurydice was dying again.

"*Orpheus!*" Eurydice screamed, her voice cracking. "*O-Orpheus, save me! Please!*" She tried to stand up but collapsed back to her knees, crawling towards him. She scraped her body across the ground as her legs stopped working. Eurydice watched in horror as Orpheus took several steps back from her, his face as pale as a ghost.

"*Orpheus?*" she gasped. Her entire chest threatened to cave in.

"*I'm sorry.*" Orpheus shook his head. Eurydice watched in horror as he turned around and sprinted for the opening of the cave, the bright light of the sun enveloping him as he disappeared completely.

"*Orpheus...*" Eurydice whimpered, collapsing to the ground as her arms gave out. She closed her eyes and started to sob, vaguely aware of Thanatos as he picked her up in his arms and carried her back to the Underworld.

21

Eurydice came back to consciousness screaming. A million memories flooded her mind. Everything she left behind in the river of Lethe smacking her upside the head.

"Eurydice? Eurydice!" Hermes's voice broke through the chaos that occupied her mind. Eurydice turned around and saw Hermes sitting next to her on the chaise in Orpheus's main hall.

Orpheus was standing behind Hermes, a concerned look on his face. He was pale. Everything about him looked muted. Eurydice's memories settled into her body like it was a physical muscle memory. There was a roaring in Eurydice's ears; she could see Hermes's mouth moving, but she couldn't hear a thing he was saying. She couldn't stop staring at Orpheus. The only thing left in Eurydice's body was rage.

Unadulterated, uninhabited rage.

All the love she had once felt for Orpheus was still there in the remnants of her mind, but it had no power over it, no potency. The only thing she could see in her mind's eye over and over again was Orpheus's face as he turned away from her and left her to die again in that cave.

"You," Eurydice growled. Rose thorns started wrapping themselves around her arms and legs; vines began creeping in from the garden outside. She stood up slowly, raising her hand and pointing a single finger at Orpheus. Hermes's eyes widened, and he held his hands up in mock surrender, jumping over the back of the chaise and taking several steps back.

"Hermes!" Orpheus hissed, staring at the god. "What the hell have you done?"

"He did exactly what he needed to," Eurydice growled, her voice dropping into a lower register. Her body was practically vibrating in holy anger. All the deceit and hurt from her relationship with Orpheus was itching under her skin like insects. Orpheus looked around the room anxiously, making a panicked, squeaking sound when he realized the room was already half overgrown with plants and vines in the matter of a few short seconds.

"Eurydice, my love," Orpheus held up his hands, "I didn't want you to know! I wanted us to have a fresh start. I thought..."

"I don't give a damn what you thought!" Eurydice snapped. Her heart was pounding, but her voice was as cold as stone. "You are a cheat and a liar, Orpheus. You thought you would just arrive in the Underworld and pick up our relationship like your betrayal never happened? Like you never left me here to die?"

"Technically, you were already dead..."

"You made me crawl up from hell to be with you again! For what?"

"She has a point." Hermes shrugged nonchalantly, suddenly very preoccupied with examining his nails. Orpheus scowled and briefly turned his attention to Eurydice.

"You fucking look at me," Eurydice snapped. Orpheus's eyes nearly bugged out of his head, and he almost broke his neck turning his attention back towards her.

"I don't even know what to do with you right now," Eurydice hissed, stepping closer to him. She was practically vibrating with her fury, but her voice remained steady. The vines creeping in from the garden were practically at the ceiling of the massive room, giving the entire house the appearance of a home that had suddenly been abandoned fifty years ago. It had an eerie effect. Orpheus swallowed thickly, and sweat broke out on his brow as he watched Eurydice step closer to him.

"Let's forget the past," Orpheus tried lamely. "I-I know I fucked up, but we were young!"

"You were a grown man," Eurydice countered, "and I was on this earth for a hundred years before you were even born."

"Good point." Orpheus looked around nervously. "Can we even try? I mean, I have been putting up with your moods ever since... Oh god." Orpheus stopped himself short, pinching the bridge of his nose as he realized his slip up.

Eurydice was silent for a perilous, disturbingly long minute. Even Hermes, who was standing in the corner with a delighted look on his face, didn't say anything.

"You have been 'putting up with me'?" Eurydice fumed. Thorny stems had started growing out of her hair, tangling with her braid.

"That's not what I meant..."

"You callous fool!" Eurydice spat. "Orpheus, you are everything that could be wrong with a man. I cannot, c-cannot..." Eurydice cursed herself as her voice broke. She didn't want to show a single stitch of vulnerability in front of Orpheus; but curse her naive heart, which had simultaneously been reminded not only of Orpheus's betrayal, but also of how much she really had loved him.

"I cannot stand to look at you," Eurydice continued. "I refuse to be in your presence, and I forbid you to ever be in mine again." Orpheus started to interrupt, but Eurydice stopped him with a glare. "If I had my way, every flower would die when you laid eyes upon it. The trees would keep the air from you; the stones would throw themselves at your body in my vengeance," Eurydice started to shout. Twisted, angry thorns started creeping in from the outside and covered the floor, effectively pinning Orpheus in a corner of the room.

"You decided that you wanted to rebuild a relationship based on lies, you used me! You wanted me to forget all about the fact that you left me to die in between worlds while you ran towards the sun. Never again, Orpheus, never again."

"If you would just listen to me!" Orpheus pleaded, dropping to his knees. Eurydice took notice of the pained look on his face when he landed in thorns.

Eurydice took one step closer, spinning her pointer finger in a small circle. The thorns responded, twisting themselves around Orpheus's wrist. Eurydice snapped her fingers, and the thorns pulled free, drawing blood from Orpheus. He howled in response, grabbing at his wounds. The foliage cleared a path for Eurydice as she stepped towards him, bending down and grabbing his chin. She forced him to look up at her, her eyes ablaze with fury.

"Orpheus, with your blood to mark this deal, I abandon you. Your god abandoned you, and now your muse leaves you bleeding in a bed of thorns. May you never sing my name again."

Eurydice turned on her heel and walked out, refusing to listen to Orpheus's cries of protest as they echoed out behind her. She waved her hand in the air, and the vines and thorns shot forward. Eurydice was content to let them overtake the entire house.

Let Orpheus pluck and prune them out of his precious estate, thorn by thorn. Eurydice's thoughts were wicked and full of vengeance while her heart was bleeding, matching each drop of Orpheus's red blood on the white marble floor, drop for drop.

Eurydice walked right out of the house and towards the garden, collapsing only when she retreated to the shade of her grove. As she wept and struggled to contain her composure, the meticulously cared-for garden started dying. Every petal fell to the ground and browned. The green grass withered underneath Eurydice's feet. Everything keeled over and dried out, a physical manifestation of the life that Eurydice had once thought she would have—now dead and dying all around her. She didn't know who she was anymore; if only she'd never met Orpheus.

"Musicians, eh?" Hermes's soft voice appeared in the fruit grove. "It seems like a rite of passage that every woman has her heart broken by a musician at least once. I know I have." Hermes shrugged.

Eurydice was silent for a moment, looking up at Hermes in a mild state of shock. Hermes waggled his eyebrows dramatically, and Eurydice couldn't help it; she started laughing. She nearly rolled over onto her side, hugging her ribs until they hurt from laughing too hard. Hermes plopped himself down in the dirt next to Eurydice rather unceremoniously, watching with a sad smile as her laughter turned into tears.

"Oh, sweet muse," Hermes sighed. He opened his arms up and pulled Eurydice into his chest. She started crying harder, every last tear wrung out of her. Hermes said nothing; he simply held her and waited for her soft cries to end. He busied himself by plucking some of the errant thorns out of her hair. Eurydice finally sat up slowly and pulled away from Hermes's grasp, wiping at her eyes.

"I'm terribly sorry. I don't want to cry any more over him, but..."

"Eurydice?" Pan's voice suddenly rang out through the courtyard. "Are you here?" Eurydice and Hermes turned around, just in time to see Pan running down the central aisle of the garden.

"What happened?" Pan took in the sight of Eurydice, red-eyed and sniffling, next to Hermes underneath the dying tree. "If Orpheus did something, I'll kill him!" Pan roared, his worry turning to rage in a matter of seconds as he comprehended the look on Eurydice's face.

"No need," Eurydice shook her head and stood up slowly. "I ended things with Orpheus."

"You... You ended things with Orpheus?" Pan repeated, his voice suddenly turning as quiet as a whisper. There was a stunned look on his face that Eurydice didn't know how to comprehend.

Did Pan never suspect I'd actually leave Orpheus?

"Pan," Hermes interjected. He stood up to his full height, looking every part the stern father. "Maybe this isn't the best time for this conversation. I was going to walk Eurydice back to her home."

"Like hell you are," Pan growled. "What are you even doing here?"

Eurydice held up her hand and silenced the two gods. "No, Hermes." She turned to Pan. "Pan and I need to have a conversation."

Pan's face morphed once more, suddenly looking concerned. He walked closer to her until he was standing in the grove between Hermes and Eurydice.

"All right," Pan nodded slowly, "I suppose we are due for a conversation. I sensed your magic and all the plants in the garden dying...and last night..."

"No," Eurydice cut Pan off with a snap, "that's not what I want to talk to you about."

Pan blanched and looked over at his father. "Can we have this conversation in private?"

"At the moment, I'm inclined to do whatever the pissed off immortal nymph wants me to do." Hermes shrugged. "I don't feel like having thorns wrapped around me between my legs."

"He stays," Eurydice ordered. She crossed her arms in a defensive manner, hating that it most likely looked as though she was trying to hug herself to feel some modicum of comfort amongst the chaos she had been dropped into that morning.

The past twenty-four hours were enough to send anyone into a downward spiral. *Fuck your best friend, drink a truth serum, discover your husband and best friend have been lying to you, ask for help from your friend's dad,* Eurydice's mind ran through everything that had happened in the past day, and it exhausted her.

"I know, Pan."

Eurydice was quiet as she said the words. She looked away, unable to make eye contact as she shuffled her feet. Not a single sound was made in the garden; only the wind moving through the dried grass made any semblance of noise. After a few moments, Eurydice picked her head up and looked at Pan. He wasn't saying anything, just staring, his mouth falling open.

"Say something!" Eurydice begged, tears welling up fresh in her eyes again. She couldn't handle the thought of losing Pan in any way, but she was furious. He had kept secrets from her too.

"You... You know..." Pan repeated, sounding like his mouth was full of wool and it was awkward to speak. "You know, and you left Orpheus."

"Of course I fucking left him!" Eurydice screamed. The last of her composure snapped, and she threw herself at Pan. He caught her before she hit the ground, and Eurydice responded by pounding on his chest. Tears were openly streaming down both of their faces now as Pan did nothing to stop Eurydice. He held her while she started to sob again, railing against his chest with tiny, balled up fists.

"You knew! You knew! You knew, and you didn't tell me, Pan! I thought we were friends."

"Gods below," Pan moaned, sounding as though his heart was equally breaking in half, "It was killing me. You have to know that, Eurydice. It was killing me inside. I couldn't sleep. I couldn't breathe knowing that you were with him, and you didn't know the truth..."

"You should've told me!" Eurydice shrieked, finally putting

some weight on her legs and standing up. She pushed against Pan's chest again and nearly sent him sprawling backward. "I can't understand why you wouldn't tell me. Make me understand!"

"It was Hades!" Pan cried, holding out his arms towards her. "It's a law—no, it's practically a covenant. We can't tell people the truth if they choose to drink from Lethe. You were in so much pain before..."

"Do you think I'm not in pain now?" Eurydice snapped back, and Pan shook his head.

"You were in pain, and you wanted to drink from the river. I tried to stop you, but it was your choice, and I wasn't going to take your choice away. But when Orpheus died, and he came back here, Hades made it very clear that there would be lives on the line if someone told you."

Eurydice started shaking. Her vision was going blurry, and she barely had the strength to stand anymore. Pan was her best friend. After last night, she realized that she also loved him more than anyone she'd ever known. Now, with the full extent of her memories back, she knew it was true.

"I've never loved Orpheus like I love you," Eurydice said the words out loud.

Pan sucked in a shuddering gasp, tears falling fresh down his face. He reached for Eurydice once more.

"Please, believe me. Everything I've done was to make sure you were happy, that you had choices. If Orpheus was going to make you happy, then I would've stepped aside..."

"It's too late," Eurydice started sobbing, sucking in air as if she couldn't get enough oxygen. Her heart was racing so quickly, she thought she might pass out. "I can't... I can't think right now. It's too much."

"We're done here." Hermes stepped in between Pan and Eurydice. He held his hand out to stop Pan from advancing any further.

"Father—"

"No." Hermes's voice was firm. He wrapped an arm around Eurydice. "I'm taking her out of here."

Eurydice hardly comprehended anything else; the last thing she remembered was floating away on a golden, glimmering cloud of power while Orpheus's dead garden got smaller and smaller beneath her.

The look on Pan's face as she floated away with Hermes was the most destroyed, despondent expression she'd ever seen on his face. Somehow, that hurt more than anything.

22

When Hermes finally landed, Eurydice blinked her eyes open as he gently set her on her feet. They were standing in the middle of a small courtyard, much quainter and more welcoming than the estate that Orpheus lived in. The small courtyard was surrounded on three sides by the house with a small altar in the middle of it. Eurydice watched as Hermes walked towards it, lighting a small stick of incense and placing it on the burning brazier. He held his finger to his lips as he stepped away from it and turned back towards Eurydice.

"You don't want Nyx to know that you're placing an offering at her altar?" Eurydice raised a brow, identifying the motifs in the mosaic at the base of the altar. Hermes shrugged his shoulders, beckoning Eurydice to walk towards the unassuming front door.

"It wouldn't be very good for my reputation, now, would it?" He gave her a cheeky wink, and Eurydice scoffed playfully.

"I don't think anyone knows what to do with your reputation," she admitted. Eurydice was relieved that Hermes wasn't treating her as though she was made of glass; his small attempts to lighten the mood pushed her impending total breakdown aside for a few short moments.

"Oh, my maiden of manslaughter? Are you in here?" Hermes suddenly called out loudly, ducking his head to not hit the low beam of the door frame. Eurydice blushed furiously, only now wondering where Hermes had brought her.

She followed him inside, where the front entrance opened into a small hallway that revealed a massive kitchen. There was a long counter, which held a mix of clay pottery and amphoras, all half-opened and spread out all over the surface. There were bundles of fresh herbs hanging from the open rafters. Eurydice brushed a sprig of lavender away from her face as she gracefully stepped around it. The opposite side of the kitchen had a roaring hearth, unlike any Eurydice had seen before.

A huge black cauldron was sitting atop a blazing fire. The flames flickered between red, green, and purple, indicating their obvious magical nature. Eurydice's face broke into a genuine smile as her eyes landed on the long kitchen table with two black dogs sitting underneath it. They cocked their ears up as they viewed the visitors, paying practically no attention to Hermes. Both of the dogs stood up from where they'd been napping and trotted over to Eurydice, shoving their wet noses against her palms.

"They know a heavy heart when they see one." A beautiful, powerful woman stepped into the kitchen. It took Eurydice one look at the bright red hair to know who she was talking to.

"Oh my gods," Eurydice gasped, "You're Hecate!"

The goddess laughed and looked between Hermes and Eurydice. "Who did you bring me this time, you fiend?"

Hermes chuckled, obviously not remotely put off by the nickname, and hopped up on the kitchen counter. He pushed a mortar and pestle out of the way, and Hecate slapped his hand.

"Don't touch my things," she quipped. Hecate settled herself at the counter near Hermes and got back to work, assembling varying ingredients from other jars and combining them before putting them in separate containers again.

"This is Eurydice," Hermes said softly, his expression gentle as he looked between the two women. "I was hoping that she could stay here with you for a night or two."

Hecate dropped the small jar she was holding, her head snapping up to take another look at Eurydice.

"Eurydice," she repeated. There was an intense look on her face that Eurydice couldn't quite decipher. Eurydice blushed furiously and looked away, scratching the dogs' ears while their tongues lolled in satisfaction.

"I can leave," Eurydice squeaked. "I didn't know where Hermes was bringing me. If it's a problem, you know. I don't want to leave. You have a lovely home." Eurydice started speaking faster; she was used to being around the gods often, but Hecate intimidated everyone. "I can leave if it's an issue, is what I mean."

Hecate smiled softly, walking briskly over to Eurydice. Before Eurydice could open her mouth to apologize for the intrusion again, Hecate opened up her arms and pulled Eurydice into a tight embrace. Eurydice only faltered for a brief moment before the overwhelming safety and warmth of Hecate's touch sent her into another bout of tears.

"There, there, sweet child," Hecate murmured. She whispered the words against Eurydice's hair, letting her cling to her bosom like a child to their mother. "There's always room for my heartbroken children here."

"I-I'm not," Eurydice hiccuped. "I'm not yours though. I'm not an acolyte."

Hecate made a soft tutting sound and pulled back slightly. She cupped Eurydice's face with her hands, her thumbs gently brushing away the tears on her cheeks.

"Every woman has the right to call themselves my child, Eurydice." Hecate was deadly serious. "Every woman needs a safe place amongst other women. Speaking of," Hecate turned around, "Hermes, get lost."

Hermes made an exaggerated gasp, licking some of the syrup off his finger where he'd been eating out of one of the jars on Hecate's countertop.

"I want to stick around for girl time." Hermes pouted. "You always kick me out."

"And why do you think that is?" Hecate countered, cocking her hip and putting her hand on her waist. She wrapped her other arm around Eurydice's shoulders and pulled her into her side. Eurydice couldn't help but feel warm all over at the receptiveness of Hecate's attitude and the warmth of her kitchen. Simply standing in such a comforting room with a genuine maternal goddess was doing wonders for her poor nerves.

"I don't know," Hermes whined again, playfully kicking his feet. "I like boys too! And I'd love to talk shit about Orpheus, personally."

"You want to hear me talk about how I slept with your son last night?" Eurydice cringed, pointing out the obvious, which Hermes seemed to be missing. He paled immediately, his face screwing up in an exaggerated expression of disgust.

"Nope, nope. I can go until the end of time itself without hearing those details." He hopped off the counter and sauntered towards them. He gave Hecate a loud kiss on the cheek and petted Eurydice on the head as though she were a small child. She didn't even mind. It was nice to feel small for a little while, to be surrounded by immortals who were older and more powerful than she was and who didn't care about the legacy of 'Orpheus and Eurydice.' She wasn't one half of a couple or Orpheus's missing piece standing in Hecate's kitchen; she was simply Eurydice.

She realized she didn't know how long it'd been since she felt like she was only Eurydice, simply and wonderfully herself. At that exact moment, admittedly, she was in knots about everything that had happened, but it felt good to be recognized as an individual after so long.

"Goodbye, Hermes." Hecate said farewell almost like a warning; Eurydice assumed that she was implying Hermes shouldn't try to worm his way back into her house.

"Goodbye, my virgin of vengeance," he grinned, waggling his eyebrows as he gave them both an exaggerated bow and departed on swift feet without a second word.

"Goodness, he never changes, does he?" Hecate smiled, her expression clearly indicating that she didn't hold any contempt or disdain for Hermes in the slightest. Eurydice didn't know if Hermes understood how warmly Hecate felt about him, but she surmised those two had a relationship that only made sense to the two of them.

"In the short time I've known him, he's been annoyingly consistent in his mischief." Eurydice nodded, and Hecate clapped her hands together.

"Yes! Annoyingly consistent," she chuckled to herself quietly. "That does explain it. Well," she raised her voice and looked at Eurydice, "take a seat, I'll get you something to drink."

She turned back to her work bench, and Eurydice got comfortable at the kitchen table, admiring the intricate carvings on the side of it. It was worn and shiny with use, and it told the story of a thousand long evenings spent with company around it. Hecate's dogs settled at Eurydice's feet, one of them plopping their head on the bench within reach of Eurydice's hand. It was clearly angling for pats, and Eurydice was in no position to ever deny them. She scratched the dog's ears absentmindedly, watching the flickering, color-changing flames of the hearth as Hecate busied herself in the kitchen.

Time didn't seem to affect Hecate's space. Eurydice was lost in her thoughts, not unpleasantly, simply enjoying the serenity. She didn't know how much time had passed before Hecate placed a steaming cup in front of her.

"Drink that, gentle one. It'll help." Hecate reached into a small satchel tied to her waist, getting a pinch of glittering powder and tossing it into the hearth. The flames popped and leaped up the chimney, licking the sides of the stone and bursting with bright pink sparks.

Eurydice squeaked and jerked away from the hearth. "Was that supposed to happen?" Hecate sat down next to Eurydice and gently patted her shoulder.

"Yes, yes, you'll have to forgive me. Getting Persephone's attention requires some dramatics. Now, drink your tea."

Eurydice's eyes nearly bugged out of her head. "Persephone?!" There was a tremor in her voice that she wasn't proud of. She remembered sitting in front of Persephone in Hades's throne room; it was the goddess's influence that got Hades to agree to let Orpheus attempt to leave the Underworld with Eurydice after all. Hecate was studying Eurydice's face, and she must have picked up on the hesitation in Eurydice's expression.

"Oh, darling," Hecate gave her a soft smile, squeezing her hand in encouragement, "don't be frightened. Persephone is no champion for Orpheus. She's just a romantic. She also likes to contradict Hades every chance she gets. She pushed Hades to offer Orpheus a deal for her own reasons, not out of any admiration for that fraud." Hecate sneered the last word, and Eurydice relaxed at seeing the goddess's response to Orpheus's name.

"I understand." Eurydice offered lamely, grabbing hold of the cup that Hecate had offered her. She brought it up to take a drink before pausing, hesitation suddenly coursing through her veins. Eurydice placed it back down on the table and grimaced, looking across the table where Hecate had taken her seat.

"I don't mean to be rude," Eurydice swallowed thickly, "but can you tell me what is in this? I've had a bit of a day when it comes to, um, ingesting things given to me by gods."

"Oh, yes, of course." Hecate didn't seem offended in the slightest to be questioned. "It's tea."

"Just tea?" Eurydice brought the cup to her face and smelled it. She was immediately knocked back by the heavy whiff of alcohol.

"Well, it's tea mixed with some ambrosia." Hecate chuckled to herself, dipping a spoon into her own cup and stirring it precisely three times. Eurydice was fascinated with everything Hecate did; every move she made seemed to be intentional. She tapped her spoon on the edge of her cup three times before setting it down and taking a long sip.

"Ah," Hecate sighed, "that always hits the spot." She looked at Eurydice and nodded at the cup in her hands. "I won't force you to drink anything you don't want to, of course, but I have always found that day drinking is really made better by drinking. According to my infinite wisdom." Hecate winked, taking another long sip.

Eurydice stared at her for a brief second before she burst into laughter; whatever she expected from the goddess of witchcraft, it wasn't this. Eurydice shrugged and knocked back half of her cup and its contents without a second thought. Frankly, there was no better way to be spending her day than getting a little shit-faced. It was well needed after finally fucking her best friend, realizing she was in love with him, discovering her husband and her best friend had lied, and she'd technically died twice.

"Fuck yes!" A cheerful, deep woman's voice echoed throughout the kitchen. Eurydice sat up straighter with a start, looking around to see where the voice was coming from. Hecate started laughing but didn't seem alarmed that a voice had called out from the ether.

The flames in the hearth crackled with pink sparks again and smoke started billowing out from the chimney into the kitchen. It was a swirling mix of pink and red, and scattered rose petals and pomegranate seeds started appearing on the floor. Hecate caught sight of the small whirlwind and rolled her eyes.

"Do you always need to make such a dramatic entrance?" Hecate called out to the ceiling, standing up from her seat at the table. She took her cup over to the counter, refilling it and filling a second cup before sitting back down. She placed the second drink across the table from Eurydice at an empty seat. The smoke continued to fill the room until Eurydice nearly couldn't see anything else; it obscured almost her entire field of vision. She was about to cry out to Hecate in confusion when all the smoke vanished just as quickly as it had poured into the kitchen.

Eurydice gasped in surprise to see Persephone sitting across the table from her. The goddess looked as picture perfect as Eurydice remembered her. She had long, wavy blonde hair that practically reached all the way to her waist, almost in the style of nymphs. She was wrapped up in a himation that was blood red in color and slowly faded out to pink. There was a thin circlet made of gold around Persephone's brow, with small, carved depictions of flowers and pomegranates. The circlet was set with black stones, which Eurydice rightfully assumed were memoirs of Hades.

"Eurydice," Persephone looked torn between grief and pleasure, "I'm so happy to see you, but not under these circumstances."

"That's why we're drinking, Persephone." Hecate smirked playfully. She snapped her fingers, and an amphora appeared on the table in the middle of the trio. "We're not writing love letters."

"Well," Persephone's smile widened. She picked up her cup and held it out towards Eurydice. "Welcome to the time-honored tradition of getting drunk in Hecate's kitchen when a man in the Underworld fucks up."

Eurydice couldn't help but start laughing, and she tapped her cup against Persephone's.

It didn't take long for the alcohol to keep flowing, and Eurydice was even more overjoyed when Persephone and Hecate didn't mention Orpheus or Pan once. They talked about anything else, from the weather to the latest in Olympic gossip. They kept going until Eurydice realized with a start that it was nearly sundown and they'd been drinking and gossiping all day. It hardly mattered; Eurydice had nowhere else to be, and the levity made her heart feel lighter than it had in weeks.

The sunset didn't stop them, and even Makaria joined them before the night was done. She also was careful not to mention Orpheus a single time, and she didn't bring up the last visit she'd made to Eurydice in Orpheus's garden. By the time it was nearing midnight, Eurydice was feeling as light as the clouds. It was partially because of the alcohol, but there was an even warmer feeling in her chest from being surrounded by strong women who didn't need to have a conversion with Eurydice around her relationship with Orpheus.

"Let's get you to bed, my child." Hecate hiccuped, still managing to sound graceful, as she pried Eurydice off the floor where she'd been dozing, using one of the dogs as a pillow. Eurydice murmured something in agreement and allowed Hecate to escort her upstairs, where she toppled into one of Hecate's guest rooms.

Eurydice was fast asleep before Hecate could even shut the door, blessedly free from the burden of wondering what mood Orpheus would be in when she awoke.

23

Eurydice woke up to the sound of arguing. A sense of fear and panic immediately started coursing through her veins. For a horrible second, she thought she was back in Orpheus's house, and there was some brawl happening outside. It took a few precious minutes for her to identify the voices; the screaming was coming from the courtyard outside. She picked up on Hecate's voice first, louder than all the rest.

"You have not been given a formal invitation or permission to enter this house," Hecate's voice dropped to a lower register and echoed, "which means you will die before the walls fall, you insolent fool."

Eurydice threw the blanket back and nearly fell getting out of bed, rushing to re-tie her chiton and go see what all of the commotion was about.

Of all the fools in the Underworld, who would attempt something so brazen as breaking into Hecate's house? Eurydice got her answer when a male's voice began shouting in response.

"Then I die! I'll go up against all the witchcraft in the world and every power of hell," the voice cracked, "but let me speak to her. I beg of you!"

Pan.

Eurydice froze on the steps, her heart leaping up into her throat. Pan was outside and was going toe to toe with Hecate's wrath in order to see her. Eurydice was nearly lightheaded with the connotations of what that might mean. She brought her hand to her chest and forced herself to breathe, taking deep breaths until she had regained some of her composure. Not all of it, but enough to head outside and to stop feeling as though she was going to pass out.

Hecate's dogs picked their heads up in curiosity as Eurydice ran past them, only pausing when she poked her head out of the doorway. Pan was standing right outside of Hecate's courtyard, down on his knees. He looked as distressed as Eurydice had ever seen him, and it made her stomach drop. He was dressed as a man, but she could see his horns nestled atop his mess of curls. His hair was all tangled, and Eurydice wondered if he had been running his hands through it excessively. His eyes were red-rimmed, and his cheeks were wet. She heard his voice hitch as he pleaded with Hecate.

The goddess herself looked like immovable stone. She was standing tall, her back straight and shoulders squared. An opaque cloud of red magic swirled around her feet like an attack dog, waiting to jump out at a moment's notice. Hecate's auburn hair had been tied back in elaborate braids, and the snakes on her golden arm bands undulated back and forth. In short, she looked furious, and even Eurydice was suddenly worried about anything she may have ever done to piss off the goddess. She was a terrifying sight to behold.

"Stunning, isn't she?" A man's voice popped up from behind her, making Eurydice gasp sharply. She spun around and got her first look at the man who must have been Hecate's consort—Aeëtes, the immortal crown prince who had been the source of the myth of the golden fleece. He shared some characteristics with Pan, from curly hair to tanned skin, except he was smiling when he stared at Hecate, even in her furious and awe-inspiring state.

"Excuse me?" Eurydice whispered, unsure of what to do.

"Hecate won't let anything come in between her and a woman she's protecting." Aeëtes nodded towards the sight unfolding in the courtyard. "If you don't want Pan to be strung up by his horns and kicked off to the titans, I suggest you intervene." Aeëtes went back to staring at Hecate like a besotted teenager. Eurydice took his words to heart, suddenly springing into action. She ran out into the courtyard, her arms raised as she called out to Pan.

"Pan!" she shrieked. "Hecate, Hecate, it's fine. It's okay. I'll speak with him." Eurydice was surprisingly breathless; it wasn't the physical exhaustion but the emotional one that was finally catching up with her.

Pan's face transformed when he saw Eurydice, and his tears started falling fresh.

"Eurydice," he practically sobbed the word out, "I needed to see you. I wanted to tell you, I swear..." Pan didn't rise from his knees, simply angling himself towards Eurydice and clutching his hands together as if he was praying. Normally, Eurydice might have found the position pathetic, but there was something about the devotion on Pan's face that made her heart soften further.

"Eurydice, are you sure?" Hecate's voice gentled as she looked between the two of them.

"Yes." Eurydice didn't look at Hecate but kept her eyes on Pan, muttering the affirmation without any hesitation.

Hecate simply nodded, all her fury dissipating in a matter of seconds. Her red magic ebbed away, and the tone of her voice lightened; even some of the red glow to Hecate's eyes disappeared. She readjusted the shoulder of her tunic and gave a short nod to Pan.

"I'll leave you both alone then. Eurydice, feel free to use the house if you need to." Hecate turned around and beckoned for Aeëtes, who had been standing in the courtyard. He practically ran to her side, kissing her cheek and interlocking his fingers with hers. Hecate gave him a smile so gentle, Eurydice suddenly got the impression she was intruding.

"If you change your mind," Hecate looked at Eurydice, "just tell the house. It'll remove anyone unwanted from the premises." Eurydice could only nod, and Hecate and Aeëtes exited the courtyard, disappearing and leaving Pan and Eurydice with the house to themselves.

An agonizingly long minute passed; Eurydice and Pan weren't able to say anything. Pan finally pushed himself up to his feet, holding his hands out to Eurydice.

"I want to talk to you, only for a minute, if you'll let me. Please." His voice was pleading, and Eurydice couldn't help herself from tearing up. She wanted to be with him just as badly, but so much had happened — so much had been revealed to her. She didn't know what was possible for the two of them.

"Come inside," Eurydice said simply, turning around and leading the way inside of the house. It felt wrong, ushering into Hecate's home, but Hecate had given her the permission to do so.

A million questions raced through Eurydice's head, and she tried to push them all aside. Pan followed her without a word, without any signs of hesitation. Eurydice didn't know where to take Pan in Hecate's house, so she settled on bringing him upstairs to the guest room. She didn't anticipate what the sight would do to her when Pan stopped at the threshold. He seemed to sense it was her space, at least for the meantime, and he leaned against the doorjamb.

Eurydice's heart nearly seized at the sight of him. Even with everything that had happened to her in the past thirty-six hours, she couldn't forget the feeling of Pan between her thighs.

"Eurydice..." Pan started, but Eurydice interrupted him.

"I don't want to hear it. I can't. I can't right now, Pan. It's not that I don't want to. I just... There's been so many promises..." Eurydice trailed off.

The atmosphere between them shifted, the air growing thick and heavy simultaneously with heartbreak and arousal. Eurydice dragged her eyes down Pan's long frame, so broad he nearly blocked out the light from the hallway.

"If you don't want to talk," Pan murmured softly, "what do you want me to do?" His voice was perfectly neutral. Even at a moment like this, he was holding it together and appearing calm for her, even if there was nothing serene about the atmosphere around them.

Eurydice sat on the edge of the bed, her breath catching in her lungs. "I don't know." Her mouth dropped open, and she watched the moment Pan's eyes lit up with his arousal. He was holding onto the door with a near white-knuckle grip.

"You've had enough promises." Pan took one step inside the bedroom. Eurydice's breath hitched. "You've heard enough sweet words." One more step. Eurydice's pulse skyrocketed. "You have to tell me what you want, my wild thing."

Pan dropped to his knees effortlessly, sinking down between Eurydice's legs. On his knees, he was still eye level with her and met her gaze with a matched intensity that lit her up from the inside out.

Eurydice leaned forward, careful to not let a single lock of hair or scrap of her garment touch Pan's skin as she whispered in his ear.

"Speak to me only the way you can." Eurydice was barely breathing. "Use the language of the trees, Pan, of the wild. Give me something that no one else can."

Pan exploded.

Before she could even blink, Pan's hands wrapped around Eurydice's waist as he tossed her onto the bed. He crawled up her body until he was suspended above her, pinning her underneath him. It reduced Eurydice's senses until all she could perceive was the heat rolling off Pan's body, the coarse feeling of his rough, hairy skin brushing up against hers. Eurydice's body reacted before her brain did, and she found herself throwing her arms around Pan's back and shifting her hips upward to feel more of him.

"Fuck, Eurydice," Pan grunted, tucking his head in between her shoulder and neck. He inhaled deeply, tracing one hand up her side until he started pulling off her chiton. "You have no idea what you do to me. You've driven me to madness for five hundred years. Do you understand that?"

He punctuated his words with a roll of his hips. Eurydice gasped and dug her nails into Pan's back when his hard cock brushed against her entrance, only thin layers of fabric separating them.

"You're Pan," Eurydice sighed on an exhale, continuing to rock her hips upward in time with Pan's movements. "You've always been mad."

Pan supported his weight on one elbow and pulled at the knot on Eurydice's shoulder, wrenching the fabric away from her body. He followed suit, and for a few desperate moments there was nothing but the awkward rearranging of limbs and discarding of clothing. Pan and Eurydice were both sweating and frantic, as confused as they'd ever been before and searching for a clarity they didn't find but were willing to burn their lives apart in the process. Nothing else mattered in those rushed, cramped movements, desperate to get closer to one another to feel something, anything, to make the raging aches in their hearts go away.

"I've always been mad because of you," Pan grunted. He grabbed one of the cushions from behind Eurydice's head and tucked it under her back. It was a subtle gesture, simultaneously arousing Eurydice further and making her want to cry harder. Even in this rush to feel one another, to lose sight of everything happening for a few moments of connection, Pan was thinking of her, always.

Eurydice was nearly going out of her mind, feeling her innermost walls clenching around nothing and practically begging to feel Pan inside of her.

"Please," she whimpered, her eyes shuttering closed, "don't say another word, Pan. I need you inside of me."

"Whatever my wild thing wants," Pan grunted in response. He grabbed Eurydice's thigh and wrapped her leg around his waist, positioning himself right at her entrance. Eurydice moaned again, and before she could open her mouth to demand he move, Pan thrust forward. Eurydice's mouth dropped open in a silent scream, and she tightened her grip on him, the blood in her veins turning to liquid fire. She relished in the stretch of him, prepared to savor the blur of pleasure and pain as her body wept to accommodate him.

Pan was panting heavily in Eurydice's ear, an incoherent babble of moans and a mess of whimpers as he refused to move until Eurydice's hands tangled in her curls.

"Please," she begged, "move, god, Pan, give it to me."

Pan only grunted in response before pulling backward and thrusting into her again. Eurydice gasped as he got a little farther, realizing that she hadn't taken him all the way the first time.

"Fuck." Eurydice pulled Pan's hair. "I don't know if I..."

"You can take it," Pan affirmed. He spoke to her in a low and soothing tone although his breath was still coming in choppy pants as he struggled to keep his composure. "I know you can take all of me, my love."

His sweet endearments mixed with the declarations he was making practically sent Eurydice over the edge right there. Pan started rocking his hips in shallow motions, working the rest of his length inside of her until finally he settled his hips against hers. Eurydice squeezed his leg tighter around Pan's waist. She knew the moment he was fully seated inside of her that she'd be ruined for anyone else.

"Move," Eurydice breathed. "Move!"

"That's my wild one," Pan exhaled, pressing a series of kisses from Eurydice's neck to her forehead. He picked up the pace again and started rolling his hips against hers with shocking dexterity, the base of his cock brushing against her clit as he ground against her with every thrust.

"Fuck!" Eurydice gasped, moving her hands from Pan's curls to his horns and holding on tightly. He was working her body over like he'd already done this a thousand times before, somehow seemingly detecting what every sigh and hitch of her breath meant.

"You feel like heaven," Pan breathed, still keeping his perfect pace. "Who would've thought I'd have found heaven waiting for me past the gates of hell?"

"P-Pan." Eurydice felt the tears start to fall down her cheeks. She couldn't handle him talking this way to her, giving her everything she'd realized she'd always wanted to hear from his mouth, not Orpheus's.

"Come for me," Pan insisted, one of his hands finding her clit. "I need to see it. I need to feel it, Eurydice, to feel how you respond to me. My love, my Eurydice."

"Oh, gods, Pan..." Eurydice's world was exploding around her, pieces of who she thought she was, her past and her future, scattered throughout the room.

"Now," Pan demanded with a sharp thrust of his hips, and Eurydice was coming. Her voice went out as her head fell back, and she screamed, her entire existence being reduced down to the overwhelming sensation of lightning and bliss pounding through her veins. Pan came with a roar, one hand grabbing out for the wooden frame of the bed and shaking the entire bed. Eurydice felt him release inside of her, and she knew for better or for worse, there would only ever be Pan for her.

Pan collapsed on the bed beside Eurydice, and neither of them said a word as they breathed through the aftershocks. Eurydice could still feel her thighs shaking. Pan seemed to notice that, and he placed one hand on her leg, gently rubbing it in a soothing motion. It did nothing to stop her body's tremors, but Pan seemed to only want to remind himself she was real. *That* had happened. She was beside him.

Eurydice knew she was going to ruin the moment, but she couldn't wait another second, keeping them both in the dark about where they would move forward after this.

"I don't know what I'm ready for," Eurydice blurted, fighting the urge to hide her face in her hands. She couldn't bear to look at Pan's face. "I don't know if I can be with you, long term. There's just been so much..."

"Stop," Pan commanded gently. He leaned over Eurydice and kissed her gently, as though he was slowly savoring every last second he had with her. "I understand."

Eurydice watched, flabbergasted, as Pan stood up and quickly dressed himself, slipping towards the door without another word.

"Wait!" Eurydice sat up, calling out to him before he could disappear. She started to cry, cursing the tears that ran down her cheeks. "I love you, Pan."

"I know." He smiled gently at her, his eyes wet and full of pain. "I love you too. When that is enough, you know where to find me."

Pan had disappeared down the stairs and out of Hecate's house before Eurydice even fully comprehended what he said.

24

Orpheus was pacing. It was a nasty habit, one that had driven his staff to fury for years. He always managed to start kicking furniture and ripping rugs whenever he got to pacing. Like everything that Orpheus touched, he lost control of his emotions and eventually ruined it in a false display of ownership. The issue Orpheus was now facing was that he had tried to own nature itself; he had tried to wrestle Eurydice, a nymph and one of Pan's chosen, into a place of submission. There was no possessing the wild. It could and would not be contained. Gaia herself would waken from the earth if anyone was ever successful.

So Orpheus paced.

He hadn't returned to his own household. Every surface was covered in dead vines and thorns, and the mess was proving impossible to clean up. Every time someone tried to clear out some of the foliage, the thorns specifically, they would magically reappear. They would never regrow—nothing was growing in Orpheus's house. They would simply reappear. Eurydice's curse was proving true; it was not an exaggeration that everything was affected by her incantation.

Even when the serving staff were bringing in food, fresh

produce died as soon as it crossed the threshold. No one really needed to eat in the Underworld for survival, but it was still regularly a part of everyone's routine for the comfort and familiarity of it. Now, Orpheus was finding no solace in his own home. The garden was a charred mess and looked as though a wildfire had ripped through it. Although Eurydice's anger could be compared to a wildfire, it was just as destructive and obliterated everything in its wake.

"Orpheus, sit down and have a glass of wine," Perseus snapped, rolling his eyes. He had been less than sympathetic to Orpheus's plight; his main concern had been the effect on both his and Orpheus's reputation.

"I will have her again!" Orpheus growled, pushing the golden hair off his forehead. His eyes were red, and there were bags under his eyes. He hadn't slept since Eurydice left, and it was beginning to show on his face and in his temperament. He was possessed with a nearly supernatural obsession for revenge. Orpheus had lost the support of his patron, his mortal life, and now his muse. He'd already lost Eurydice once, and this time around, people wouldn't be sympathetic about it. When he'd returned to the mortal world without Eurydice, it only pushed Orpheus's fame higher. There was nothing the Greek people loved more than a tragedy. Now the citizens of the Underworld wouldn't be as forgiving.

Everything hinged on getting her back. Orpheus's thoughts shifted to a dark, angry place, which was a more ominous side effect of Apollo's influence.

"I'm sure you will," Perseus rolled his eyes, "but drink something to take the edge off because you're going to make a hole in my floors."

Orpheus grunted angrily in return, plopping himself down on one of the chaise lounges. He snapped his fingers, and a serving girl practically leaped to hand him a glass of wine.

"You're being no help," Orpheus snapped angrily, gulping down half of his wine in one sip. "If you aren't going to contribute anything other than sarcasm, I'd rather drink alone."

"You're in my house," Perseus reminded him with a sneer. "Yours is covered in thorns because you couldn't keep you woman under control."

"Fuck you," Orpheus hissed, nearly spilling the rest of his goblet. "You try marrying a muse and see what that gets you."

"No, thank you. I decided to eliminate the women in my life that were threats."

"I never understood that." Orpheus rolled his eyes. "I'm not sure how a woman hiding in a cave was a threat to you. Unless you're that fragile."

"Watch it," Perseus growled. He jumped to his feet and stalked over to where Orpheus was sitting, jabbing his finger in Orpheus's face. Orpheus dropped his cup, sending a crimson red stain splattering across the pristine floors. Orpheus was on his feet in a second, responding by shoving Perseus's shoulders. Perseus went sprawling, landing in the puddle of spilled wine.

"All right, cut it out!" Perseus snapped, holding his hands up in mock surrender. Orpheus and Perseus were already breathing hard, both of them frustrated and already fairly well imbibed for the time of day. "I'm not your enemy here. I'm only saying that drinking in my house and moping aren't going to do anything. Why don't you just let her go? She's one woman, for fuck's sake." Perseus rolled his eyes and pushed himself up, wiping at some of the wine on his tunic.

"I wish I could," Orpheus grumbled, plopping back down on the chaise rather unceremoniously. "You know that my reputation wouldn't take it well. Everyone is expecting me to be with Eurydice now that we're both in the Underworld."

"All right." Perseus crossed his arms across his chest, trailing his thumb across his lip as he began to think. "So you need her to play house with you. You don't actually have to be in a relationship, but for all intents and purposes, you need people to assume that you are. You need her complicit."

"Yes, alive would be helpful." Orpheus grumbled again, motioning for the serving girl to bring them another round of wine. "I'm so glad that you're here to help."

"Hear me out," Perseus groaned. "No wonder Eurydice left you. You can't listen for shit. I'm starting at the beginning. It's called making a plan. You should try it," Orpheus said nothing but handed Perseus a glass of wine apologetically, motioning for him to go on.

"We know that murder and maiming are out of the question if we need her alive and willing to play house with you. So the question becomes—how do we get Eurydice to go along as your wife?"

"Blackmail, I'd assume is the answer you're looking for." Orpheus took another sip of his wine and began pacing again, except this time Perseus joined in. They began mulling over all of the ways they could try to get Eurydice in line, but every idea came up short when dealing with the premise of an enraged muse and nymph.

"What does she love? Flowers, the fucking trees?" Orpheus quipped frustratingly. "We can't exactly set a field of flowers on fire and expect her to pretend to be my wife for all eternity."

Orpheus and Perseus went back and forth long into the night. They practically held their own caucus, debating every which way they could try and get Eurydice under their thumb. The wine continued to flow as they ate and drank their way through their scheming, until finally, they were both half-collapsed on the floor in the early hours of dawn.

Orpheus was propped up by the leg of a chair, and Perseus was lying on the ground. The early rays of dawn were starting to creep into the great hall, and the conniving duo was nowhere closer to hatching any sort of scheme that would help them get Eurydice under Orpheus's control.

"If only we could call on H-Hermes," Orpheus hiccuped. "The trickster would know of a way or two to sort this out."

"Can we not call on him? There's nothing keeping us from petitioning the gods. If he runs his mouth about it, we can always pass it off as a trick of Hermes's." Perseus picked his head up from the floor, his eyes brightening as he thought of asking a god for assistance.

"Hermes won't work." Orpheus shook his head. "Eurydice is one of Pan's creatures. Hermes won't do anything that could or would affect his son. He's sneaky, but he has loyalties." Perseus made a discontented sigh and lay back down on the floor.

"Well, then I don't know. Apollo is gone, and he is the only one who ever showed you favor."

"Oh, blame me for that," Orpheus snapped. "If you want to start talking about ushering in the gods' favor, why don't we call Zeus? Or are you no longer his favorite bastard hero?"

Orpheus rolled his eyes and propped his head up a little higher, just so he could finish off his wine. He still managed to spill some, staining the front of his tunic and coloring his lips dark purple. He looked like a disgruntled child who'd gotten into a grape harvest and spent the afternoon gorging themselves on sweet grapes; it was hardly the polished, beautiful picture of the infamous poet people had come to expect.

Perseus hauled himself up to a sitting position, and his eyes widened. He snapped his fingers and pointed towards Orpheus.

"Don't bring me into this if you're not able to handle the heat. I'm the one who has spent my evening trying to come up with ways for you to keep your wayward wife under your thumb. Zeus won't mess with matters of the Underworld; we know that."

"Well, by that logic, Pan shouldn't even be able to visit here either," Orpheus deadpanned.

As soon as the words were out of his mouth, he sat up a little straighter and wiped the wine from his mouth.

"Pan shouldn't be able to visit here," Orpheus repeated himself, his voice getting louder. "Pan shouldn't be able to visit here!"

"You said that already." Perseus looked bored. "Besides, didn't Hades already grant Pan permission permanently to visit here because the forests were his territory?"

"He most certainly did," Orpheus's sly smile started growing across his face, "because of a loophole. It would be a shame if someone exploited the same logic for their own benefit."

"What are you saying?" Perseus picked his head up as his attention started to pique. "You want to go visit the mortal realm?"

"No." Orpheus shook his head. "However, what would happen if all the gods were able to come and go between the Underworld and the mortal world as they pleased? What if Demeter was able to come down here and visit the fields, the forests, anywhere the plants grow like Pan is allowed to?"

Perseus's eyes widened as his mouth dropped open. "Demeter would never leave. She'd be in the Underworld all the time to keep an eye on Persephone."

"Which would..." Orpheus encouraged Perseus to finish.

"Which would infuriate Hades. He'd do anything to keep that from happening and to protect his wife from her mother. There's no love lost between Persephone and Demeter."

"Who do you think he'd choose then? Pan or Persephone, his wife?" Orpheus practically clapped his hands together in glee. Orpheus and Perseus both stood to their feet.

"Hades would choose his wife, no questions asked. He'd revoke the special privileges that he's given Pan because he'd never want Demeter looming around in the Underworld that often!"

"Exactly!" Orpheus crowed in victory, and they nearly

chipped their cups slamming them together in a toast. "With Pan forced out of the Underworld, Eurydice won't have a friend left. She'll have the nymphs and a goddess or two, surely, but her distraction will be gone."

"Do you think she'd come right back to you if she knew you were responsible for getting Pan exiled from the Underworld?" Perseus questioned.

"She can never know," Orpheus agreed. "It's not a perfect plan. I'll have to lay it on thick once Pan is banished and go to her to offer support."

"It's risky." Perseus shrugged. He walked over to an end table and poured himself another glass. Orpheus extended his hand out in a silent question, and Perseus refilled his glass too.

"It is, but it's the best plan we got. Murder and maiming aren't viable options, as we established, which means eliminating the competition is the next best thing." Orpheus chewed on his lip, starting to pace back and forth, although his steps were noticeably wobblier after hours of consumption.

"It also relies on you being charming to a weeping Eurydice, who will have been ripped apart by losing another 'love of her life.'" Perseus pointed out.

Orpheus was not immune to the flaws in his plan; it was fallible from the start, as there was no guarantee Demeter would help them either. There was, however, a very good chance that she would for the opportunity to get unfettered access to the Underworld.

"If I don't manage to get Eurydice under my thumb," Orpheus grunted, "everything is lost for me anyway. Do you have any other ideas?"

"No." Perseus shrugged, tipping the last of his cup's remnants into his mouth.

"Well then," Orpheus clapped his hands together and looked out at the rising sun, "let's try and summon a goddess."

25

Orpheus walked through the double-door entrance to Hades's receiving hall with the most bravado than any of the other times he'd entered.

The braziers that lined the door were fully ablaze, causing Orpheus to break out in a sweat as he approached the dais. Hades regularly appeared in the receiving hall to speak to the citizens of the Underworld; it functioned much more similarly to a mortal kingdom than others would realize. Orpheus didn't take the time to set up an appointment or forewarn Hades of his arrival even though it would've been the polite thing to do.

Orpheus was arriving with another goddess after all.

Hades was sitting on his black throne, carved from bone and dotted with gemstones embedded into it. He consistently wore the same thing, his thick hair curling down towards his shoulders and heavy black chiton nearly sweeping the floor. His face was pulled down in a tight scowl, and even without the crown on his head, he would've exuded nothing but dominance and total control. If Orpheus didn't have another Olympic deity on his side, he would've been far more anxious strolling up the carpeted aisle.

"Orpheus?" Hades turned his attention to the poet, and his

scowl deepened. "I had rather hoped that you wouldn't ever grace my halls with your presence again. I certainly don't understand what else you could possibly want." Hades's voice was tense, and Orpheus broke out in a sweat. He didn't know if it was the blazing braziers at his back or the intensity of Hades's un-approving gaze, but he didn't wait around to find out. He shuffled his weight between his right and left foot, clearing his throat before he spoke.

"I come with someone else to speak with you on the matter of how you're running your kingdom, Lord Hades." Orpheus tried to input a sense of calm and authority of his own into the words, but his voice still shook as he said them. He watched as Hades sat up straighter, his brow furrowing as his lip curled. He slammed his fist down on the arm rest.

"You wish to speak to me about how I'm running my kingdom? You're fucking lucky I run it the way that I do, or my adherence to the ancient rules of Lethe would've been broken to tell Eurydice what you've done."

The floors shook when Hades spoke, and Orpheus tried not to drop to the floor in fear. Thick, black clouds of smoke started to congregate around Hades's feet, his power rising as his agitation with seeing Orpheus again grew.

"I don't come to speak to you on the matter of Eurydice," Orpheus managed to say. "I wish to discuss Pan."

"Pan?" Hades grumbled, leaning forward in his seat as he evaluated Orpheus, taking delight in how he squirmed under the attention. "Should Pan be here for this? If you are to speak ill of him, then everyone deserves their chance to speak out against the charges."

"N-no." Orpheus shook his head. "I want to speak to you regarding..." Orpheus swallowed thickly, his anxiety more apparent as he got closer to revealing his plan.

"I don't have all day," Hades sneered, his voice sounding as slick as oil. He had reclined in his seat ever so slightly, which was an insult in and of itself. Hades was posturing; he was proving to Orpheus that he didn't find him a threat. Except it was hardly posturing when it came to Hades, the god who arguably had the most power in the entire pantheon and the eldest of the three brothers who ruled their world. He truly had no reason to be intimidated by Orpheus, and Orpheus knew it.

"Why is Pan allowed in the Underworld?" Orpheus nearly vomited out the words. "He's not a creature of the Underworld, and even Hermes, his father, doesn't live here all the time..."

"Hermes lives wherever he pleases. He is the god of messages and a psychopomp. There is no place in the world that is off limits to him," Hades interrupted sharply. "Do not lecture me on the positions and jobs of my family." Hades's voice dropped an octave. "I know them and all their movements well."

The color drained from Orpheus's face, and he took a deep breath, trying to summon what little courage he needed.

"So why is Pan allowed in the Underworld?" Orpheus pushed again. Hades rubbed his hands together as if he was using all of his strength not to get down off his dais and punch Orpheus clear across the face.

"I don't take well to dead mortals asking me why gods are allowed in my realm." Hades cracked his knuckles. "But if you are perturbed over his presence, he is allowed here because he is a god of forests. The Underworld has forests. Hermes brought this to my attention, so special permissions were given to Pan to allow him to cross through the gates of Hell. Does that answer your question, poet?" Hades's words were clipped, and his mood was growing more sour by the minute as evidenced by the growing clouds of smoke that were now trickling down the dais and towards Orpheus.

"By that logic...other gods whose territories also exist in the Underworld should also be allowed to come and go as they please, correct?"

Hades's eyes narrowed as he stood to his full height, coming down off the dais and crossing the distance between him and Orpheus. Orpheus couldn't help but fall backward in a desperate attempt to put more space between them. Hades looked as furious and vengeful as he had ever seen him, his expression stone cold and power radiating off him.

"Why do you meddle in the affairs of gods?" Hades demanded, his voice plummeting into its lower register. The rafters and walls shook with the force of his power as the dark smoke began filling up the receiving hall.

"I'm only following your logic, Lord of the Dead." Orpheus bowed his head with a mocking tone of voice. "You wish to follow the rules so closely. There is another god who intends to take advantage of your benevolent ruling."

"Then let them speak for themselves," Hades growled, his bident appearing in his grip out of thin air, "and do not show up here speaking of games that you do not understand, foolish poet. Remember that you are nothing but a shade in my kingdom of shadows."

"I have arrived to speak for myself," a disembodied female voice filled the hall. "You know I always like to send my messengers ahead of me, Hades."

Thick, green smoke started to pour through the windows, and it began mixing with the black clouds scattered across the floor. The entire room was almost immediately completely obscured by the foggy displays of the gods, their power made manifest. While Hades's power smelled of smoke and cedar, this new, invading emerald magic smelled of rotten vegetables and mildew. Orpheus found himself coughing and covering his face with his arm as he scrambled backwards towards a far corner, hoping to find a pocket of fresh air.

"Demeter!" Hades bellowed, his rage exploding out of him like a canon. Orpheus heard one of the windows shatter from the force of his anger. All the black smoke evaporated from the room in an instant. Hades was now dressed for battle, the edges of his bident dipped in flames and armor strapped across his chest and arms. Orpheus started shaking, his face nearly frozen in fear. He would've never brought this loophole to Demeter's attention if he knew it meant seeing Hades's anger unleashed.

"How dare you even set foot in my dominion!" Hades growled, sending another shockwave over the stones. "Show yourself, you precious bitch."

The green smoke in the room started to coagulate and twist upwards, forming a tornado of clouds as they spun faster. Moments later, they parted, revealing Demeter standing in her physical form in the middle of Hades's hall. She was swathed in shades of green and emerald from head to toe, and her himation was accompanied by an additional shawl. Her body was tall and lithe, without an extra curve on her. She was hauntingly beautiful but looked as though she might blend in with the stalks of wheat she so watched over. Demeter's hair was so dark brown, it was nearly black, but it glimmered in the firelight when she turned her head. She wore no circlet but had a laurel made of wheat stalks tucked into her hair.

"Oh, Hades," Demeter cooed mockingly as she held her arms out wide, "is that any way to greet your mother-in-law?"

"You don't deserve the right to call yourself a mother," Hades spat. He pointed his bident towards her. "What are you doing here? It's bold of you to cross the Styx, knowing what I told you I'd do to you if I ever saw you again."

Orpheus might have been out of his mind with cowardice, but he could swear he heard the river Styx answer from beyond the palace windows, its currents picking up speed in protest.

"I'm simply here to take advantage of your generosity." Demeter offered Hades a half-bow that was more mocking than respectful. "If Pan is allowed into the Underworld to visit his forests, surely, I must be granted those same rights to visit the fields of Asphodel."

Hades turned his head slowly, his eyes fully black and glowing with power. Orpheus trembled when Hades's gaze landed on him.

"I see," Hades nodded once, studying Orpheus, "I have to admit, this is rather well played. You told Demeter about my bargain with Pan, it seems."

"He most certainly did." Demeter offered Hades a warm and patronizing smile. "If you are going to allow Pan access to the Underworld's forests, then certainly, you have no issue allowing me access to what is mine."

Orpheus thought he might pass out as another ripple of palpable power tore free from Hades. It was clear that Demeter had meant Persephone when she referred to 'what is mine,' and Orpheus suddenly found himself wishing he hadn't played the games of gods.

"Everything in the Underworld is mine!" Hades exploded, black flames pouring out from his back and underneath his chiton. He leaped forward in the blink of an eye and pinned Demeter against the stone wall, pressing her against the stone with his bident encompassing her neck.

"Everything, *everyone*," Hades growled, his lip curling, "in the Underworld is mine."

Orpheus thought for a split second that Hades was going to murder Demeter right where she stood. The color drained from her face, and her bravado dissipated. Demeter swallowed thickly and forced another smile on her face.

"It is your honor on the line, dear Hades. What chaos would erupt if the gods discovered that their eldest, the powerful ruler of the dead, wasn't playing by the rules he so closely cherishes?"

"Fuck honor!" Hades shouted, slamming his fist against the stone, dangerously close to Demeter's face. "I'll release the titans and turn all of Greece into the Underworld before I let you anywhere near my wife again."

Demeter stuttered, the fear apparent on her face. "Y-you

know how many innocents would get caught in the crossfire if you did that, Hades." Demeter's voice quivered. "You wouldn't allow that to happen."

For a tense moment, Orpheus was convinced that Hades was indeed going to go ahead and murder Demeter on the spot. He squeezed his eyes shut and prepared to run through the doors and flee as soon as Demeter hit the floor. Instead, Hades released the goddess and took several steps backward as though he was disgusted to be near her.

"The choice is yours, Hades." Demeter cooed, some of her bravado returning. "You either have to abolish Pan from the Underworld or allow me to enter of my own freewill. As often as I like."

Not a single sound could be heard in the receiving hall. Orpheus finally dared to look directly at Hades, who was staring at Demeter and looked like he was imagining all the ways he could kill her. When he finally spoke, his voice was like stone. It was cold and calculated, and the air around them reverberated with every syllable that came out of Hades's mouth.

The fires in the braziers suddenly went out, casting the room in darkness. Orpheus tried to scramble further into his corner, hiding from Hades's wrath. He could barely see anything through the shadows, only the gleaming fury in Hades's eyes as he spoke to Demeter.

"No one shall enter the Underworld except through me. All the gods of Greece, the deities of the pantheon, and immortals of heaven, all must seek me out for admission to the land of the dead. The titans, the fates, and the shades have more rights than the Olympians between the boundaries of my realm."

The entire Underworld started to shake with the force of Hades's declaration, his power and magic making it celestial law as soon as the words left his lips. Black and blue flames erupted from the braziers, casting little to no light but filling the room with the heat of the fires of hell.

"Anyone here who is not of my flesh, born from my power, or shares my bed, if they have immortal blood, shall perish upon their entry to the Underworld without my explicit permission. I revoke all visitors forthright, lest they plead their case to me." Hades's voice morphed from being full of gravel and brimstone to sounding like silk and oil. "And they shall plead their cases to me on their knees, for whether they rule the skies or the grain or the earth..." Lightning and thunder started to crack and roll from the ceiling above them. "they all become my subjects in the end of their days."

A massive cracking noise shattered Orpheus's eardrum as he rushed to cover his ears, curling up into a ball. A huge flash of light accompanied it, and then there was silence. Orpheus waited for a few precious seconds to see if he was still in one piece, but then he finally opened his eyes out of morbid curiosity.

Hades was sitting on his throne, looking as cool and calm as ever. He didn't have a single hair out of place or a drop of sweat on his brow. All his armor had disappeared alongside his bident. On the floor in front of the dais, Demeter was on her knees. Her hands were bound behind her back with tendrils of smoke and another one was tied tightly around her head as a gag. Her eyes were wide with fear as she trembled before the Lord of the Underworld, all of her previous bravado gone.

"You do not have my permission to be here," Hades cocked his head as he looked at Demeter, his expression suddenly bored. "So be gone."

There was another flash of dark smoke, and Demeter vanished entirely from the hall.

Orpheus leaped to his feet and ran as fast as he could out of the room, too occupied with the fear Hades would destroy his shade to realize his plan had worked.

26

Eurydice was staring out the window of Hecate's bedroom, unable to pull herself away from the view. She had been consumed with the thought of her and Pan together ever since he'd left, unable to get any sleep whatsoever. She had the opportunity to make a decision that was utterly selfish...to choose Pan and her own heart over the overwhelming weight of the expectations of being a part of a famous couple. For the first time in her life, she wondered what it would be like to be selfish.

She didn't take another second to think about it. Eurydice ran straight downstairs and disappeared out Hecate's front door, knowing exactly where she could find Pan.

She journeyed quickly through the Underworld to the forests, praying that Pan was still somewhere in the Underworld. Eurydice breathed a sigh of relief when she stumbled into her favorite clearing, her eyes drifting straight past the flowers she loved so much and landing on Pan. He was sitting with his back towards her, leaning against the oak tree that had sprung up after their full moon spent together.

"Pan!" Eurydice's voice cracked when she called out to him, and she realized her cheeks were wet with tears.

Centuries of longing were held in the close gap between them. Pan turned around, and his mouth dropped open in surprise. He smiled at her but quickly faltered, regaining his composure as he walked over to her. He was walking slowly, but his entire body was tense as if he was holding himself back.

"Eurydice..." he whispered the word like it was holy. "Does this mean...?"

"I love you," Eurydice cried out to him. She crossed the short distance remaining between them and jumped into his arms. "I love you. Gods, I love you, Pan. It's enough. It's always going to be enough."

Pan's smile was so bright that it could've outshone Helios himself. It made Eurydice giggle, and her entire body felt lighter than it had in years. Everything about Pan felt right as he wrapped his arms around her waist, holding her to him.

"Are you sure? If you need time, I understand."

"Please stop talking." Eurydice shook her head. "I know what I said, but I was scared. I was scared, and I don't want to be afraid anymore. I don't care what other people think, what anyone has to say. I just want you."

Pan's smile turned devious as he started to lower them both down to the soft earth beneath them.

"Then stop thinking." Pan grinned as he laid Eurydice on her back. Arousal was already running hot through her veins. All it took was the feeling of Pan's body on hers, and she was on fire.

"How come the past couple times I've seen you, I always end up in this position?" Eurydice smirked, watching Pan's playful expression as he kissed his way up her center line until he was suspended above her.

"God of fertility, remember?" He winked, kissing Eurydice again. There was nothing tentative or gentle about it; it was claiming and possessive. Pan kissed like a god who had finally found something he'd wanted, and he was never going to let that go.

Eurydice moaned into the embrace as Pan nipped at her lip, tracing his tongue along the seam of her mouth until she opened up for him. He started grinding against her core, his hips already moving at a devastating, even rhythm against her as she cursed.

"Fuck you," she gasped playfully. "You don't play fair at all." Eurydice's hands came up and gripped Pan's horns as he laughed louder, trailing one hand down her torso. He left goosebumps in his wake, and Eurydice's back bowed as her nipples went taut under the thin chiton she had thrown on. Pan's expression went hot as he tugged the fabric down, his eyes lighting up as she was revealed to him.

"Of course I don't play fair," Pan chuckled. His hot breath ghosted over her breasts, and Eurydice whined at the teasing sensation. "Now that I've got you in my arms, saying that you love me, I'm going to use every trick in the book to remind you why you should've come to this realization a long time ago."

Eurydice started to laugh before it devolved into another gasp as Pan sucked one of her nipples into his mouth. He bit and sucked at her with just the right amount of pain and pleasure, and Eurydice's thighs clenched tighter around nothing.

"I thought you said you didn't want me to t-think," Eurydice panted, letting her head fall back as Pan switched to her other breast.

"Oh, sweet Eurydice," Pan ripped the rest of her tunic off her body, "my tricks don't involve 'thinking' whatsoever."

Eurydice gasped as Pan continued his perfect assault on her breasts, switching back and forth between them until she was practically begging for more. Pan was hellbent on worshipping her body and getting to know every square inch of it, even though he already seemed to know everything about Eurydice's arousal as if he'd been handed a map.

Eurydice's eyes fluttered closed as Pan reached down and started rubbing firm circles on her clit, bringing her right to the edge as he left another love bite on the swollen flesh of her breast.

"My wild thing," he purred. Pan's beard scraped against Eurydice's overheated skin. "Come for me, Eurydice," Pan whispered the command, and Eurydice's first orgasm shot through her like wildfire, turning all the blood and bone in her body to liquid heat. She collapsed against the ground and tried to catch her breath, watching as Pan gently licked each of his fingers clean. The sight was so erotic that it lit Eurydice up from the inside out, and she was desperate to get a taste of him.

"Is that so?" Pan raised one brow, and Eurydice realized she said the last part out loud. Her brain was pleasantly muddled from her last orgasm, and she wasn't processing through a filter.

"Yes," she nodded, biting her lip. Pan sat up on his knees and fisted his cock, already hard and dripping at the tip. He moved forward up Eurydice's body, his skin flushed with sweat and arousal.

"Then be good and open your pretty mouth for me, Eurydice," Pan cooed in a sweet tone of voice that was in direct opposition to the dirtiness of his words. Eurydice clamped her legs together as another wave of heat rushed through her body.

She obeyed immediately, and Pan kept a grip on the base of his cock, feeding it past her swollen lips.

"Fuck," Pan swore, his head dropping back. "Just like that, Eurydice. That's it. Get me nice and wet."

Eurydice moaned around him, causing Pan's entire body to shiver and go taut. She sucked him down until he hit the back of her throat, causing her to gag as spit pooled at the corner of her mouth. Eurydice went to quickly wipe some of it off her cheek, but Pan caught her wrist.

"Absolutely not," Pan chided, slowly starting to rock his hip, shallowly thrusting in and out of her mouth. "I want you to make a mess of me, Eurydice. Cover my cock in your spit so I can thrust it right back into your weeping cunt."

Eurydice cried out around him and hollowed out her cheeks, sucking Pan down as far as she could take him, lying on her back. As he pulled out, she flicked her tongue around the head and savored the salty flavor of him. Everything around her had been reduced to one singular point, and that was Pan. Nothing in her life had ever made as much sense as feeling him on top of her, both of them wild for one another in ways that she had never understood before then.

"F-fuck," Pan cursed again. "I'm close," he warned her, his thrusts becoming more erratic. Eurydice only sucked harder in response, reaching her hand up between his legs to cup his balls in one hand. Pan came with a shout, and Eurydice swallowed everything she could, some of his come mixing with the spit dripping off her lips as he pulled away.

"Gods be damned," Pan panted, staring down at Eurydice as if she was the sun and the stars. "You look utterly debauched right now, my love, and never more stunning." Pan leaned down and kissed her, not even hesitating for a moment.

Pan pulled away, and Eurydice whimpered at the loss of contact.

"Don't worry. I'm hardly done with you." Pan chuckled. "Get up on all fours." Pan got off Eurydice and helped her into position, her coordination thrown off with the strength of the need coursing through her.

"Pan, I need you," Eurydice gasped as she settled into position. Pan leaned over her body, pressing gently down on her shoulders until Eurydice rested her head on her arms with her back arched.

"You'll have me soon," Pan promised, sounding equally out of breath. "If I die, the last thing I want to see in this world is your dripping pussy with your ass up in the air for me." Pan delivered a sharp slap to Eurydice's ass, causing her to moan obscenely and rock her hips backwards.

"My gods," Pan exhaled heavily, running his fingers through her core. "You're soaking wet, Eurydice. And to think

I thought your pretty face streaked with my come was a beautiful mess, but your flushed cunt is just begging for attention, isn't it?"

"I swear to the gods, Pan," Eurydice snapped, "if you don't fuck me, I'll find someone... Oh, fuck!"

Eurydice cut herself off with a scream as Pan grabbed her hips and thrust his cock to the hilt inside of her. Eurydice cried out in relief as he stretched her open, pounding into her with a devastating and dominating pace. She couldn't formulate a single thought besides the delicious ache and pleasure of Pan fucking her on all fours like they were no better than animals in the woods themselves.

Pan bent down until his chest was pressed against Eurydice's back, wrapping one hand around her throat and squeezing gently. Eurydice let out a sound that was somewhere between a cry and a moan. Pan cursed as Eurydice fluttered around him in response.

"Hear me now," Pan grunted, his breath hot in her ear. "I'm not like anyone else you have ever dealt with, Eurydice, and there will be no escaping me." He punctuated his words with well-timed thrusts, as if he could drive home his point to the very core of Eurydice.

Her eyes burned as her heart seized in her chest, an overflow of emotions threatening to come out of her as Pan kept up his brutal, delicious pace. Orpheus had wanted to possess her, to keep her like a trinket; Pan wanted her to be his, not in ownership, but in something more equal altogether. He started speaking again as if he heard the thoughts running through Eurydice's head.

"You're mine, Eurydice, but don't forget that every inch of me has always belonged to you. Every hair on my head and every breath in my lungs."

Pan pulled Eurydice up to her knees so her back was flush to his chest, tightening his grip around her throat and dropping his other hand to rub gentle circles around her clit. He felt even bigger inside of her this way, making Eurydice cry out. She dropped her head to his shoulder, the overflow of arousal and emotions making her sob.

"Let it out, my love, my heart," Pan was panting heavily and rocking his hips against hers. "Come for me. Let it all go." Eurydice's body tightened up, and she screamed, her release pummeling through her like she had been run over by a herd of wild horses. Pan's hips stuttered, and he was coming a second later, his release spilling into her.

Eurydice nearly collapsed to the ground, but Pan caught her, holding her in his arms as he gently lowered them both down to the earth. He rearranged them until Eurydice was nestled on top of him, Pan on his back, resting her head on his chest. Eurydice dozed for an undetermined amount of time until she felt like her capacity for thought had come back.

"Pan..." she started slowly, and Pan made some sort of chuffing sound underneath her.

"If you are about to express some sort of sentiment of regret, I would like to inform you that I simply won't be accepting it." He opened his eyes and winked at her, his playful countenance always putting Eurydice at ease. Pan had been her best friend for centuries. She knew that he would listen to anything she had to say with sincerity.

"No, I don't regret it," Eurydice laughed. "I don't think anyone could regret sex like that."

Pan preened with obvious pride. "I'm flattered."

"Don't take it too seriously, god of fertility. I'm not sure if that means you're talented or just lucky in the sex department."

"Do you care enough to make the distinction?" Pan quipped back.

"Not at all." Eurydice gave a little shrug, propping her chin up on Pan's chest so she could look him in the eye. "I don't know if this feels too fast, too slow, or too...anything. I've known you for ages, but now that I've realized I love you, it feels like everything clicked into place all at once. I can't imagine going a day without you now. Is that insane? I know I should probably take some time, reflect on everything that happened with Orpheus..."

"Eurydice," Pan interrupted her gently, "you have spent centuries wondering about what the *right* thing is. You always think about other people and what their thoughts are. You stayed with Orpheus for as long as you did because you were worried about what people would say. Am I wrong?"

Eurydice flushed. "You're not wrong."

"Anyone in your position would've done the same thing. It's daunting." Pan pushed some of the hair off Eurydice's forehead. "Just answer one question. Do you love me? Do you want to be with me?"

"You know I do."

Pan smiled. "Then don't worry about anything else. If you feel later down the road that you want to take some time apart or you feel differently, we'll cross that road when we come to it."

"You'd let me go if I told you that I wanted some space?" Eurydice raised a brow and looked at Pan with a healthy dose of skepticism. Pan chuckled in response.

"Oh, sure. I'd let you go all the way into the next room over, if you really needed it. Might even let you go outside for a few hours if you really needed space."

Eurydice burst out laughing and tumbled off Pan's chest, landing on her back next to him. He laughed alongside her and found her hand, intertwining their fingers together.

"I'm serious, though. Whatever you need, I'll find a way to give it to you. Even if it means one day that you want some space. I just won't be happy about it, unfortunately, but I won't apologize for missing you."

Eurydice blushed bright red, kissing Pan's cheek and curling into his side. "You'll never have to."

III

27

For the first time in a long time, Eurydice woke up with a smile on her face. It was better than being content; she was happy. She'd spent years in the Underworld without a complaint, but everything else was different when she woke up next to Pan.

He was still fast asleep, his broad body curled around her protectively as if he was worried, she'd try to sneak away.

As if there will be any getting rid of me now, Eurydice thought to herself. Her heart was so full, it was going to burst. She had loved Orpheus in a way for a time, but that time was over. She had crawled through hell, very literally, to understand the love she had with Pan was only actualized when she leaned into what she wanted. Eurydice was no longer sitting idly on the sidelines of her own life. She was no simple muse; she did not exist for the inspiration of others. She was going to grow and cultivate her life the way she wanted it, an ironic lesson to learn after you were dead, and that life included Pan.

He looked every inch the god of fertility as he made soft snoring sounds in his sleep. The late afternoon light was coming into the room, illuminating the wide shape of his shoulders and the dark hair that covered his olive skin. His warm, big hands traced over Eurydice's body, reaching out for her even in his subconscious. Eurydice shifted slightly to get closer to Pan, relishing the soreness in her limbs.

Eurydice's eyes fluttered closed, and she was prepared to doze off again, wrapped in her lover's arms, when a rush of golden magic rippled through Hecate's home. It woke Pan instantly, and they both sat up in bed, recognizing the potency of Hermes's power. There was something urgent and anxious in the magical signature, which was uncharacteristic for Hermes.

"What do you..."

"Do you think we should..." Pan and Eurydice both started at the same time, and Eurydice motioned for Pan to continue. He smiled gently and kissed her softly, trailing his way down her throat in a series of kisses. He acted like he couldn't get enough of her, and Eurydice relished in the sensation of being adored for who she was, not for what she could do or inspire for others.

"Let's go see what your father wants." Eurydice grinned, unable to somber completely. Pan groaned exaggeratedly, kissing Eurydice once more before he got out of bed and gave her a delicious view of his bare ass.

"Now I see why everyone complains about him interrupting," Pan grunted. Eurydice said nothing as they both got dressed quickly, too happy to ruin the moment with any more words. Pan grabbed her hand and led her down the stairs to Hecate's kitchen where Hermes was sitting on the countertop.

"If Hecate knows you're sitting on the counter..." Pan cautioned. Hermes hopped off with a smirk on his face, but something was off about his countenance. It set Eurydice on edge. She found herself standing closer to Pan and intertwining her fingers with his.

"What bothers you?" Pan cut straight to the quick, sensing the tense atmosphere emanating from Hermes's power that ebbed throughout the kitchen.

Hermes sighed heavily. "Pan, you've been summoned to Hades's throne room for an audience with the Lord of the Underworld."

A twinge of panic twisted in Eurydice's gut. In her experience, it was always an unknown being summoned to the Lord of the Dead's hall. Pan's expression darkened further, and he pulled Eurydice closer to him. His voice had dropped to a growl when he addressed his father.

"For what purpose?"

"I wasn't told." Hermes bit his lip. It was strange for Hermes to be requested to summon an audience and not know what it pertained to. It made Eurydice even more nervous, and she started shifting her weight back and forth. Pan sensed her discomfort and squeezed her hand tightly. Pan looked pensive for a moment, and Eurydice was surprised when he nodded in agreement without asking any additional questions.

"Then we'll go." Pan nodded his head solemnly, and Eurydice's chest tightened. There was no way she was going to let him do this alone, and she appreciated that he'd said 'we.'

The journey to Hades's estate was quick and silent. Eurydice could feel her anxiety growing as they got closer and the manor carved out of the side of a mountain of obsidian loomed over them. She never seemed to care too much before in her life, whether it was when she was alive or dead, but now that she had finally pushed past the voices in her head, she had found things worth fighting for, and she was afraid to lose them. If she lost the flowers or the trees, they would always come back to her as the world turned. The fields died every year, and they always returned.

Pan was as wild as the nature that functioned as an extension of his will, but he could be taken from Eurydice in a way that flowers could not.

Hades's dominion loomed over them, imposing as ever, a constant watching eye over the Underworld. As the massive double doors to the estate swung open for Pan and Eurydice,

Eurydice's breath hitched. Pan's arm slipped around her waist, and he squeezed her as close to his body as possible as they walked through the halls. Pan stopped her outside of the great room.

"Hades is a fair god." His voice was steady. "Don't be frightened."

"I can't help it." Eurydice shook her head. "I feel like I just got you back in my life, for some reason, and now you're going to be taken away from me. I know it doesn't make any sense."

"You've been through a lot, Eurydice." Pan kissed her forehead softly, pinching her chin gently between his fingers and tilting her head up to look at him. "I'm not going to let anything else happen to you, okay? I understand if you don't want to trust Hades, but will you at least trust me?"

Eurydice nodded, going up on her tiptoes to kiss Pan soundly before she turned and shoved open the doors to the receiving hall, marching through without another second of hesitation with her head held high.

Hades was alone; the second throne on the dais sat empty. Eurydice's stomach sank a little further; she wished Persephone was there. The goddess had a romantic heart that might be used to sway things in Eurydice's favor...if she even knew why they had been called there in the first place. The braziers weren't lit, and there was no obvious incense smoking throughout the cavernous room, making Eurydice feel slightly less intimidated. It didn't seem as though Hades had pulled out all the stops to intimidate them.

Hades was sitting on his throne with his back straight and a completely neutral expression. If he was surprised to see Eurydice when only Pan had been summoned, he didn't show it. It took a minute for Eurydice to realize Orpheus was also in the room, half hidden by a column on the exterior. Her heart rate jumped, and she pushed back against the urge to start screaming and demanding he be thrown out. The dread in Eurydice's stomach calcified. If they had been summoned for anything good, Orpheus wouldn't be in the room.

"Hades," Pan greeted calmly, stopping a few feet from the dais. Eurydice was practically frozen to the spot. Pan squeezed her hand gently, and it pulled her back to the present. She nodded her head once in Hades's direction to mimic Pan's greeting.

"Pan." Hades's voice was calm. He was as still as stone and not even a single twitch in his expression revealed anything about his mood or what they were about to endure. Intense flashbacks started rolling through Eurydice's mind as she found herself leaning on Pan for support, no longer subtly.

At the sight of a clearly distressed Eurydice, Hades's face finally softened, but it was twinged with regret. He opened his mouth to speak, and Eurydice's world shattered once again.

"Pan, your privileges to visit the Underworld have been revoked. The forests of Asphodel and Elysium belong first and foremost to the Underworld, not to you, which makes them a part of my domain..."

"That's not fair!" Pan shouted, stepping towards the dais. His face contorted in anger, but Eurydice dropped her gaze to the floor.

This can't be happening. This can't be happening, not again...

"You are to leave directly from this hall and proceed to Greece. Thanatos and Hermes will accompany you as my representatives of the Underworld..." Hades kept on talking over Pan's outburst, who looked prepared to jump up onto the throne and strangle Hades with his bare hands.

"You rotten bastard!" Pan was furious, his face beet red and spit flying from his mouth as he yelled. "How dare you go back on your word, the infallible honor of Hades..."

As soon as the word 'honor' left Pan's lips, Hades exploded. He jumped up from his throne and made it down the dais steps in the blink of an eye, grabbing Pan by the shoulder and giving him a hard shake. Black smoke started to pour in from the windows, and the sound of thunder shook the rafters. Eurydice fell to her knees and extended a hand out towards Hades and Pan.

"Pan, stop!" she screamed until she thought her temples might burst. "Hades, don't hurt him!"

"You know nothing of which you speak," Hades growled, his voice shaking the entire room. He released Pan, who stumbled backwards but managed to keep his footing. Hades looked prepared to fight Pan on the spot, and Eurydice prayed that Pan wouldn't choose now to make a stand. There was something in Hades's eyes that Eurydice couldn't quite place. Even though she didn't know the god very well, none of this was worth dying for in the middle of the throne room.

"Pan, please." Eurydice found her voice and was surprised at how calm she sounded. She stood up carefully and held out her hands toward him. "It's not worth it. We'll... We'll figure something out... Just go."

The look on Pan's face shattered Eurydice, sending pain and discomfort rattling through her body and down to her bones.

"I'm not like that son of a bitch," Pan sneered, his attention turning to Orpheus. Orpheus was cowering in the corner of the room, keeping one eye on the chaos. "I'll fight for you, Eurydice. Do you understand that? No one will keep me from —"

"I'll keep you wherever I damn well please," Hades snapped, "and that means not in my Underworld."

"Hades, you—"

"Stop!" Eurydice called out again, getting Pan and Hades's attention back on her. She walked over to Pan and threw her arms around his neck, pressing a kiss to his cheek as she did so. Her voice was muffled when she spoke, keeping her words quiet and just for him.

"I know, Pan. I know. I can fight for myself though, okay?" She released a shaky breath, her previously calm voice starting to sound breathier and more upset. "I need you to respect that. It's about time everyone understood that Eurydice can fight her own battles. We'll find a way to be together. I promise. Can you trust me? Can you do that?" Eurydice pulled away from Pan, placing her hands on either side of his face. They were both crying, and for once, Eurydice found herself hoping that no one would try and save her...and Pan would do exactly as she asked.

It was silent in the throne room for a perilous minute, even the thunder and clouds of Hades were deathly still. Eurydice was barely breathing until Pan let out a deep exhale and nodded his head solemnly. He didn't look at Hades as he pulled Eurydice close to him and kissed her soundly. It didn't matter who else was in the room; all that mattered to him was that this might be the last moment he had with her, and he wasn't going to let it go.

"We're not done. Do you understand me?" Pan whispered against Eurydice's lips, their tears mixing with one another's. She released a shaky sob, agreeing with him.

"I know, Pan. I know. But we can't find a way together if you're dead. Just listen to Hades for now."

"Fine," Pan acquiesced, kissing Eurydice one more time before she released him.

"She stays this time," Hades interrupted, seemingly reading Eurydice's thoughts as she prepared to walk Pan to the gates of hell. "There's no need for Eurydice to walk another suitor to the edge of the Underworld."

Whatever decimated pieces of Eurydice's heart were left dissolved into oblivion. She was surprised that she was able to stay standing as Pan spat at Hades's feet and turned on his heel, marching towards the hallway where she could see Thanatos and Hermes waiting in the wings. Before he left the room, he found Eurydice, mouthing the words 'I love you' before Thanatos's hand appeared on his shoulder.

"I love you too!" Eurydice sobbed, her voice sounding as

wrecked as she felt. All her previous attempts at calm and bravado were ripped to shreds like torn clothing, but she knew it was up to her now to find out why there had been a sudden change in Hades's ruling.

Eurydice had had enough of deciding whether or not she could be with this suitor or that immortal. The romantic games of deities had put her in the crossfire for too long. Now it was the time for everyone to understand just how much of a problem it was going to be for anyone who stood in her way. As Eurydice watched Pan disappear down the long hallway, flanked by gods on either side, her mind was made up.

I'm no longer a muse. I'm going to become a fucking problem.

28

Eurydice stared at the empty doorway, Pan's frame long having disappeared from sight. A shaking hand appeared on her shoulder, trying to turn her in its direction.

"Eurydice?" Orpheus's voice was shaky as he implored her. "Why don't you come home? It was a dreadful revelation, I'm sure, collecting all your memories, and Pan took advantage of that..."

Eurydice spun around, fury in her eyes. Thorns started appearing all down her arms while vines shot out from her hair.

"How dare you?" Eurydice shouted. She was ready to strangle Orpheus until the light drained from his eyes. Never before had she felt so much fury towards a living being. "You want to talk about taking advantage of me? You tried to hide the fact from me that you abandoned me in the Underworld!"

"We can make it work," Orpheus argued, "if you would just be more like... Oomph!" Eurydice cut Orpheus off with a sharp slap to the face. She didn't think; she just swung with an open hand and smacked him as hard as she could.

"You little prick," Eurydice's lip curled, "get the fuck out of my sight. I never want to see you again. We will not be 'making it work' and I will never be synonymous with someone ever again. Even if I love them. The muse is speaking for herself now."

Orpheus had stumbled away, clutching his cheek with an appalled and shocked expression on his face. Some of the thorns had sliced through his cheek, dripping crimson blood on his pristine white tunic. Orpheus turned around and started searching, whining when he saw Hades sitting on his throne, looking bored again.

"Hades! Did you see..."

"Do I look like a house maid or a midwife to you?" Hades growled, raising one dark brow. He had his bident sitting across his lap, and he picked it up. "You sound like a squabbling child."

Orpheus looked outraged. "But Eurydice..."

"Your plan worked, Orpheus." Hades stood up and crossed his arms over his broad chest. "You pushed me until Pan got exiled, but you have to live with the consequences. Eurydice is not beholden to you in the slightest. You will certainly find no champion in me for your cause." Hades's voice dropped lower as he spoke, making the atmosphere in the room drop a little bit more.

Orpheus looked like a petulant child. Eurydice shivered at the change in temperature and also in remembrance of the time she had spent together with Orpheus. Everything about him now repulsed her; she could not believe that there was a time when she thought he was the be-all and end-all when it came to men.

"Eurydice..." Orpheus whimpered, looking towards Eurydice with a broken look on his face.

"Get out," Hades commanded, pointing one finger towards the door. "Before you are removed, and I promise I will not make it polite."

The thunder rumbled again, and Orpheus turned on his

heel and ran out of the room without a second glance. Eurydice was once again slightly stunned at how quickly he would abandon her after trying to declare his fealty. There was a heavy silence in the room, and Eurydice realized she didn't quite know what to do next. There was no one beside her that she needed to consider, only herself.

The only thing I want to consider is how to get Pan back. Her thoughts were turned towards him. Maybe she was running into one relationship after another, but this one was her choice. Pan loved her; he'd always had. It was the kind of love that made her want to be better in spite of everything, to make decisions that benefitted herself for once.

"I am sorry for what happened." Hades's voice broke Eurydice's train of thought. She jumped a little, momentarily forgetting that she was standing in Hades's great hall with the infamous god.

"Lord Hades, why—" Eurydice turned around and was about to ask Hades why Pan had been banished when the doors to the room flung open. They slammed against the walls and sent cracks up to the rooftop, echoing throughout the cavernous room. Eurydice ducked and covered her head out of habit, but Hades only looked embarrassed.

"Hades! What in the fuck is going on in here? I have left you alone for two days and now... Oh, hi, Eurydice, darling." Persephone stormed into the room. Her hair and tunic were whipping around her as she stormed through the doorway. As she walked, the pink swathes of fabric morphed to a darker red color, then crimson, and then black. Eurydice watched in equal parts admiration and horror as her crown of flowers died and the petals fell off, revealing a crown of open-mouthed skulls.

Persephone stopped in front of Eurydice, pulling her into a tight hug without a moment's hesitation.

"I'm so sorry about this, lovely child." Persephone made a tutting sound and turned around, pointing her finger at Hades. "Would you like to explain yourself to me?"

Eurydice had never seen the fearsome Lord of the Underworld look afraid before, but Hades sat back down on his throne and blushed. Eurydice was watching one of Greece's most fearsome gods blushing under the interrogation of his wife.

"Do you want to speak about this over dinner, my sweet wife?" Hades reached up and undid the knot in his hair, turning on the charm. He smiled warmly, his dark eyes glowing. "I haven't made that smoked fish for you in a few months..."

"Do not try to distract me, Hades Aidoneus Plouton Clymenus!" Persephone snapped. "This conversation is relevant to Eurydice, anyway."

"Honestly, I am dying to hear why this happened." Eurydice shrugged, looking between Persephone and Hades. "And I've done a lot of dying." She pinned her gaze on Hades. "I can't fucking imagine why you've let this happen."

As soon as the words came out of her mouth, Eurydice's eyes widened, and the color drained from her face. Perhaps she was emboldened by the appearance of Persephone, but Eurydice suddenly remembered she still didn't have any place reprimanding the god of the dead. Persephone giggled, grabbing hold of Eurydice's hand and giving it a squeeze.

"Don't worry, love. He doesn't mind it when women speak back to him."

Eurydice's mouth dropped open in surprise, and Hades groaned exaggeratedly, covering his face with his hand.

"Hades, please," Persephone implored him, her expression softening. "I can't believe you would do this, after everything that's happened."

Hades stood up and crossed the room until he was standing next to Persephone. He wrapped an arm around her waist and tugged her closer to him, Eurydice letting go of Persephone's hand. There was a tenderness in the gesture that she didn't imagine that Hades was capable of, even though the stories of how much he loved his wife stretched far and wide. It made her heart ache when she thought of Pan on his way to the gates of hell to be escorted out of the Underworld.

Hades told them both the story of what happened with Orpheus and Demeter, especially how he threatened Demeter and refused to let her run amok in the Underworld. Persephone's anger ebbed and flowed with the story, her magic spiking every time she heard the mention of her mother's name. Eurydice's anger ebbed away. Orpheus had discovered the loophole, and she understood why Hades had to make the decision that he did. She just wished that it didn't involve her losing the love of her life mere moments after they had finally come together. It was like dying on her wedding day all over again.

Eurydice turned away and walked towards one of the low benches along the wall, sinking down onto it as she tried to process the bevy of emotions that ran through her head. Persephone was now embracing Hades, and he was running a hand through her golden hair. Her anger had seemingly dissipated. While Eurydice was glad they had come to some sort of reconciliation, a placated Persephone was probably not going to fight for Eurydice like an angry one. To her surprise, Persephone picked up her head and looked directly at the nymph.

"How do we help Eurydice and Pan then, beloved?" Persephone grabbed both of Hades's hands and raised a brow. "We can't leave everything like this."

"I don't know," Hades admitted, stroking a hand through his beard. "I didn't want you to get stuck in the crossfire, Eurydice, but there was nothing I could do at the time. I couldn't let Demeter have free reign in the Underworld."

Persephone visibly shuddered at the mention of it, and Eurydice knew that she didn't blame Hades for his decision. She was heartbroken over what it meant for her, but he had done it to protect his consort. Even Eurydice could see what kind of chaos it would cause if all the gods suddenly started using the loophole that Pan had been provided.

Hades opened his mouth to say something when a breeze fluttered through the door.

"What now?" Hades groaned, pinching the bridge of his nose. Makaria drifted in a moment later, the sweet smell of her magic and soft sparkling clouds accompanying her presence.

"Eurydice," Makaria offered up a sad smile. She crossed the room and went straight to Eurydice's side, sitting down on the bench and wrapping an arm around her shoulders. "I came as soon as I heard. Thanatos told me. He's ushering Pan to the gates with Hermes." Makaria narrowed her gaze and stared at Hades with a venomous expression. "What the hell did you do?"

Hades grunted and threw his hands up in exasperation. "Are there any other goddesses who have an issue with the way I'm running my Underworld? Do you want to poll Nyx and Hecate?" Hades paused. "On second thought, no, never mind. Let's not. Let me have it, Makaria."

"Your Underworld?" Persephone interrupted Hades first, tilting her head to the side and pursing her lips.

"I'm starting to see why Cronus wanted to eat everyone," Hades grumbled under his breath, making his way back to his throne and collapsing down onto it. He said nothing as Persephone brought Makaria up to speed, who didn't comment until Persephone was done speaking.

"But how do you feel, dearie?" Makaria turned to look at Eurydice first, her eyes filled with concern.

"I want Pan," Eurydice sighed, looking at the trio of gods before her. "I don't know how, and I understand why Hades did what he had to do, but...it seems horrific if I'm staring down at a future without him."

Persephone, Hades, and Makaria nodded in agreement, all of them looking imploring at one another as if one of the gods would have an answer to their problems.

Eurydice was horrified when she realized she had started to cry again, quickly wiping away at the tears on her cheeks. Makaria leaned over and helped her, using the hem of her own chiton to help Eurydice. Persephone looked between Eurydice and Hades, her expression changing from sorrowful to inquisitive.

"Hades," she looked up at her husband, "you're open to some suggestions on how to fix this mess, correct?"

Hades stared down at his wife with a deadpan expression. "Persephone, what makes you think that you wouldn't tell me your ideas anyway, and when have I not listened?"

Eurydice couldn't help but chuckle a little under her breath at how Persephone had Hades wrapped around her little finger. Makaria nudged her shoulder, apparently picking up on the same thing.

"Well," Persephone looked at Eurydice, "everyone should have a fair chance in life, don't you think?"

Hades's mouth pulled into a thin line. "Yes, I'd like to think that's how this realm has been governed since long before you came along." Persephone glared at him, and Hades held his hands up. "But you have made such great improvements. Carry on."

Persephone smiled. "Orpheus had the same chance as Pan when he exploited the loophole regarding the Underworld. Shouldn't Pan have the same chances as Orpheus?"

Total silence fell over the room. Eurydice was trying to figure out what Persephone was talking about. Surely Pan didn't want to become a poet or have his chance at being an acolyte of Apollo.

"Are you talking about trying to curry favor with Apollo?" Makaria interrupted. "That would be rather impossible since he's dead. I can't say that I feel sorry about that either."

"I'm well aware," Persephone and Hades answered at the same time. Hades immediately motioned for Persephone to continue.

"I'm not talking about Apollo," Persephone said, her smile growing across her face. "I'm talking about the chance to lead Eurydice out of hell."

You could hear a sewing needle drop in the great hall. Eurydice's heart jumped up into her throat. Could Persephone be suggesting what she thought she was? Would Hades give her a chance to follow Pan out of the Underworld, the way she had tried to follow Orpheus? Eurydice almost didn't dare to hope. She wasn't breathing as she stared at Hades's face.

He looked stunned, deep in thought as he looked at Persephone and then Eurydice. Finally, when Eurydice thought she might be sick, Hades started nodding slowly.

"It would only be fair." His grin turned into a wide smile. "Pan should be allowed the opportunity to succeed where Orpheus failed. Eurydice, do you have any objections to the proposal?"

Eurydice thought she was going to faint. Could she do this again? Would she be able to make that journey? She loved Pan more than she had ever loved Orpheus, but that journey was not for the faint of heart. She had nightmares about it until the day she drank from Lethe and forgot about it entirely.

Isn't it worth it, though? For Pan? Eurydice realized that her mind was already made up; she was just nervous about it. She slowly started nodding her head, her hands trembling in her lap. Makaria held her tighter.

"Yes." Her voice was barely a whisper. "I would do it again. If it was for Pan... I trust him. I would make that journey for him again."

Hades turned to face Eurydice, offering a slight bow of his head. Persephone clapped her hands together in joy as Hades decreed it. Eurydice felt the words of another bargain with the Lord of the Dead sink into her skin.

"Eurydice, nymph of the forests, twice now you have died and been sent to my realm. For the third and final time, I offer you the opportunity to escape the Underworld. You can follow

SONG OF MEMORIES

Pan out of the gates of hell. If Pan does not look back, if he does not look behind even once to confirm that you are there, then you shall step into the sun and become an immortal, living nymph of the green earth above again. Do you accept?"

Eurydice's nervousness was suddenly gone, replaced with a warm, gooey feeling of memories of Pan and running in the sunshine of the mortal realm. She saw the excited and supportive smiles of Persephone and Makaria, both of them who had been alongside her almost every step of the way.

Eurydice stood up and took a deep breath. She squared her shoulders back and looked at Hades, meeting his gaze.

"I accept."

Eurydice was going to crawl up from hell for the second time.

29

Eurydice expected to feel a deep sense of anguish and anxiety douse her system, but instead, she only felt a stoic sense of calm. That journey haunted her nightmares until the day she swore herself off those horrors and drank deeply from the river of Lethe. But this was not that memory, and she was not that woman who'd suffered at the hands of Orpheus's ego.

Eurydice took a long, steadying breath and looked around the room. Makaria, Persephone, and Hades were all staring back at her with either warm or neutral expressions. She was suddenly overwhelmed with the realization that she had found the favor of the gods all on her own. While Orpheus had only ever had the favor of Apollo, she had stumbled into the support of three of the Underworld's most infamous keepers.

"Well," Eurydice smiled with a calm shrug, "what are we waiting for, I guess?"

Hades nodded in agreement and held his hand out towards the open door, retreating towards the dais. Persephone clapped her hands with glee and took Eurydice's arm while Makaria flanked her other side, both goddesses escorting her towards the door. As they were about to cross the threshold, Hades cleared his throat, effectively stopping them.

"Eurydice?" Hades settled back down on his throne. "I do hope that you shall never return to this realm, as much as your presence has blessed it. Go well. Have faith."

Tears sprang to Eurydice's eyes as she grappled with the weight of such good wishes from an immortal as powerful as Hades. What he said was true; if she made it out of the Underworld this time, as long as there were no 'incidents' like the snake on her wedding day, Eurydice's immortality in the world above would be returned to her. It was an insurmountable offer that Hades had extended to her.

"Thank you for your stewardship, Lord Hades." Eurydice gave him a formal curtesy, feeling in the moment like it was the most appropriate form of gratitude she could offer him. Persephone started giggling, urging them along down the hallway.

"He's such a sap." She winked. "As long as you can appeal to his side of fair judgement, you can get just about anything past him."

"Is that so?" Makaria piped up, her grey eyes sparkling behind her white hair. "I'll have to file that away for the future."

"To be fair," Persephone smirked, "I don't know if it will work as well for you or Thanatos since you aren't sharing his bed."

Eurydice blushed at the insinuation, and all three of them laughed harder, making quick work to catch up to where Thanatos and Hermes were escorting Pan to the gates.

The closer she got, the more Eurydice had to fight the temptation to kick up her heels and start running. What a world of a difference it made to be tackling the challenges of the Underworld with someone that she trusted. If this entire situation had proven anything to her, it had shone a bright light on how little she had truly loved or trusted Orpheus to begin with.

As they rounded the corner and the massive gates of hell came into view, Eurydice caught sight of Pan ahead of them. He was flanked on either side by Hermes and Thanatos, very much mimicking the position that Eurydice found herself in now. Persephone saw her face light up and released Eurydice, nodding in the direction of Pan.

"Go on, young nymph." Persephone winked, and Eurydice froze for a brief second, her heart jumping up into her throat. Then, she was off. She started running, feeling as free as she had felt in eons. There was nothing chaining her to any one place or person anymore; only her choices dictated who she was or what she wanted to do.

And she wanted to run to Pan as fast as her legs could carry her.

"Pan!" Eurydice cried out, her voice echoing off the boundless hills around them. "Pan!" Eurydice started giggling like a child, her feet barely touching the ground as she moved as fast as she could. The wind whipped through her hair, and flowers sprung up in the footprints she left in the soft dirt. Pan halted and turned around, his face wet with tears that he had been freely shedding in Eurydice's absence. When he looked at her, Eurydice could practically feel the warmth of the sun and smell the sweet air perfumed with blossoms as he smiled. Pan dropped to one knee and held out his arms for her, just in time for Eurydice to crash into him at full speed.

They were delirious with laughter, Pan easily accepting the weight of impact and rolling them into the grass. Somewhere above them, Eurydice could hear the small chorus of gods now cheering at their reunion. She tuned it out, settling on top of Pan and cupping his face with her hands.

"My love," Eurydice gasped, trying to catch her breath. "We've done it. We've done it. Hades said..."

"What did he say?" Pan sat up straight, and Eurydice shifted in his lap. He searched her face for any indication of what Hades had decreed.

"He said that you are to be offered the same chance as Orpheus," Eurydice breathed. Her smile was so wide, she thought her face might split in two. "If I can follow you out of the gates of hell, and as long as you don't look back... I can come back to the mortal world with you."

Pan's face morphed from sorrow to glee and back again. A myriad of emotions ran across his face until he shook his head, almost as if he was trying to clear the excess of feeling from his thoughts.

"Are you serious?" Pan looked from Eurydice to the two goddesses she came with. "That is what he said?"

"Every word." Persephone held up her hand as if she was taking a solemn vow.

"I can attest to it." Makaria smiled, finding her way over to her consort. Thanatos kissed her hair and smiled widely back at Pan and Eurydice on the ground.

"About damn time!" Hermes crowed with delight. The wings on his sandals fluttered to life, and he clapped his hands in glee. "I knew that old tyrant had a soft spot for love stories."

"Don't we all?" Persephone looked pointedly at Hermes, who blushed, and Eurydice assumed there was a story there. Pan looked at Eurydice, gently running his thumb over her cheek.

"Are you sure?" His voice was quiet, meant only for her as he ignored the chorus of gods around them. "I don't want to have to put you through that again if you..."

"No, no," Eurydice shook her head and cut him off. "I want this. I want the chance to do this with you. I'm not scared of it." Eurydice started to cry. "You've already followed me to hell and back. The least I can do is make the journey with you one time."

Pan responded by kissing Eurydice, pulling her as tightly to him as possible. He ignored completely that they were being watched; all of his love and undying affection for her poured out into the embrace. That was something about Pan that

Eurydice never knew how much she'd appreciate; he put everything in action. While Orpheus had been entirely comprised of words and sonnets, Pan was nothing but action. If he meant something, he proved it to Eurydice without a second thought. It never left her guessing or worrying about his intentions, and that relief alone made Eurydice feel light enough to float.

"Then let's go." Pan grinned, pulling away from Eurydice and leaving her with swollen lips.

Pan helped Eurydice stand to her feet as they were surrounded by the bevy of gods, all of them piling on good wishes and luck.

"You'll do fine!"

"Don't worry about it for a moment. You've already done it once before!"

"If you fuck it up, I'll disown you." Hermes added with a smirk, which Pan didn't seem to take to heart, and Eurydice assumed that was a glimpse into how Hermes preferred to parent. Persephone hugged them both tightly, patting Pan on the head affectionately. Persephone shared a special kinship with Eurydice and Pan, all of them having some sort of sacred connection to the nature they were born from.

"I'm glad it worked out, old friend." Persephone winked at Pan and looked at Eurydice. "You are a perfect fit for each other."

"It hasn't worked out just yet," Pan quipped, eyeing the long, cracked path that disappeared into the wall of stone past the gates. The gates themselves were intimidating enough, carved from wrought iron and obsidian stone, with the faces of some of the Underworld's more infamous inhabitants, including the titans. Cerberus's post just beyond the gates was empty, which meant he was likely off at home, scamming the staff for extra food. This entrance was not used for mortal souls who were arriving to the Underworld. That was handled by Charon, and this entrance was infinitely more intimidating.

Eurydice was already catching whiffs of the sour scent of sulfur.

"It'll be fine." Persephone was elated as if she was already planning the wedding.

"Are you ready?" Pan helped Eurydice to her feet, and they both turned to look at the winding path ahead of them. Eurydice was looking at it with fresh eyes, every part of her feeling the need to run towards it and not look back—as long as Pan didn't either.

"As ready as I'll ever be." Eurydice's expression was tender. Pan grabbed hold of her hand and squeezed it, saying their final farewells to the gods. They were inundated with another round of well wishes, and Pan set off walking. He would be allowed to hold her hand until the path started to ascend, and he took advantage of every minute.

Eurydice didn't dare to look back herself at the fading landscape of the Underworld. She had discovered parts of herself in her journey through the land of the dead that she didn't know existed; she'd lost part of herself, too, that she wouldn't miss. Eurydice truly had died to find herself, and while she wasn't full of optimism in this moment, she was full of peace. After a lifetime and a stint of being dead, of optimism and false promises, peace was the most valuable thing in the universe to Eurydice.

The landscape around them slowly started to die; the grass withered, and the intense smell of sulfur got thicker. The shadow of the gates ebbed away until it disappeared into the darkness that was slowly consuming everything around them. The soft earthen path decayed into a cracked road of sharp stones. Eurydice sucked in a sharp breath and forced herself to exhale slowly as the memory of those jagged rocks across her skin came tumbling back. The road to the mortal world continued through a small crevice in the stone wall in front of them. As soon as Pan stepped into it, there would be no speaking to him, and he couldn't turn around until they both reached the sunlight. Pan gave Eurydice's hand another tight squeeze, without turning around, as she fell into place behind him.

"Any last minute doubts?" he asked softly, and Eurydice's heart swelled. Pan was constantly checking in with her, making sure that this was something she was willing to go through again. Even as he spoke, his eyesight stayed dead ahead.

"Not a single one," Eurydice whispered back. Pan nodded his head and stepped forward, stepping out of his sandals as he did so.

"Step into those," he commanded gently. A fresh round of tears started to gather in Eurydice's eyes. Pan noticed her determination to always be barefoot and knew she'd woken up that morning, and like every other morning, she refused to put on sandals. "And follow me."

Eurydice did as he instructed, carefully slipping on the much larger leather sandals Pan left for her. He dropped her hand and walked forward with his head held high. Eurydice took a deep breath, steadied her nerves, and ducked inside the tight crevice and followed Pan.

The darkness enveloped her entirely, and Eurydice found herself waiting yet again for the chaos to descend. She was prepared for the panic to grip her heart now that she was actually consumed in the recesses of the deep, but it never came. The rocks didn't hurt her feet and maybe it was in her imagination, but the air was sweeter too. The sulfur didn't sting her nostrils or make her eyes water. Even the ground felt smoother as she made her way triumphantly forward.

Time started to lose all of its meaning, but Eurydice was prepared for that side effect of the path to hell. She simply surrendered to it instead of fighting it, focusing entirely on her memories of Pan and the concrete knowledge that he was walking in front of her. In the darkness, a soft, gentle sound started to separate itself from the silence. It was melodic, haunting, and Eurydice was captivated by it; it moved her forward, refreshing her hopes. Eurydice didn't know how long the music continued until she recognized the voice—Pan was singing to her.

With a melody more beautiful than anything she'd heard from Orpheus himself, more melodic than a single note from Apollo's lyre. Pan sung to her, helping Eurydice weave her way through the path and the dark caverns of the roadway. She couldn't help it; her heart swelled, and she started to smile. She knew that he wouldn't be able to hear her if she responded, but he sang; he sang nonetheless, and Eurydice knew he was doing it to remind her that he was there. Eurydice's smile grew even wider, and she laughed, the joyful, happy sound almost completely at odds with her surroundings. But then the atmosphere got a little lighter.

The dark, pitch-black world she was walking in began to turn blue, then grey. Eurydice didn't put a single boundary around the hope exploding in her chest. She had done this before, but it was going to end a second time.

Soon, before she could even realize it, Eurydice was blinded by a bright light that filled the entire cavern. The rock pathway opened up into a massive cave with a mouth that would hold half a battalion. Eurydice started runnin,g and she ran until her entire body was bathed in sunlight. The stones beneath her turned into grass—warm, soft grass that had been touched by the sun!

Eurydice looked up and as her eyes adjusted to the light... There was Pan. He was still walking, refusing to look back, until he crossed the mouth of the cave, and he was completely clear of its confines.

Eurydice's breath caught in her throat as she picked up her pace.

Not now, not now. I have to get there too... She prayed that he wouldn't slip up on the instructions. But Pan was steadfast. He didn't even look like he was breathing.

Eurydice let out a joyful shout as soon as she crossed the threshold, practically jumping onto Pan's back.

They went tumbling into the flower beds surrounding the cave entrance, laughing like children. Eurydice was so full of joy, she thought that her chest might explode. Pan rolled them over until he was on top of her, cradling her face gently and looking her over for any injuries.

"Wild one, are you all right?" Pan inquired, pressing a series of kisses to her face. Eurydice flopped back in the grass and grinned, closing her eyes as she let the warmth from the sun and Pan's love flood her senses.

"Oh, Pan..." Eurydice smiled. "I'm better than I have ever been."

30

SIX MONTHS LATER

Eurydice leaned over Pan's shoulder and grabbed an overflowing goblet from his hand. She ignored his squawks of protest as she sipped from it, gulping half of the cup's contents in one sip.

"Hey!" Pan whined playfully, slipping his arm around Eurydice's waist and making room for her on his lap. They were sitting at a long table set up in the middle of a field, every seat filled with a nymph, dryad, or acolyte of Dionysus and Pan. It was the full harvest moon and one of Eurydice's favorite times of the year to celebrate. The field was full of fresh grain, and the squash blossoms scattered across the table smelled delightful. The light of the moon illuminated all their bright and shining faces, and a massive bonfire was stoked to great heights just beyond the end of the table.

"You don't mind." Eurydice smiled. She kissed him on the cheek and finished off the rest of the wine. "Is there more of this?" Eurydice looked around absentmindedly for another fresh amphora on the table. The moment the words left her mouth, her cup refilled, and she squeaked in delight.

"Oh, I'll never get tired of that." Eurydice smiled, taking

another sip. Some of the wine dripped down her chin, and Pan leaned forward, cheekily licking some of it off.

"Careful, my love." Pan waggled his eyebrows suggestively. "If you spill any more wine, I'll have to clean it up."

Eurydice raised an eyebrow in challenge and looked at him with a smirk on her face, purposefully making eye contact with him as she turned her glass upside down and poured it out in her lap. Pan yelped as it splashed on their legs, jumping up from the chair and managing to keep a hold of Eurydice in his lap.

"Oh, you cheeky thing." Pan chuckled, setting Eurydice up on her feet. She started laughing, her head falling back as she tossed the cup on the table. Pan never looked as good as he did in those moments, all wild and free, lit by the fire and his cheeks ruddy with alcohol.

Eurydice had never known what it was like to live. The past few months had taught her more about being alive than anything else in either of her previous lives—both in the mortal world and the Underworld. Part of her was a little afraid that the magic would ebb once she and Pan fell into a rhythm together, but the opposite was true. Their friendship didn't really ever end; it just continued to grow with the romantic affection between them. He consistently surprised her with all of the ways he paid attention to the little things she did and said.

There was a sudden burst of wind that sent some of the dishes flying off the table. Everyone jumped out of the way except for Pan and Eurydice, who recognized the golden magic.

"Hermes!" Eurydice smiled, grabbing a fresh cup and holding it up in salute. "I was wondering when we'd see you again."

Hermes materialized from a glittering golden cloud of magic, the wings on his helmet and sandals fluttering. He landed on the middle of the table, making an exaggerated bow and a wink in Eurydice's direction.

"Hello, darling muse. How are you doing today?"

"I'm right here," Pan deadpanned playfully. Hermes grinned and jumped off the table, pulling his son into a hug.

"I already knew you were doing wonderfully with this goddess at your side, so I didn't need to ask."

"Good save," Pan chuckled. He returned the embrace and clapped his father heavily on the back in greeting. Hermes pulled away with a mischievous glint in his eye and conjured a pheasant leg from the table, digging into it with abandon.

"I will say, Olympus certainly does love their ambrosia, but no one caters a party like Dionysus."

Eurydice shrugged. "It's to counteract all the alcohol."

"As if you'd want to counteract it!" Hermes acted scandalized. "I'm sure you both will be happy to know that you made a delicious stir in the Underworld. So much gossip! The scheming! The trickery of it all." Hermes looked enamored. "It's been a delight to see it all unfold."

Eurydice and Pan had willfully been living in their own little world since returning to the mortal realm. They cavorted with Pan's creatures of the wild and acolytes of Dionysus, but as much as they could, they avoided the gossip and rumors surrounding Eurydice's second—successful—departure from the Underworld. Eurydice's ears burned for the first time since she left.

"Did... Are they saying horrid things about me?" Eurydice stepped a little closer to Pan and couldn't help but feel some of her old tendencies come through. She hated disappointing people after all; it was one of the reasons she had even been involved with Orpheus as long as she had.

Hermes shook his head and started to laugh. "Oh, by the gods, absolutely not. Everyone loves a decent drama. Pan, the infamous fertility god, being in love with one of his nymphs for years, unrequited? While the love of his life was one half of the 'Orpheus and Eurydice'? Plus, he," Hermes pointed dramatically at Pan, "is the one who actually succeeded where Orpheus failed, escorting you out of the Underworld!" Hermes let out a joyous scream and tossed his hands up. "Gods, everyone was going on about that Oedipus guy for a while, but this is the thing that plays are made of." Hermes threw back another goblet of wine, and Eurydice sighed in relief, laughing and turning to kiss Pan on the cheek.

"He certainly did succeed where Orpheus failed. He's succeeded in a lot of areas where Orpheus failed." Eurydice laid the innuendo on thick. Hermes made a dramatic retching sound and pretended to step away until Pan waved him back.

"But tell us because I'm dying to know above all else... What happened to Orpheus?" Pan looked calm, but Eurydice could see the gleam of vengeance in his eye. Pan was keen on making sure that Orpheus got what was coming to him in the end.

"Oh, that is a story." Hermes plopped down on the table and started kicking his legs back and forth. "For starters, he was pretty quickly run out of the social groups he cavorted in. His reputation no longer worked for them, you know? Then there was something about him trying to get too close to a maiden at a dinner party. Dionysus and Hecate got involved before sunrise. Hecate had him sent to Tartarus before Hades could even get out of bed."

The blood drained from Eurydice's face. She wasn't bothered that Orpheus's soul was banished to the pits of the Underworld; it was overdue, quite frankly, but she hated the idea that he almost hurt someone else before his misbehavior finally caught up to him. Pan was right there, stepping in between Hermes and Eurydice, so all she could see was his face.

"Do you want to go somewhere quieter?" Pan asked gently, rubbing his hand across her shoulder comfortably. Eurydice breathed easy as soon as Pan was around, his wild presence and quick to action mannerisms always made her feel safe. It might be too chaotic for other women, but Eurydice wasn't even a woman, anyway; she was a nymph with all the chaos and wildness it entailed.

Eurydice looked around the party. There were already intoxicated guests happily lounging across the table; food was being shared, and the wine was pouring fresh with every jar and amphora. The fire was stoked even higher, and she caught the warm smell of frankincense as someone tossed incense into its flames. Eurydice much preferred the wild noises of a party under the stars than the haunting silence of an empty house with only Orpheus's melodies cutting the gloom.

"No," she smiled softly, "I don't think I do." Someone in the distance picked up a flute and started playing; Hermes made an excited wiggle and disappeared off to follow the music.

"Do you want to dance?" Pan offered, eyeing the nymphs that had already started to swing around the bonfire.

Eurydice turned, and her heart lit up. Gone were the days where she was scolded for being too improper. She nodded and kissed Pan quickly before heading off towards the dancers.

"Are you coming?" she asked excitedly, bouncing her weight from foot to foot. Pan sat back down on his chair and angled it so he was staring at the fire.

"You go on." He grinned. "I want to take in the view for a while."

Eurydice's smile was dazzling as her chest expanded further; every day she learned that she had a new capacity for happiness, and Pan was determined to set the record every day. Eurydice ran towards the circle of nymphs and jumped in, spinning wildly around the flames without a care in the world. Petals sprang up in her footsteps, and roses wove their way through her hair.

Eurydice surrendered herself to the sensation of being free

and alive and in love. Utterly, irrevocably in love—the greatest song she'd ever heard.

Sign up for my newsletter to get updates on *The Dread Queen's Bargain*, the next novella in the Asphodel series featuring Persephone and Hades's story. Read on for a sample of *The Trickster's Heart*, out now!

THE TRICKSTER'S HEART
CHAPTER ONE

"Keep going... Yes, that's it. There's only one road. You can't miss it. You're on it now. That's...great. Have fun!" Hermes waited patiently while giving directions to a freshly dead mortal soul. He did this everyday but always took time to remind himself that humans didn't.

The apparition disappeared down the short sandy path towards Charon. As soon as it vanished, Hermes released a long exhale and let the smile drop from his face. It was becoming more and more exhausting to keep up appearances —a fact that frightened him more than it should have.

Hermes always did his job without complaint, and he knew that it was best for everyone if he avoided boredom. It was one of the reasons he took on so many jobs. These days, none of them seemed to have the same effect they once had, and he found himself struggling to keep up with the workload. He wasn't tired; it was just dull now. It was as though everything he'd once loved was slowly slipping away from him, and it was driving him nearly insane to figure out why.

Hermes disappeared on the wind, leaving behind a slight smell of crocus flowers and a pale cloud of golden magic. He hurtled through the Underworld with one destination in mind

—the only place that still welcomed him with an open door and only one raised brow instead of two.

Okay, maybe 'welcome' is a strong word.

All the same, when Hecate's courtyard came into view, Hermes felt part of the knot in his chest begin to loosen. The unpretentious home was probably the smallest out of all of the god's residences, but it was the most comfortable—only Hestia was a better host. The courtyard was framed with columns, with a small lit altar in the very center. It was surrounded by mosaicked tile that gleamed in the fire's glow. Hecate maintained the last ritual space for Nyx, the Goddess of Night and her closest friend. Hermes prepared to drop down in front of the altar. The moment he pulled back his magic and started to descend, he slammed into an invisible wall.

Hermes let out a surprised yelp and went flying through the air, landing in the soft earth a stone's throw away from the courtyard's entrance. He picked himself up slowly and shook out his limbs, smirking as he dusted dirt off his shoulder.

"That was a cruel trick, putting up wards!" Hermes sauntered towards the archway. "You know an aerial descent was my preferred entrance. Doors are for mortals!"

As he approached the house, he conjured a stick of incense from thin air and tossed it into the altar basin, but not before making sure no one saw him. Three large black dogs came running out of the main house, jumping up on Hermes and fighting for attention while covering his face in kisses.

"Oh, who's a good boy?" he cooed to each of the massive hounds while scratching behind their ears.

"It looks like they're finally getting used to you, Trickster," a deep male voice yelled out to him from the house's doorway. Hermes turned his attention from the dogs and caught sight of Aeëtes, Hecate's consort, leaning against the archway.

Aeëtes was the only immortal, of the god or demigod variety, who matched Hermes in feigned nonchalance. He was taller than Hermes, with tanned skin and a short beard, and he perpetually looked like he had stepped off a beach. There was a tightness around his eyes that was uncharacteristic of his permanently sunny demeanor, and Hermes's brow furrowed as he closed the gap between them.

"What's wrong with you then?" He tilted his head to one side, not bothering to push the golden curls out of his eyes.

Aeëtes looked surprised before shaking his head and letting out a rough, quick laugh.

"You cut right to the point, don't you?"

Hermes shrugged. "If Hecate's no longer satisfied with you warming her bed, she should know that I'm more than happy to take your place." He winked at Aeëtes and snickered when Aeëtes's expression darkened.

"Careful, Hermes."

"You're simply *so* easy to rile up, my dear friend." He clapped a hand on Aeëtes's shoulder and steered him inside. "Who am I to deny myself all of life's little joys?"

Aeëtes scoffed, "You're a real piece of work, you know that?"

"You say that as if you don't love that about me." Hermes winked and strolled into Hecate's kitchen like it was his own. He hopped up on the massive counter and started swinging his legs back and forth like a child.

Hecate's kitchen was legendary, and deep down, Hermes knew his nearly unfettered access to it was rare. He appreciated it, even if he didn't mention it.

The dogs had filed in after them, collapsing down in front of the lit hearth in a heap of fur and tails. A large pot was simmering over the fire, with dark purple smoke snaking up towards the ceiling. Bundles of herbs hung from the rafters, and a thousand tiny jars and clay pots littered the table and workbenches that took up the rest of the kitchen's space. It was the apothecary of the mother of witches, the goddess of dogs and women, and Hermes knew where the limits were when he was lucky enough to be there.

Hermes looked around. "Where is my lovely night terror?"

Aeëtes sat down at the table and ran a hand over his face before letting out a long sigh. "I'm not entirely sure, to be honest. I hoped you would know."

"What do you mean, she's gone?" A rush of anxiety ran through Hermes, and he hopped off the counter. Hermes straightened up to his full height, and a pulse of magic flickered over his skin, the wings on his sandals coming to life as his scepter appeared in one hand.

"Easy there." Aeëtes held up a placating hand, slightly surprised at how quickly Hermes jumped to revenge and reconnaissance. "She's not missing in that way. There was a disturbance near one of her temples. Some mortal men were harassing her acolytes. It pissed her off to the point where she decided to go handle it...*personally.*" Aeëtes shuddered.

It pleased Hermes to see that even though Aeëtes loved Hecate, she still scared him a little.

She scares me, too, honestly.

"Ah, I see." Hermes's battlements vanished, and he leaned against the counter, appearing entirely relaxed again. "You don't know which temple?"

"No," Aeëtes sighed, leaning his head against his hand. "She didn't say when she left. She only managed to get a few sentences out before she disappeared. She was spitting mad."

"I believe it." Hermes grimaced. "I haven't led anyone to the banks of Styx recently that had Hecate's signature on them, so I don't think she's finished them off quite yet. How long ago did she leave?"

The god snapped his fingers, and two cups of wine appeared. He handed one to Aeëtes and knocked his cup against it in a hearty cheer. Aeëtes nearly drained it in one sip. His desolation was written all over his face, and while Hermes couldn't understand it fully, he tried to lighten the mood.

SONG OF MEMORIES

"Careful, big boy. I'd tell you to go slower, but there's more where that came from. I'm happy to warm your bed, too, if that's what it takes to stop your moping." His tone was equally suggestive and playful. Aeëtes rolled his eyes.

"Cut it out. Can you be serious for once, please?"

A sharp pang of rejection flooded through Hermes, but he was quick to bury it. From the day he was born, fully-formed and already in a role he'd had no choice in, Hermes had never stayed in one place for long. His relationships with the gods of the Underworld were the strongest ones he had, and he wasn't exactly forthcoming with them.

Hermes would listen to anyone's secrets—and for the most part, contrary to his reputation, he would keep them—but hardly revealed his own. He got through most of his relationships with a quick wit and quicker comedic timing, assuming that was the most value he would ever be to anyone. When his efforts were met with a sharp tongue, he didn't blame Aeëtes, but felt rejected all the same.

Hermes didn't answer Aeëtes's question and repeated one of his own. "Tell me, how long ago did she leave?"

Aeëtes let out a long sigh, finishing his drink. "Two days, maybe?"

Hermes froze with his cup halfway to his mouth. A sense of mild disbelief and annoyance crept into his expression as he narrowed his gaze towards Aeëtes.

"She's been gone for...two days," Hermes deadpanned. Aeëtes nodded woefully, now resembling a child who wasn't allowed to have more sweets than an immortal demigod and son of Apollo. Hermes put his cup down and crossed his arms over his chest. "Two days?"

"Yes!" Aeëtes sounded close to tears.

"Oh, for the love of the gods. For the love of *me*," Hermes griped, sounding exasperated. He went to Aeëtes and pulled him up to his feet. "I'm going to say this as rudely as possible." Hermes grinned. "Pull yourself together!" He gave Aeëtes a little shake and sat him back down while Aeëtes allowed himself to be maneuvered like a training dummy.

"She's never taken off like this before! I don't know where she is or how long she'll be gone. I know Hecate can take care of herself—"

"You have no idea," Hermes interrupted, a sly smile on his face that alluded to a more illicit memory. Aeëtes ignored him; he knew that Hermes and Hecate shared a bit of a past, but every immortal had a past with Hermes.

"She can take care of herself," Aeëtes continued, "but that doesn't mean I'm not worried about her. I don't know how this works when she disappears."

Hermes studied Aeëtes, feeling a little perplexed himself. He had no experience with whatever it was that Aeëtes was feeling. It was common for people to come in and out of his life, take what they needed or what he was willing to give, and then leave again. Hermes had never come close to what Aeëtes was describing, this feeling of loss or want, especially with a permanent partner. It was easier that way.

Hermes leaned back against the kitchen counter, his white tunic stretching across his chest. He managed to look positively devious and cherubic at the same time; it was an innate talent.

"She's going to be fine. It's *Hecate*." Hermes stressed her name. "I promise, she's taking her time getting her revenge and is going to spend a few days getting wine-drunk with her acolytes, castrating rapists, and adopting stray dogs. Girl stuff." He winked at Aeëtes and managed to get a smile out of the brooding demigod.

"I suppose you're right." Aeëtes's expression lifted slightly. "You must think I'm insane."

"Entirely so," Hermes answered honestly with a shrug. "I'm going to chalk this up to being another human emotion and blame it on the fact that you were raised by mortals."

It was Aeëtes's turn to chuckle as he held up his cup in Hermes's direction. "You say that now, Trickster, but no one falls in love like the gods. Hades talked a big game before Persephone. Thanatos did too."

"Ha!" Hermes snapped his fingers again, and their cups refilled. "That was because they were bored."

Aeëtes shook his head slowly, the smile on his face utterly disbelieving. "You really think that Hades and Thanatos were *bored*?"

"Emotions are for mortals. They're pointless. You can always pick up more jobs. Look at me."

"So you admit it. You stay busy instead of ever considering the idea of settling down? You're honestly telling me that you aren't looking at me right now, in my desolation," Aeëtes jested, "and you don't wonder what it feels like? To care about someone that much? To miss them?"

Hermes feigned a shocked expression, but a very real anxiety came to life in his chest as he struggled to keep his tone playful.

"And you call me a trickster! Excellent wordplay, I'll give you that. Alas, you're wrong, young man." He held his hands out as his scepter reappeared and his helmet settled atop his curls. "No one could ever keep up with me."

The wings on Hermes's sandals and helmet fluttered rapidly as if to prove his point, and without another word, Hermes vanished from the kitchen.

ALSO BY MOLLY TULLIS

The Asphodel Series

Consort of Darkness

Don't miss the first story in the Asphodel series: the story of Nyx and Erebus.

Lost to Witchcraft

Hecate, Nyx's best friend, fights her heart's attempt to fall in love.

Enamored in Death

Thanatos, the god of death, has to work with a partner for the first time.

The Trickster's Heart

Hermes, the world's trickster, becomes victim to the greatest trick of all—love.

The Romanov Oracle

A fantasy stand-alone based on the story of Anastasia Romanova.

ABOUT THE AUTHOR

Molly Tullis would have picked the Phantom of the Opera over Raoul and named her French bulldog Jean Valjean. She only believes in black clothing, red lipstick, and never turns down an iced coffee or tequila. She enjoys writing fantasy, romance, or any genre with an opportunity to insert a dark-haired, morally grey man.

When not identifying as an author, she identifies as a woman with bangs, finger tattoos, and a nose ring, who can tell you what planets are making you sad.

Her DMs are always open on Instagram (@thebibliophileblonde), and you can get information on all upcoming projects at www.thebibliophileblonde.com.

Made in the USA
Las Vegas, NV
03 February 2025